2

SHAMAN
PASS

SHAMAN PASS

a Nathan Active mystery

Stan Jones

Published by
Soho Press, Inc.
853 Broadway
New York, NY 10003

Library of Congress Cataloging-in-Publication Data

Jones, Stan, 1947–
Shaman pass : a Nathan Active mystery / Stan Jones.
p. cm.
ISBN 978-1-56947-413-6
1. Police—Alaska—Fiction. 2. Inupiat—Fiction.
3. Alaska—Fiction. I. Title.
PS3560.O539 S48 2003
813'.54—dc21   2002042624

10 9 8 7 6 5 4 3 2

To the people who define my life:
Rufus, Etta, Susan, Paul, and Sydnie

ANNA

ACKNOWLEDGMENTS

FOR THE DETAILS OF the search technique used in the closing chapters of this book, I am in debt to Bill Hess, a longtime friend, Arctic journalist, and photographer. He describes its use during an actual search on Alaska's North Slope in his lovely and fascinating book, *Gift of the Whale*, and he generously added much useful information about it in a series of e-mail interviews.

The description on page 127 of the fate of Chukchi's last "devil-doctor" is drawn from the diaries of Charles Brower, a Yankee whaler who settled in Barrow in the late 1800s and spent the rest of his life there. The entry I relied on is recounted in *Sadie Brower Neakok: An Inupiaq Woman*, by Margaret B. Blackman.

Also, my thanks to Dr. D. P. Lyle, who provided advice on the causes, care, and feeding of dislocated shoulders.

Finally, my deepest gratitude to my editor, Laura Hruska, for the skill, insight, and dedication she brought to the task of helping me tell this story.

In the olden days, the Inuit slew those who killed their kinsmen. One vengeance followed another like links in a chain.

—Nuligak, in *I, Nuligak*

Beware the fury of the patient man.

—John Dryden

A NOTE ON LANGUAGE

"ESKIMO" IS THE BEST-KNOWN term for the Native Americans described in this book, but it is not their term. In their own language, they call themselves "Inupiat," meaning "the people." "Eskimo," which was brought into Alaska by white men, is what certain Indian tribes in eastern Canada called their neighbors to the north; it probably meant "eaters of raw flesh."

Nonetheless, "Eskimo" and "Inupiat" are used more or less interchangeably in Northwest Alaska today, at least when English is spoken, and that is the usage followed in this book.

In formal or public speech—such as journalism—"Inuit" is probably the most widely accepted collective term for the Eskimo peoples (not all of whom are Inupiat) in Siberia, Alaska, Canada, and Greenland. But it is not an Alaskan word and so is not much used by the Inupiat of the state's northwest coast. Accordingly, it appears rarely in this book.

The Inupiat call their language Inupiaq. A few words in it— those commonly mixed with English in Northwest Alaska— appear in the book. They are listed below, along with pronunciations and meanings. As the spellings vary among Inupiaq-English dictionaries, I have used spellings that seemed to me most likely to induce the proper pronunciation by non-Inupiaq readers.

A Northwest Alaska Glossary

aaka (AH-kuh): mother

aana (AH-nuh): grandmother; old lady

akhio (AH-key-OH): a low fiberglass cargo sled that slides on its belly; unlike a dogsled, it has no runners

amaguq (AH-ma-GUK): wolf

anaq (AH-nuk): excrement; dirt

angatquq (AHNG-ut-cook): shaman

Aqaa (ah-CAH!): It stinks!

arigaa (AH-de-gah): good!

Arii (ah-DEE): I hurt!

ataata (ah-TAH-tah): grandfather

ee (E): yes

inuksuk (in-UK-suck): a manlike figure made of stones; the Inupiat used them as trail markers and as bogeymen to frighten caribou into lakes or traps

Inupiaq (IN-you-pack): the Eskimo language of northern Alaska; an individual Eskimo of northern Alaska

Inupiat (IN-you-pat): more than one Inupiaq; the Eskimo people of northern Alaska

kikituq (KICK-ee-took): a monster; the spirit familiar of an *angatquq**

kunnichuk (KUH-knee-chuck): storm shed

kuspuk (KUSP-uk): light parka

malik (MULL-uk): accompany or follow

masru (MOSS-rue): Eskimo potato

miluk (MILL-uk): breast

---

* Here, I confess to taking creative license. In actual fact, an *angatquq*'s spirit familiar was called his *angatquq*. I thought this would be hopelessly confusing in fiction, and so substituted *kikituq*, a word of somewhat similar meaning, to serve as the *angatquq*'s spirit familiar.

muktuk (MUCK-tuck): whale skin with a thin layer of fat adhering; a great delicacy in Inupiat country

naluaqmiiyaaq (nuh-LOCK-me-ock): almost white; an Inupiaq who tries to act white

naluaqmiu (nuh-LOCK-me): a white person

naluaqmiut (nuh-LOCK-me): more than one white person; white people

nanuq (NA-NOOK): polar bear

natchiq (NOTCH-ik): seal

pukuk (PUCK-uck): pry, poke around, get into things

quiyuk (KWEE-yuck): sex

siksrik (SIX-rik): squirrel

taggaqvik (ta-GOG-vik): place of shadows

ugruk (OOG-rook): bearded seal

ukpeagvik (OOK-pea-OG-vik): place of snowy owls

ukpik (OOK-pik): snowy owl

umiaq (OOM-ee-ak): whaling boat, made of a wooden frame and covered with the thick, tough hides of walrus or bearded seal

Village English: a stripped-down form of English used by the Inupiat of Northwest Alaska, particularly older people and residents of small villages

Yoi! (rhymes with "boy"): So lucky!

CHAPTER ONE

"SHOULD I TAKE IT OUT?"

The paramedic from the Chukchi Public Safety Department dropped to her knees beside the mortal remains of Victor Solomon, then looked up at Alaska State Trooper Nathan Active and repeated the question with her eyes.

Active snapped the cap into place over the lens of his Nikon, tucked the camera inside his parka, closed the zipper, put his mittens on, and considered the paramedic's question as he gazed around Victor Solomon's sheefish camp on the ice of Chukchi Bay. Active hated moments like this even more than most moments at a death scene. Instinct told him the proceedings ought to be as solemn as the event itself, the questions as profound as the fact of a human soul moving on to the hereafter, if there was one.

Instead, it always came down to this kind of niggling decision: Should the shaft protruding approximately four feet from Victor Solomon's chest be left in place? That way, the pathologist who would do the autopsy could remove it himself, noting whatever needed to be noted about its relationship to the wound and Victor's death.

Or should it be removed to facilitate the body's transportation by snowmachine and *akhio* from Victor's sheefishing camp across eight miles of sea ice to the village of Chukchi? Active turned and looked. The town was just discernible through the milky air as a line of dark rectangles on the horizon.

Vera Jackson, the paramedic, pointed at the fiberglass *akhio* hitched to the back of her snowmachine, a blue-and-black Arctic Cat. "He'll get a lot of bouncing around on that. It might make the wound bigger. Or the harpoon might fall out and get lost." The wind whipped her hair, raven black with streaks of ice gray, into her bright, dark eyes. She blinked and tucked the hair into her parka hood.

Active turned back to the corpse and studied the harpoon shaft. The upper section was of dark, weathered wood, very old from the look of it. The wind had dusted it with snow since Victor's killing an undetermined number of hours earlier, but it was still obvious the wood had been worked to make the shaft round and smooth.

The lower section was ivory, lashed to the wood above it with some kind of tough-looking handmade thong—rawhide or sinew, probably. The ivory section disappeared into Victor's chest just below the breastbone.

Active stamped his Sorels on the snow-covered ice, pounded his mittened hands together, and turned his back to the bone-saw wind rolling in from the west. Why would anyone kill an old man like Victor Solomon, and why with an old harpoon, if that's what it was? Why not something quick and sure, like a gun?

And why not on a warmer day?

"Maybe we could take it apart right above the ivory piece there," Active suggested. "Saw through those thongs holding it together?" That, he thought, would preserve the evidence and solve the transportation problem, too. "You bring a saw, Vera?"

The paramedic rose from her kneeling position by Victor and wrinkled her nose in the Inupiat no. "When they said he was just lying by his sheefish hole, I didn't bring anything like that. We only bring the saw if we have to cut them out of a car or airplane or something."

Active looked at the two civilians within earshot and lifted his eyebrows in question. "You guys got a saw?"

One was an Inupiat teenager named Darvin Reed, the sheefisherman who had found Victor dead on the ice and reported it by cellular telephone to the dispatcher at the Chukchi Public Safety Building. Active couldn't help considering the cellphone aspect of the case mildly remarkable. Sure, there was no reason the Arctic or the Inupiat should be any less accessible to the reach of modern technology than anyone else. Or any less susceptible. But still.

The other civilian was Darvin's sheefishing partner, a white kid. His name was Willie Samuels. Active had asked the two to wait and they were watching the proceedings from the seats of their snowmachines. Both shook their heads no in answer to Active's question about the saw.

A half-dozen other civilians watched from about fifty yards away. Some had been on the scene when Active and Vera Jackson arrived. The rest had shown up since. Active had taken their names and phone numbers, or house numbers if they didn't have phones, and chased them back once it was established that Darvin and Willie were the actual discoverers of the body.

Active was considering whether to canvass the hangers-on for a saw when Willie pulled out a clasp knife and opened it. "I guess you could try this if you want."

Active looked at the knife. The blade was at least four inches long, much bigger than the Leatherman on his own belt. He looked at Vera.

"I think cutting it with that knife might jostle it around as much as taking him to town like he is. Those thongs look like *ugruk* hide to me. Real tough." She looked at Victor. "But I could try pulling it out. Real careful and slow. Maybe I could work it loose without messing up the wound too much."

"It's not frozen in?" Active asked.

Vera shook her head. "I don't think so, except a little bit around the hole maybe. He didn't freeze much yet, from having his warm clothes on. This must have happened last night, I guess."

Active considered the pros and cons for a few moments. "Try not to touch the shaft any more than you have to," he said finally. "We still have to go over it for fingerprints."

He wasn't too worried. Considering the temperature was barely above zero now and had been a few degrees lower during the night, it seemed highly unlikely the killer had wielded the harpoon bare-handed. Fingerprints were a long shot.

Vera nodded and knelt again by the corpse. She opened a case she had brought to Victor's side earlier, slipped off her gloves, and took out a pair of scissors. Victor's heavy parka had evidently been unzipped when he was impaled by the thrust up into his chest cavity, but Vera had to cut through a down vest, a plaid wool shirt, and an undershirt, all soaked with frozen blood, to expose the entry wound.

She laid the scissors aside, put her gloves on, and gripped the shaft with both hands, rocking it gently. "Feels like the head is stuck," she said. "Must have gone through him and got in his rib cage in the back. Or his spine."

She rocked the shaft again, then applied a little twisting motion and that was enough. The shaft popped out of Victor's chest with a wet slurp. Vera rocked back and caught herself, and suddenly they were looking at ten or twelve inches of bloody ivory.

Vera pointed with a surprised expression at the tip, which was not a head at all, but a nicely tapered cylinder, squared off at the end as if to fit in a socket. "I guess the head came off inside him."

Active heard the buzz of an approaching snowmachine and turned, prepared to shoo away another curious civilian. But no. He recognized the red parka and wide middle-aged shape of Jim Silver, the city police chief of Chukchi.

The chief pulled up, shut off his snowmachine, and stepped over to Victor Solomon's corpse. He motioned to the harpoon in Vera's hands. "OK if I take a look?"

Active studied the chief's pockmarked face for a moment. "Sure. But we are outside the city limits."

Silver grinned. "Easy, Nathan, I know it's trooper jurisdiction, but I got a feeling when I heard about the harpoon."

"Harpoon? How—"

"There was one taken in the museum burglary," Silver said. "You knew that, right?"

Active stared at the police chief, then at the shaft. "No, I didn't know. I thought all they got was Uncle Frosty."

"Nah, there were some other odds and ends, too, according to the paperwork from the Smithsonian," Silver said. "A mammoth ivory amulet with an owl's face on it, and a harpoon."

"This harpoon?"

Silver shrugged. "It sure looks like the picture the Smithsonian sent. There aren't a lot of harpoons around nowadays, especially with ivory at the business end. Like I said, I got a feeling."

Active nodded to Vera, and she handed Silver the shaft. He brushed away the snow and frost at the joint where the ivory and wooden sections were lashed together, and squinted at a little collection of scratch marks thus exposed. He grunted, and shook his head. "Shit, I was afraid of this. It's Uncle Frosty's harpoon, all right. Fucking Calvin."

CHAPTER TWO

UNCLE FROSTY HAD ARRIVED by air on another windy, milk-skied morning three days earlier, while Nathan Active was being teased in timeless Eskimo fashion about his new snowmachine.

"So you decided on the Yamaha." Jim Silver strolled around the machine in question and stopped at the handlebars. His parka was open as usual, his paunch bulging out between the flaps. Unlike Active, Silver never seemed to feel the cold. He rolled back the gauntlets covering the Yamaha's handlebars and whistled in mock admiration. "Heated grips, ah? *Yoi!* You'll be so warm on the trail."

It was Silver's lapse into Village English, the "*yoi!*" in particular, that warned Active he was in trouble. "*Yoi!*" meant "So lucky!" or "So nice!" but carried an undertone of the sly Inupiat ridicule of which Silver, though white, had become a master during his long years in Chukchi.

Active wriggled his toes in the cold and tried to work out a defense. "The heated grips were included. I didn't order them," he said at last.

"Uh-huh." Silver took another turn around the Yamaha, then stepped back a pace, his face split by a huge, malicious grin. "But why the ladies' model?"

Active said a silent "Fuck!" and an audible "Yeah, right." He huddled a little deeper into his parka against the wind scraping across the Chukchi airport, and against whatever it was that Silver was about to spring on him.

Silver touched the Yamaha's cowling with a gloved hand. "I'm not saying it's not a lovely shade of purple, because it is."

Active waited in misery, his breath coming in visible puffs. The wind lashed the long guard hairs on the wolf fur of his parka ruff into his mouth. He huffed them out.

"It's just that around here . . ." Silver paused, as if pondering how to administer the kill shot as humanely as possible. "Well, around here, purple is a ladies' color and anything purple is known as a ladies' model. Purple four-wheeler, purple pickup, purple boat, purple airplane, purple snowgo, that's a ladies' machine in Chukchi. I thought you'd know that."

Silver left his orbit around the Yamaha and sat down on it, facing the rear. "Nice soft seat, too." He leaned back, rested his head on the handlebars, and sighed, then looked at Active. "Usually, the dealers have to mark down the purple ones before they can move 'em. Hector didn't by any chance give you a special deal on it, did he?"

Active gave Silver the finger—a gloved finger.

Silver smiled and wagged his head. "Thought so. But I take this as a good sign. Even with a discount, a new snowmachine is a major financial commitment for you, Nathan, cheap as you are. You've decided to stay in Chukchi after all, I take it?"

"No, I just need something to get around on till my transfer comes through. I'll sell it when I go."

Silver smiled again. "Uh-huh." Then he sat up and swiveled around to stare east along the main runway of Chukchi's airport. "I think I hear him."

Active peered east through the haze that came with a springtime west wind, and finally picked up the rumble of old-fashioned propeller engines. Then he spotted the Arctic Air Cargo DC-6. It was just a speck over the tundra east of the gravel spit that contained Chukchi and its straggling dirt streets and mostly unpainted wooden houses. He pointed across the lagoon. "That him?"

Silver nodded. "Yep, Uncle Frosty's finally here, looks like."

Three handlers came out of the Arctic Air Cargo office. One climbed on a forklift and hit the starter. The engine turned over a few times, then caught, coughing and grumbling in the cold.

The other two walked over to the purple Yamaha, boots crunching on the snow that covered the tarmac. "Hey, Billy, Horace," Silver said as the ancient freighter labored toward the runway.

Horace, the older of the two, looked at Active's snow-machine, then at Active, then away, a slight smile on his lips.

"Horace is too polite to say anything," Silver whispered to Active. "Your older Eskimos are like that. Very gracious."

Active knew that, and Silver knew he knew it. He didn't say anything.

Billy, on the other hand, was young and, Active judged, only half-Eskimo at most.

"That Hector stick you with a ladies' model, ah? Too bad." Billy grimaced in mock sympathy. "Somebody sell my uncle one of them once. He get so mad when he find out what purple mean, he take that snowgo out on the ice and shoot it, just leave it there."

Billy turned to study the approaching DC-6 for a few moments, then swung back to Active. "I feel bad, though, *naluaqmiiyaaq* like you getting stuck with ladies' model. Maybe I'll swap you my old Polaris, give your Yamaha to my girlfriend, ah? She really like purple." He pointed at a battered relic parked outside the chain-link fence surrounding the tarmac.

Half the Polaris's windscreen was gone, and the seat was so

patched with silver duct tape that none of the original Naugahyde was visible. Two red bungee cords held down the engine cowling.

Horace smiled again and Silver chuckled.

As the tires on the DC-6 chirped onto the runway, Active reflected on the injustice of still being known after all this time as the village *naluaqmiiyaaq*—the Inupiaq word for an Eskimo who tried to be like a white man.

Sure, he had been raised in Anchorage. But he had been born in Chukchi and was, in fact, a full-blooded Inupiaq. He had been taken out of the village at the age of eighteen months when his adoptive parents, two white schoolteachers, had burned out on the Bush and decided to give Alaska's largest city a try.

True, he was back in Chukchi only because his bosses at the Alaska State Troopers had posted him there for his first assignment. And sure, he would be on a plane home to Anchorage the moment the troopers gave him a transfer. But it had been two years now. How long before he stopped being the *naluaqmiiyaaq*?

It was at that moment the right retort came to him like a gift from some ancient god of Eskimo teasing. He looked at Billy. "If your girlfriend likes purple, maybe I'll give it to her myself," Active said. "Ah?" He lifted his eyebrows with a grin that said, "Your move."

This time Silver laughed out loud and even Horace chuckled. Billy got a thoughtful expression on his face, then frowned and walked over to stand beside the forklift. Horace walked over, too, and shouted something to Billy that sounded like, "That *naluaqmiiyaaq* act like a real Eskimo sometimes, ah?" But Active couldn't be sure, over the cough of the idling forklift.

"What brings you out on a day like this anyhow?" Silver

asked Active as the DC-6 taxied in. "I thought Uncle Frosty was going straight to the tribal museum, no fuss, no muss. How did the troopers get involved?"

Active grimaced. "Beats me. All I know is, the state has to sign some kind of receipt and disclaimer of interest, then turn Uncle Frosty over to the museum to make it all legal and keep the Smithsonian happy. And somebody in Juneau apparently decided the troopers were the right agency to do it. We got a letter from the attorney general saying to meet Uncle Frosty and sign the papers, so here I am. In about five minutes, Uncle Frosty will be Malcolm Anirak's problem." He pointed at a red Ford pulling up to the chain-link beside Billy's snowgo. A magnetic sign on the pickup's door said CHUKCHI TRIBAL COUNCIL.

The DC-6 braked in front of Arctic Air Cargo and the four big propellers shuddered to a halt. The cargo door swung up to disclose a crate with SMITHSONIAN INSTITUTION stenciled on the side. The forklift rolled toward the plane, forks rising as it went.

Roger Kennelly, the newsman for KCHK, Chukchi's public radio station—known as Kay-Chuck—pulled up to the fence on a four-wheeler and rushed onto the tarmac. As the driver got his forks under the crate, Kennelly pulled a camera from his backpack and began shooting pictures, presumably for his side job as stringer for the weekly *Chukchi Bay Times*.

"How about you?" Active asked Silver. "Does the city have to sign for Uncle Frosty, too?"

"Nah, I'm just here to make sure the Inupiat Republican Army doesn't do anything any crazier than usual." Silver jerked his thumb at a skinny, intense-looking Inupiaq in mirror sunglasses climbing off a snowmachine just outside the fencing. The cold didn't seem to bother him, either. He wasn't even wearing a parka, just a snowmachine suit, a headband

around his ears, and gloves that looked too thin for the
weather. And his snowmachine looked too old for heated
grips. The machine, a trail-worn Ski-Doo, was a fraternal twin
to Billy's Polaris. The dogsled hitched on behind was a
ramshackle collection of splintered hickory spliced into
continuing service with driftwood, wire, scrap lumber, and
duct tape.

"Ah, the famous Calvin Maiyumerak," Active said.

Silver nodded with a wry grin.

Maiyumerak spotted the two lawmen, raised his right fist in
a power salute, then went to the dogsled and pulled a picket
sign from under a blue tarp held down with bungee cords. FREE
UNCLE FROSTY! the sign said in red Magic Marker lettering.
Maiyumerak put it on his shoulder and headed for Malcolm
Anirak's pickup.

"Oh, shit, I gotta keep those two apart." Silver, moving fast
for a man of his bulk, galloped out of the gate in the chain-link
fence and reached the pickup just as Maiyumerak rapped his
sign on the pickup's roof over Anirak's window. Active headed
over to watch.

"Free Uncle Frosty!" Maiyumerak shouted at the window of
the pickup, which was so frosted over that Anirak could barely
be seen inside as he pounded the horn and motioned for Silver
to do something. Maiyumerak whacked the truck with his sign
again. Anirak jumped out.

Silver arrived just in time to step between them. He grabbed
Maiyumerak's sign in one hand, his collar in the other, and
backed him up two steps. "Calvin, what did I tell you about
this?" the police chief was saying as Active reached the fence.

Anirak slammed the pickup door and examined the roof
over the window. "He scratched my paint!" Anirak said.

Kennelly panted up, stuffing the camera into his backpack
and pulling out a tape recorder. He slung it over his shoulder

on a strap, and held a microphone between Silver and Maiyumerak. Silver swatted the microphone aside. "Christ, Roger, how many times have I told you not to put that thing in my face?"

Kennelly stuck it back into the space between the two, but farther from Silver. "This is a public facility. I have a right to record these activities," he said. Silver sighed and looked tired. But he didn't swat the microphone again.

Kennelly was white, very young, very serious, and, Active feared, might be in Chukchi to save the Inupiat from Western civilization. He was devoid of humor, with one remarkable, near-brilliant exception: He had, as far as Active knew, coined the name "Uncle Frosty" for the unidentified Inupiat mummy the Smithsonian was shipping to Chukchi. At any rate, the first time Active had heard it was when Kennelly used it during a call-in show on Kay-Chuck. Kennelly had somehow tapped into the cheerful fatalism with which the Inupiat seemed to arm themselves against the perplexities of life, and the nickname had caught on instantly. From then on, the Smithsonian mummy was Uncle Frosty.

Silver turned his attention back to Maiyumerak. "I explained this to you yesterday, Calvin. You can walk around and shout your slogan and wave your sign. But you can't hit anything with it. If you do, I'll have to put you in jail for interfering with these activities."

"I got my free speech right to express my opinion that Uncle Frosty should be left out on the tundra like them old Inupiat used to do." Maiyumerak shook his sign. "That's where them *naluaqmiut* from the government found him anyway."

"Yes, we've all read your letters to the editor and heard you calling me names on Kay-Chuck," Anirak said. "But our tribal council has the right under the Indian Graves Act to receive Uncle Frosty's remains and care for them as we see fit." The executive director of the Chukchi Tribal Council was about forty, Active guessed, pudgy with black-frame glasses. He wore a shirt and tie even today, and only a windbreaker over them. Presumably Anirak was relying on the Ford's heater for protection from the elements during this brief excursion out of the tribal offices. Active had talked to him a couple times about the handoff of Uncle Frosty, and had heard him being interviewed on the radio about the mummy's impending arrival. Malcolm Anirak might have been born Inupiaq, Active had concluded, but he was now pure bureaucrat.

"Care for them! Ha!" Maiyumerak raised his sign as if he would now whack Anirak over the head with it, caught a warning look from Silver, and instead thumped the butt of it on the snowy gravel beside the fence. "You're gonna put Uncle Frosty in a glass case in your museum so them *naluaqmiut* tourists can look at him."

"That's what my council directed me to do and that's what I'm going to do. It'll be a very tasteful educational display and it's not just for visitors. Our schoolchildren and other local people will also learn about how we lived before the *nalua*—" Anirak glanced at Kennelly, who was not only white but also a reporter, and shifted gears. "Before we adopted Western ways."

"It's still not right!" Maiyumerak shouted. "You should put him on the tundra, let the animals take him. That's the Inupiat way. Back to the earth, like a great big circle."

"That's the old Inupiat way." Anirak climbed into his truck and spoke through the open door. "Things are different now. We need the money Uncle Frosty will bring in if we are going to keep our tribal school open. Our bingo games alone can't do the job and picket signs won't either." Anirak slammed the door and glared at Maiyumerak through the frost on the window.

Maiyumerak looked for a moment as if he would whack the Ford again, but he lowered the sign and walked to his snow-machine. Kennelly trotted over and interviewed Maiyumerak as he bungeed the sign onto the dogsled.

The forklift driver deposited Uncle Frosty on an Arctic Air Cargo flatbed truck as Horace walked up to Active with a clipboard. "I guess you're supposed to sign this, ah?"

Active took the clipboard, fished inside his parka for a pen, and signed quickly before the ink could congeal in the cold air. Horace walked out the gate and took the clipboard to Anirak, who rolled down the window of his pickup to sign.

Silver came back through the gate and stopped beside Active's Yamaha. "Coming down to the museum? My guess is, Calvin has some more fireworks planned."

"What, the Chukchi Public Safety Department can't handle the IRA? You're calling in the troopers?"

Silver turned a withering look on Active's purple Yamaha, smiled, and climbed into the green-and-white Chukchi Police Department Bronco parked inside the fence.

CHAPTER THREE

WHEN THE FLATBED WITH its entourage of police, press and Malcolm Anirak reached the museum, Maiyumerak was already there. He was, Active saw, in the process of chaining his Ski-Doo to the hasp that held together the swinging doors of the museum's shipping dock. The FREE UNCLE FROSTY sign was bungeed upright to a stanchion on Maiyumerak's dogsled.

The museum was a brown two-story humpbacked wooden building designed, Active had heard, to resemble an inverted *umiaq* or whaleboat. Silver pulled up, parked the city Bronco, and, with an expression like an army private sentenced to latrine duty, hurried over to Maiyumerak. "Look, Calvin, fun's fun but enough's enough. Unlock that damned thing and get out of the way or I'll arrest you right now."

Kennelly rushed up with his camera and microphone, and Maiyumerak grinned in pleasure, exposing a black hole where one of his front teeth should have been.

"Go ahead if you want a political prisoner in your jail. Under the United Nations Charter on the Rights of Indigenous . . ." Maiyumerak trailed off to watch Silver's back as he stalked over to his Bronco.

The police chief threw open the door, grabbed a microphone, and shouted at the dispatcher who answered his call. "Lucy, get somebody from the city shop over to the museum with a set of bolt-cutters, will you? And tell 'em to be at least reasonably quick about it! Cop time, not village time!"

He pulled a pair of handcuffs from the seat of the Bronco and walked toward Maiyumerak, who now had a look of alarm on his face. "You can't cut that chain! It's for Kobuk."

"This is Kobuk's chain?" Silver put his hand on it and his face lit up.

"That's right, he'll have to stay in the house without it," Maiyumerak said. "That's where I left him when I took off the chain but he's not a house dog. My grandma can't handle him, she's too old."

"I'll say he's not a house dog. He's a fucking wolf, except about twice as big." Silver glared at Maiyumerak. "But you should have thought of that before. Even if I don't cut it, that chain is evidence now. You're going to be sitting in my jail and Dolly's going to be trapped in the house with that damned monster of yours. Now put out your wrists."

Maiyumerak put his hands behind him and backed away. "Wait a minute, maybe I could unlock it."

Silver dropped the handcuffs to his side. "All right. Do it."

"In fifteen minutes I could."

"Fifteen minutes?" Silver's smile vanished. "Why not right now?"

"Fifteen minutes." Maiyumerak's lips took on a stubborn set. "That's my protest. Fifteen minutes."

Silver glanced at his watch, started to say something, checked himself, and looked at Malcolm Anirak.

Anirak, who had his window down and was watching from the warmth of his pickup, shrugged. "I guess I could go get a cup of coffee."

"OK." Silver turned to Maiyumerak. "You can have your fifteen minutes, but none of your bullshit when I get back. You take off that chain and clear out, or you're going to jail. Just like when you put seal oil on the seats of the tour bus, remember?"

Maiyumerak showed them the gap in his teeth again. "Smell good."

"Not to tourists," Silver said. "To tourists, seal oil smells like dead fish."

Maiyumerak grinned again, then looked stubborn once more. "But you have to pull your gun on me, too."

Silver groaned. "I pull my gun when I'm going to shoot somebody. You want to get shot?"

"You have to make me stop with your gun. So I can put it in my petition to the United Nations."

Silver swore and stuck out the handcuffs. "All right, damn it, the deal's off. Gimme your wrists."

Maiyumerak put his hands behind his back, looking more stubborn than ever.

"OK, how about this?" Silver made a pistol with his hand, pointed it at Maiyumerak, and jerked his thumb up in a cocking motion. "Symbolic gunpoint, will that work?"

Maiyumerak relaxed, grinned, and behind the mirror glasses lifted his eyebrows in the Eskimo yes.

Silver dropped his hands to his side, drew himself up to full height, and put on a stern expression. "Calvin Ray Maiyumerak, in the name of the Chukchi Public Safety Department—"

"And against the United Nations Charter on the Rights of Indigenous Peoples," Maiyumerak said.

"— and in possible violation of the United Nations Charter on Whatever, if there is such a thing, I hereby order you, at symbolic gunpoint, to unlock your damned snowmachine and vacate these premises within fifteen minutes or you will be arrested and incarcerated in the jail of the Chukchi Public Safety Department for an indefinite period of time."

Silver raised his right hand, turned it into a pistol again, cocked his thumb, and put his index finger to the middle of Maiyumerak's forehead. "OK?"

Maiyumerak grinned and lifted his eyebrows again.

Silver pinched the bridge of his nose for a moment, then turned and strode toward his Bronco. "Just another day in the annals of Chukchi law enforcement," he said as he passed Active.

"I'm speechless with admiration," Active said, straddling the purple Yamaha.

Silver turned for another look at Maiyumerak, who had unbungeed the FREE UNCLE FROSTY sign and was waving it while he marched in circles before the loading door as Kennelly snapped away with his camera.

Then Silver swung on Active with a suspicious frown. "Of whom?"

Active grinned and shrugged.

"Fucking Calvin," Silver said. "You wanta get some lunch?"

ACTIVE WAS working at his desk shortly after noon two days later when Silver stepped into his office.

"Fucking Calvin," the police chief said. "You hear?"

"Hear what?"

"The museum was burglarized last night, and guess what's missing."

"Wha—you mean Uncle Frosty?"

Silver nodded grimly.

"No kidding. And Calvin did it?"

"Who else?"

Active couldn't help smiling a little. "And what does he

have to say for himself? Just exercising his indigenous rights under the U.N. Charter on Whatever, was he?"

"He says he didn't do it."

"And what does the evidence say?"

Silver grimaced in disgust. "Very damn little. Almost nothing, in fact. Somebody broke the padlock on the loading-dock door, probably with a crowbar, went inside, and snapped the bands off the crate, pried it open, grabbed Uncle Frosty, and took off. Probably in a snowmachine and dogsled, but the snow around that door is so hard-packed he barely left a trace."

"Calvin got an alibi?"

Silver scratched his scalp at the hairline, a habit of his. "His grandmother says they watched TV together last night and went to bed around eleven or twelve. He was still asleep when she brought him his morning coffee around nine."

"Hmm. Kind of iffy."

Silver nodded. "Dolly could be fudging to protect her grandbaby, like any self-respecting *aana*. Or Calvin could have gone out while she was asleep, stolen Uncle Frosty, hid him on the tundra somewhere, and snuck back into the house without her knowing. She's pretty deaf when she takes out her hearing aid."

"So what now?"

"So nothing, unless somebody turns up who saw him do it. Or Calvin has an attack of conscience and confesses."

Active grinned in sympathy. "Uh-huh."

Silver sighed heavily. "Fucking Calvin."

CHAPTER FOUR

THE NEXT MORNING, THE cell-phone call had come in on the 911 line from Darvin Reed. And Active, instead of coasting peacefully through Friday into the weekend, now found himself on the sea ice beside a dead man in a sheefishing camp. The identification of the murder weapon made it clear that the museum burglary hadn't been just the final act in an unusually entertaining piece of Chukchi street theater after all. But Calvin Maiyumerak?

Silver said it again: "Fucking Calvin." His words came out in puffs of steam that rode away on the wind as he handed the harpoon to Active.

"You think Calvin did this?" Active gestured toward Victor Solomon's body, still lying in the snow pit surrounding his sheefish hole. "That clown?"

"You know how that clown makes his living?"

Active shook his head.

"Among other things, he's a dog trapper."

"What?"

"We used to have a terrible problem here with loose dogs, always mauling little kids and chasing the *aanas* around and stealing meat. It finally got so bad the city council ordered my officers to start shooting them on sight. But Roger Kennelly put it out on public radio and *All Things Considered* picked it up. Then one of those animal-rights groups from Outside got hold of it and that was the end of our dog-control program, or so we thought. Next thing you know, Calvin moves down from Ebrulik. Pretty soon the loose-dog problem is going away, Dolly's turning out wolf ruffs and mittens right and left, and everybody's happy."

"Calvin shoots them? Doesn't that spook people a little bit?"

"No, he doesn't shoot them," Silver said. "Exactly how he does catch them is a bit of a mystery. He doesn't put out traps, otherwise he'd catch more kids than dogs. Some people say he carries rotten meat around in his pockets to attract them, then breaks their necks with his bare hands."

Active winced, then had a thought. "What about the carcasses?"

"Kobuk takes care of them."

"Kobuk? Who—oh, that dog he was talking about at the museum?"

Silver nodded. "That's the word, anyhow. I doubt even a monster like Kobuk could eat more than a dog or two a week but of course most of the huskies around here are your compact little trail dogs. You never know."

"You ever check up on it?"

"God, no, why would I? The council's happy, I'm happy, and what the animal-rights people don't know won't hurt me."

Active turned the harpoon in his hands and examined the scratch marks. "Wait a minute, didn't you say there was an owl's face on the amulet? Isn't that what this is?"

He turned the marks up for Silver's inspection. Two circles with a vertical stroke, slightly curved, beneath: ᐃ. "Two eyes, with a beak in between?"

"Could be," Silver said. "The Smithsonian called it a property mark, but it does look like an owl, all right."

"A property mark?"

"Yeah. Like a brand. The old-time Eskimos used to scratch

out some kind of symbol on their harpoons before they learned to write. That way, if a weapon got stuck in a seal or a whale and turned up later, everybody would know who it belonged to. The whaling captains still do it today."

"Makes sense, I guess," Active said. "But why would Calvin use this thing to kill Victor Solomon? I can see him harpooning Malcolm Anirak, maybe. But this old guy?"

"Victor Solomon is, or was, chairman of the tribal council. You didn't know that?"

Active shook his head. "The attorney general has made it clear that we trooper types should steer clear of tribal politics."

Silver grunted in acknowledgment. "Wish somebody would give us city cops the same order. Anyway, Victor was the one who pushed the council to get Uncle Frosty and put him on display."

"And Calvin knew that?"

"You bet he did. Victor summoned our guys down to a council meeting last month to throw Calvin out, he was raising so much hell about it. And Victor was all over me to lock Calvin up for stealing Uncle Frosty. Threatened to go to the city council as soon as he got back from sheefishing if I didn't have Calvin behind bars."

"I better call in and have him picked up," Active said. "If he's still around. You got a radio along? I tried mine already. It won't reach."

Silver pulled a walkie-talkie from inside his parka, tried unsuccessfully to raise the dispatcher in Chukchi, and shook his head. "Too far."

"I got my cell phone," Darvin Reed said. He pulled it out, flipped it open like a communicator on *Star Trek*, and brought it over to Active.

Active looked at Silver. "I think all of our guys are in the field, except maybe Carnaby. Maybe your guys could go get Calvin."

Silver nodded and took the phone. "I wish the city would get me one of these." He turned his back to the west wind to dial, then worked the phone up into the side of his parka hood to talk.

While the chief told Lucy Generous, the dispatcher, to send two officers to Dolly Maiyumerak's house to bring Calvin in for questioning, Active looked again at the harpoon in his hand. It needed to be wrapped in something, in case the killer had left a fingerprint, but nothing in the evidence case strapped to the cargo rack at the back of Active's purple Yamaha was big enough.

"You bring any trash bags?" he asked Vera Jackson. She nodded and brought a roll from the *akhio*. Active wrapped the harpoon in two trash bags and laid it across the seat of his Yamaha.

"Should we put him in the sled now?" Vera asked.

Active nodded and went to Victor's shoulders while Vera took his feet. Victor lay on his back in a washtub-sized pit scooped out in the snow around the sheefishing hole in the ice, which Victor would have drilled with the gasoline-powered auger lying in the basket of his dogsled. They heaved together but Victor's shoulders wouldn't budge. Vera dropped Victor's feet and frowned.

"Looks like his parka froze in," Active said. "There was probably some water around the hole."

They knelt in the pit and worked the dead man out of his parka, then carried him to the *akhio*. Vera dropped to her knees to bag the body and strap it to the sled.

Active found an ax in the jockey box at the back of Victor's sled and used it to chop the parka out of the ice, finally exposing the round, six-inch hole through which Victor had done his sheefishing.

His fishing rig—a boomerang-shaped piece of driftwood, some monofilament line, and a silver jigging lure—still lay on the snow at the edge of the pit. Victor apparently hadn't been using it at the time of his death, as the line was wrapped around the driftwood and the lure was snagged into it by a barb of its treble hook.

Active knocked as much ice as he could off the parka, then rolled it up, stuffed it into a trash bag, and bungeed it and the harpoon onto the cargo rack of his Yamaha.

"All right if I take him to town now?" Vera asked.

Active nodded. "Put him in the morgue at the hospital till we can get him down to Anchorage for an autopsy."

Vera lifted her eyebrows, hit the starter on the paramedics' snowmachine, and drove off, swiveling her head to watch how the *akhio* was towing.

Silver returned Darvin Reed's cell phone, and listened as Active interviewed the two sheefishermen. They had found the body about two hours ago, they said, just before Darvin had called in, and the scene had been the same then as it was now. Except for the fact that other civilians had stopped by before Active arrived, leaving footprints and snowmachine tracks everywhere. Active could see no hope of getting a cast or a photograph of any of the killer's tracks.

Active looked at Silver. "You want to ask these guys anything?"

Silver shook his head.

"All right, you can go," Active told the sheefishermen.

"We never fish yet," Darvin said.

"Yeah, we spent all morning here with you," Willie said.

"So go drill yourselves a hole and fish."

Darvin pointed behind Active. "What about Victor's hole? Can we use it if you're done?"

Willie nodded in support. "Yeah, Victor always knew where the best holes were. Besides, we don't have an auger and this one's already drilled."

Active shook his head. "No, this hole is evidence. You stay away from it."

"What about them? Are they evidence, too?" Darvin pointed at a stack of frozen sheefish beside Victor's tent. "Maybe we could take them."

The fish were big, two or three feet long, Active estimated. He counted—there were nine, looking almost like fireplace logs, except for tails and the glazed eyes staring sightlessly over the ice. They were lightly dusted with snow and it was clear they had been there all night, untouched by the killer or anyone else.

"Victor got no family around here," Darvin said.

Active glared at Darvin for a moment, then walked over, broke the pile apart, and checked the sheefish for anything resembling evidence. "Yeah, OK, take them."

Darvin grinned as he and Willie began hauling the sheefish to the dogsleds behind their snowmachines.

Active glanced around the camp, then went into Victor's tent again. He had searched it soon after arriving. Now as then, nothing in it looked significant. A cot with some caribou hides and a sleeping bag, cooking gear, supplies, a rifle. Nothing disturbed, nothing obvious missing, no sign the place had been ransacked or robbed. He pulled the Nikon from inside his parka and fired off several shots with the flash, then went outside and photographed the sheefishing hole where Victor had fallen.

There wasn't much to go on. The only sign of himself the killer had left was the harpoon and the hole in Victor Solomon's chest. Active looked at Silver. "We better get back and talk to Calvin."

"What about this stuff?" Silver waved at Victor's camp.

Active frowned in perplexity, then looked at Darvin and Willie, who had divided up the sheefish and wrapped them in the blue tarps that, along with duct tape, made life possible in the Bush. They were now bungeeing the fish into the baskets of their sleds. "Hey, you two. I'm deputizing you. I want you to break up this camp and bring it to me at the troopers'."

Darvin frowned. "*Arii*, we never fish yet."

"All right, tonight, then. You can take it in when you're done fishing and bring it to me tomorrow at the troopers'. And don't mess with Victor's stuff. Just load it up and bring it in."

"*Arii*, it'll take too long to pack. We gotta go make our hole still." Darvin gazed at Active with an innocent air.

Active looked at the sheefishing hole. With Victor's body gone, it would freeze over soon. Already the west wind was brushing tendrils of snow into it, smoothing the jagged edges left when he had chopped Victor's parka out of the ice.

"All right, you can use Victor's hole." Active shook his head and tried not to think what his instructors at the trooper academy would say if they knew about the Arctic version of crime-scene management.

"It's not evidence?"

"Not anymore." Active swung his leg over the Yamaha and turned the key. Silver followed suit, and they headed for Chukchi.

CHAPTER FIVE

SILVER MADE IT TO the village first and was already hurrying out of the Public Safety Building when Active pulled the purple Yamaha up in front.

"No Calvin," Silver said as Active turned the key and the snowmachine coughed itself into silence. "His grandmother told my guys he's out hunting caribou."

"Hmmph." Active pulled off his sunglasses and stowed them in a shirt pocket. "Since when?"

"Since early this morning."

"Hmph."

"Yeah."

"Let's go talk to her."

"Yeah."

Active unlocked the trooper Suburban nosed up to the Public Safety Building, reached in, and started it. While the elderly rig warmed up, he put Uncle Frosty's harpoon and Victor Solomon's parka on the floorboards behind the driver's seat. Then he took off his own parka and tossed it on the front seat. Then he took off the Refrigiwear overalls and tossed them on the backseat. Then he put the parka back on and saw Silver watching the performance.

"You ever notice," Active asked, "how even the simplest thing gets complicated in the Arctic?"

"Goes with," Silver said as he climbed in the Suburban's

passenger door. "You're so busy taking care of the little shit, you never have time to worry about the big shit."

"You get used to it after a while?" Active slid behind the wheel, slammed the door, and turned on the heater. The engine was still too cold to provide any warmth, but the blower did produce a loud squeal.

"Resigned is more like it," Silver bellowed over the noise. "You should have plugged in the engine heater." He pointed at a row of electric sockets set along the side of the Public Safety Building.

"The troopers are conserving energy this week," Active said.

SILVER DIRECTED him to Dolly Maiyumerak's place, a tiny house with dark green tar paper on the walls and roof. A pony-sized husky emerged from a snow-covered oil drum with one end sawed off, and rumbled deep in his throat as they got out of the Suburban. The limit of his chain was marked by a circular archipelago of yellow stains cobbled with brown droppings on the hard-packed snow.

"That Kobuk?" Active asked.

Silver nodded. "Mackenzie River husky. They're about half wolf."

Active looked at the gigantic husky. There were a few bone splinters on the hardpack around his barrel. They could have been anything from chicken to seal to caribou. Or dog. "I can see how feeding him could get to be a problem."

Silver chuckled and they started for the house. Kobuk's rumble escalated to a snarl and he lunged toward them, stopping dead just before the chain jerked him up. Up close, Active could see that Kobuk had a lot of silver-gray fur, and yellow wolf eyes.

"Thank God that chain's not any longer," Silver shouted over Kobuk's roar.

They skirted the husky's circle and went in through the *kunnichuk*. Active knocked on the inner door.

There was a stir inside, a pause, and then the door creaked open a few inches and an old woman with a cigarette and a hearing aid glared out at them. She swung her gaze from Silver to Active and then back to Silver, to whom she nodded curtly. "I tell them other guys already, Calvin's not here. You could come back later."

Active flipped back his parka hood, introduced himself, and put out his hand. The old woman took it with great reluctance, and no pressure. It was like shaking a glove full of loose bones.

"You're that Eskimo trooper, ah?"

He nodded and lifted his eyebrows, hoping the Eskimo yes would get him a few points with Dolly Maiyumerak.

"You're just like *naluaqmiu* trooper, that's what I hear." The glare deepened.

"Can we come in, Mrs. Maiyumerak?" Active asked. "So we could ask you a few questions?"

"I told you, I already talk to them other guys."

"It won't take long. Can we come in?"

The old woman was silent a long time. Then, "You could ask 'em out here."

Active pulled his hood up. It was cold in the *kunnichuk*. Their breaths made plumes in the air. "Calvin went hunting this morning, you said?"

The woman lifted her eyebrows.

"And when did he leave?"

"I don't know, seven-thirty maybe. 'Mukluk Messenger' is on Kay-Chuck when he's leaving, I think."

"Do you know where he went?"

She shrugged. "Wherever them caribous are, I guess. I tell him we need some meats, he just say he'll get some caribous. He never say where he go."

"What about last night? Did you see him last night?"

"Why you ask all these questions? He already tell them other cops he never take that Uncle Frosty."

Apparently she hadn't heard about Victor Solomon's murder. Active glanced at Silver, who gave the tiniest of nods. Active calculated for a moment, then concluded there was little reason to conceal the already too-public details of the murder.

"This isn't about the burglary. Last night Victor Solomon was killed with a harpoon that was stolen along with Uncle Frosty."

He watched as Dolly Maiyumerak's frown vanished, her face locked into a mask of inscrutability, and she gazed silently out the window of the *kunnichuk*. Active had seen the mask before. It appeared when an Eskimo confronted a *naluaqmiu* who asked too many questions.

"Mrs. Maiyumerak?"

She took a deep drag on her cigarette, exhaled, took another, swung her gaze to the two men and spoke, her words wreathed in smoke. "My grandson's home all day yesterday till maybe five or six in the afternoon. Then he's over to his girlfriend's till after I go to bed. I guess I hear him come in little bit after midnight maybe, then he get up around six-thirty to go hunting. He never kill Victor Solomon."

Silver spoke now. "It's common knowledge they didn't get along, Dolly. Victor always called your grandson *anaq*."

She squinted in negation. "Maybe Victor need killing then. But Calvin never do it."

"Who's his girlfriend?"

"That Queenie. What's her last name?" The old woman looked at Silver. "You know, she call bingo at the Lions Club?"

"Buckland? Queenie Buckland?"

The old woman lifted her eyebrows.

"Could we come in and look through your grandson's room?" Active asked.

She looked at Silver and rolled her eyes. Active turned in time to see that Silver was doing the same.

She opened the door wide and gestured at the interior of the house. It was a single room, and not a very big one at that. One corner was closed off with a curtain that concealed, judging from the smell, a honey bucket. Otherwise, the space was undivided.

"That's my room over there." Dolly pointed at a single bed against one wall. "And that's Calvin's room." Now she pointed with a shiny, smoke-yellowed finger at a sofa against another wall. "And this my kitchen." She pointed at a two-burner camp stove sitting on a scarred plywood counter under some equally scarred plywood cabinets. "You done looking now?"

Active thought for a while about what to say. "I'm sorry for your trouble" came to mind but didn't quite seem to fit.

"Thank you. Will you call us when your grandson gets home?" He handed her a business card.

She squinted a no and pushed it away. "I'll tell him to call you if he want to."

Active put the card in his pocket, and followed Silver out of the *kunnichuk*. "Your guys talk to the girlfriend already?" Active asked when they were back in the Suburban.

Silver shook his head. "Just Dolly. Queenie's virgin territory, so to speak."

THEY FOUND Queenie Buckland stocking the Pepsi machine at the Lions Club bingo hall in preparation for that night's game. She was tall, fat, and broad-shouldered, like a linebacker with breasts. A heavy jaw gave her face a certain menacing gravity, redeemed only by laughing eyes. She wore sneakers, jeans, and a T-shirt that said IF YOU LIKE MY HEADLIGHTS YOU'LL LOVE MY BUMPER. Like Maiyumerak, she had a tooth missing in front, and Active found himself wondering how it affected their kissing.

When they asked if she had seen her boyfriend the day before, her answer matched Dolly Maiyumerak's account: Calvin had shown up around six with a sheefish and she cooked it for dinner.

"How long did he stay?" Active asked.

Queenie popped a Pepsi and took a swallow. "Let's see, seem like we watch that Millionaire program, then we you-know couple hours, then he go home around midnight, maybe one o'clock."

"You-know?" Active asked.

"Uh-huh." She lifted her eyebrows and smiled a big smile that showed them the gap where her tooth had been. "You know. *Quiyuk*."

"A couple of hours of *quiyuk*," Silver said when they got to the Suburban. "You wouldn't think it, the scrawny little shit."

Active grunted. "You believe her?"

"About the two hours?"

"About the rest of it."

Silver shrugged. "She could be lying for him. Just like Dolly could."

Active turned it over in his mind, thinking of Victor Solomon dead on the ice, of Calvin Maiyumerak's rusty snowmachine and ramshackle dogsled, and the one-room home of Dolly Maiyumerak. "What's the deal with Dolly and Calvin anyway? Why do they live like that? Where are his parents?"

"They live out in Ebrulik. I guess when Dolly got too old to take care of herself, Calvin's dad, Dolly's son, sent him down here to live with her. Apparently Calvin's mother can't stand the old lady so she couldn't move up to Ebrulik. You know how it is with mothers-in-law and daughters-in-law."

"I've heard."

"But Calvin's basically feral," Silver said. "He likes to live the old way as much as he can, won't take a regular job. Except for this business about Inupiat sovereignty, I don't think he has much idea what goes on in the outside world. He traps in the winter and commercial fishes in the summer. Dolly gets some social security and some welfare and sews the mittens and ruffs from whatever it is he catches, and they get by. Somehow."

Active started the Suburban and headed for the Public Safety Building. "If you could call it that."

Silver nodded. "Tough life. They're tough people, I guess."

"Tough enough to kill Victor Solomon?"

Silver was silent, thinking it over. "Yeah, I believe so. I think Calvin just plain hated old Victor. And, you know, there's the talk about him killing dogs with his bare hands." Silver shook his head.

"Victor used to call him *anaq*, huh?" *Anaq* was included in Active's limited but growing vocabulary of Inupiaq words. It meant shit. "To his face?"

Silver nodded. "And in public. Like when Victor had us throw Calvin out of that tribal council meeting. 'Haul away this piece of *anaq* before I throw it in a honey bucket' is what Victor said when we showed up."

"Well, that's pure Eskimo."

Silver nodded. "Plus, Calvin probably figured Victor would go out and find Uncle Frosty on the tundra and bring him back and then work out some way to get Calvin thrown in jail for the burglary. He had to know it wouldn't end as long as Victor was alive."

Active thought it over as the Suburban rolled smoothly up

Third Street, the only paved road in Chukchi. "I have to find Calvin," he said finally.

"Yeah," Silver said. "I guess you do."

"So, that's about it," Active said an hour later as he finished his briefing, closed his notebook, and looked up at Captain Patrick Carnaby, commander of the Chukchi detachment of the Alaska State Troopers. "We obviously have to find Calvin."

"Obviously." Carnaby chewed his lower lip for a moment. "Calvin Maiyumerak, huh?"

"You know him?"

"A little. Seen him around town, heard him ranting on the radio about Inupiat sovereignty . . . kind of a hothead, I guess."

"There was definitely that bad blood between him and Victor," Active said. "Nobody likes being called *anaq* all the time."

"Yeah, I guess old Victor could be a real son of a bitch." Carnaby nodded, seeming lost in thought.

"And Silver says Calvin kills dogs with his bare hands, so that old Dolly can sew them into ruffs and mittens for the tourists."

"Really?" Carnaby said. "Who'd a thunk it? So how you gonna find Calvin?"

"I guess I don't see any point in going after him."

"Oh?" Carnaby lifted his eyebrows in the white expression of inquiry.

Active shook his head. "There's two possibilities. One, he's out hunting caribou, like Dolly says, even though she professes not to know where. If that's true, he'll come back on his own."

Carnaby nodded. "And?"

"And possibility two is, he's not hunting caribou, he's running."

Carnaby nodded again, and grinned. "And where's he going to go?"

Now Active nodded. "Exactly. I think he only has three real choices, all bad. A, he can hide out on the tundra, but eventually he'll run out of supplies and have to come into a village, or maybe somebody will just run into him out there."

Active pointed at a map of Alaska on the wall behind Carnaby's desk. "B, maybe he can make it on that wreck of a snowmachine to someplace where he can catch a plane, but we'll be waiting."

Another nod from Carnaby.

"Or, C, he can hide out with a friend or relative in one of the villages, maybe Ebrulik, where his parents live."

Carnaby grinned again. "In which case it'll be all over town in about five minutes."

"So we wait," Active said. "We watch Dolly's house here. I already put the word out to the airlines, the public safety officers in our villages, and to the troopers and city cops in Nome, Barrow, Kotzebue, Fairbanks, and Galena. And I put a message on Kay-Chuck saying the troopers need to contact Calvin Maiyumerak and anybody encountering him should let us know. He's bound to turn up."

"Sounds right." Carnaby's grin was bigger than ever. "Low-impact police work. Low impact on our travel budget, low impact on the manpower situation in this office."

Active grinned, too, at how cheap Carnaby was. Still, the Republicans in the legislature were always pounding on state agencies to do less with more, and Carnaby seemed to find ways to put life into the vapid political cliché. "Plus which, Chukchi P.D. is carrying part of the load on this one because of the museum burglary," Active said, to make Carnaby feel even better.

"What about the harpoon?" Carnaby said. "Any fingerprints there?"

"Didn't check yet. You want to?"

Carnaby nodded, grinning in enthusiasm. He was known to the officers beneath him—and those above—as the Super Trooper. That wasn't just because, at six-two, square-jawed and broad-shouldered, he was a walking recruitment poster. It was also because he had some kind of ESP about cases and could normally juggle intradepartment politics with his left hand while juggling local politics with his right.

Besides which, he was a fingerprint expert. Not just an expert, but an enthusiast also, who wrote papers about cold-weather fingerprinting for law-enforcement journals.

Active went to his office and brought the harpoon to Carnaby. "I'll let you know in a couple of hours," the captain said.

Active trotted downstairs and stopped at Dispatch to see if he and Lucy Generous were still on for lunch.

They were, she told him with a huge smile, so they drove to the Arctic Dragon in the trooper Suburban.

After they ordered—Szechuan beef for him, teriyaki salmon for her—he sketched the Victor Solomon murder for her. That was one of the advantages of having a dispatcher for a girlfriend. You could discuss cases with her. Plus, Lucy was a lifelong resident of Chukchi. She normally knew more about a breaking case than most of the cops in town, including himself.

"Do you know either of them?" he asked when he was finished. He dipped a spoonful of the Arctic Dragon's miso soup and waited for her reaction.

She frowned for a moment, then squinted a no. "Not really.

Victor lived alone and didn't have many friends that I ever heard of, except maybe a few at church. I think maybe he was too mean to have friends. And Calvin only moved down here from Ebrulik a couple years ago. I don't think I ever met him."

She giggled, covering her mouth in that way she had, her loveliness momentarily distracting him from what she was saying. "But I did dispatch on him a couple times. Like when he put the seal oil in the tour buses. *Aqaa!*"

Active refocused and grinned. That was another word in his small but growing vocabulary of Inupiaq. It meant "Stinky!"

"So Victor went to church?" he asked.

She nodded. "All the time, pretty much. He was Catholic, a parish deacon, I think."

Active frowned. "Hmph."

"What?"

"I'm surprised to hear he was so churchy."

"Why?"

"He sounds a little un-Christian. Had no friends, always called Calvin *anaq*."

"Is that why Calvin killed him?"

"I don't know. Maybe. Do you think your grandmother knew him?"

"Aana Pauline? I don't know, she goes to the Friends Church and they don't mix with the Catholics too much. But I could ask."

He lifted his eyebrows and they moved on to a discussion of that night's dinner.

She would be in class at the community college when he got home from work, but she would leave something in the oven for him. Pauline had traded some mittens she made for half a caribou and the roast was from that. It would still be hot when he got there, and he could eat that, but he had to promise to eat some salad with it. He bobbed along pleasantly on the flow of her chatter, then lifted his eyebrows again when she was done.

As always, he felt slightly guilty about the marriage-like state they shared. He was getting what a man normally got out of marriage—sex, food, and laundry. But she was not getting what a woman normally got: commitment, children, and financial support.

He gazed out the Dragon's picture window, which over-looked Beach Street and Chukchi Bay. Under the bright, hazy sky and a dim red eye of sun, the west wind was still rolling in. It must have picked up a little—now it was sweeping before it a thin layer of snow that undulated over the sea ice like fog.

It was not exactly the imbalance in the relationship that made him feel guilty, he thought as he watched the snow ripple toward them. It was his knowledge that she disliked this imbalance, but was too uncertain of his affection to challenge it.

"What?" she was saying when he came around to the conversation again.

"Nothing. I very much enjoy your company, is all."

"And I love you," she said.

He had no comeback to this, so he smiled and busied himself with his Szechuan beef. Lucy lowered her eyes and concentrated on the last bites of her salad, then started on the salmon.

CHAPTER SIX

"IT'S JIM SILVER."

Active struggled to swim up from his recurring bullet dream and take the phone he sensed had trilled a few seconds earlier. But he drifted down into it again, jerking the trigger of the useless gun pointed at the shadowed figure coming at him with a butcher knife. The knife was hard to see this time, though. Perhaps it was something else, a—

Lucy Generous poked him in the shoulder with the stubby antenna of the cordless. "Wake up. It's Jim Silver."

He started, awake at last, and rolled onto an elbow to take the phone. "Yeah, this is Nathan." He was panting as usual from the bullet dream and Silver picked it up over the phone.

"Hope I'm not interrupting anything," the chief said.

Active got his breathing under control, then forced out a chuckle that he hoped sounded lewd enough to confirm Silver's mistaken guess. "Nothing that won't keep," he said. "What's up?"

"One of my officers just called in," Silver said. "He cruised past Dolly Maiyumerak's house a minute ago and Calvin's snowmachine was parked in front."

Active cleared his throat and walked into the bathroom as he spoke. "Your guy talk to him?"

"No, he called in for instructions."

Active filled a glass under the faucet and took two quick swallows. "Anything going on inside the place?"

"Doesn't look like it. The lights are all out."

"OK, I'll get right over there," Active said. "Ask the officer to wait and keep an eye on things, will you?"

"Maybe I'll cruise on over there myself."

"Sure," Active said. "You know Calvin already."

He clicked off the phone, stepped out of the bathroom, and looked at Lucy, who was staring at him with the familiar mixture of reproach and anxiety. He looked away.

"It was the bullet dream, wasn't it? And you'll go see Nelda Qivits again."

He was silent. These charges no longer required a plea.

"Do you want to talk about it?" Her voice was soft now, caring rather than challenging.

"I just can't. You know that."

"Well, have fun then! God knows we haven't been having much of that in this bed lately!" She rolled onto her right side and pulled the quilt up until it just covered her left ear, which was how she slept.

He stood frozen, not wanting to leave it like this but unable to think of a way out. Maybe a joke.

"You're not worried Calvin Maiyumerak might harpoon me?"

"Don't change the subject."

Active shook his head and returned to the bathroom to rinse his face in the bathroom sink, inspected the result, and decided the image of the troopers would not be tarnished beyond repair if he didn't shave today, as it was a Saturday.

He went out to the kitchen of the trooper bachelor cabin and tried to think of a breakfast that wouldn't take long to make or eat. Since Lucy had moved in more or less full-time a few months ago, he had lost what little knack he ever had for food preparation. Lucy bought the groceries and cooked them, and only she could cook what she bought. Her groceries were too complicated for him—they had to be mixed, blanched, blended, basted, battered, marinated, and subjected to other procedures he couldn't name—which was probably why they were delicious when she cooked them.

He rummaged in the refrigerator and came up with a slice of caribou roast from the night before. He put it on a pilot bread cracker, poured ketchup on top, and thought about coffee.

There were grounds in the freezer compartment of the refrigerator, he knew, and a gleaming black-and-chrome Mr. Coffee on the counter by the microwave. But it seemed like too much business for so early in the day.

Then he remembered that he had not emptied and washed the Mr. Coffee from yesterday morning. He shook the urn and heard the blessed sound of sloshing. He poured a cup, set it in the microwave, punched in ninety seconds, and hit the start button. He hoped, as he recalled that he hadn't closed the bedroom door, that the sound of the microwave's fan wouldn't wake Lucy.

"That's not yesterday's coffee, is it?"

Well, at least she was letting go of the bullet-dream thing and willing to argue about something normal. He looked through the glass of the microwave door at the cup, which was sending up the first tendrils of steam. "No, I'm just heating up some of that leftover caribou." He held his breath to see if her truth radar had kicked in yet. When she hadn't answered after fifteen seconds, he released the breath.

When the ninety seconds were up, he wolfed down the pilot cracker and caribou, went outside, set the coffee in the Suburban's cup holder, and started the rig. Then he unplugged the cord for the Suburban's engine heater from the electric socket under the light outside his *kunnichuk*, coiled the cord, and looped it around the radio antenna. When he got in and turned on the blower, it produced a little heat and no squeal, making him glad the Trooper energy-conservation program didn't extend to living quarters.

It was a little after seven, the haze gone, the west wind gone, the new day coming on clear and sharp as broken ice. The sun was just above the eastern horizon and throwing shafts of yellow and blue over the village as he drove to Dolly Maiyumerak's cottage. Silver was there in his Bronco, stopped driver-to-driver beside a green-and-white Chukchi Police Department pickup.

Both men had their windows down and were talking as Active pulled the Suburban over and parked on the side of the street. He walked to Silver's Bronco, opened the passenger door, and leaned in. "I see the lights are on now. Any other sign of life?"

Silver nodded and looked at his watch. "Dolly looked out the front window beside the *kunnichuk* there and waved at us four minutes ago. That's it so far."

"You been up to the door?"

Silver shook his head.

Active studied the scene. Maiyumerak's snowmachine was parked to the right of the *kunnichuk*, just outside the circle marking the radius of Kobuk's chain. The sled, Active saw, was empty, with no sign of blood or hair in the basket. "Look at that," he said. "No caribou."

"Nope," Silver said. "Guess the hunting wasn't so hot."

"Guess not," Active said.

Kobuk sat on top of his oil-drum house, watching the three visitors without much interest. Active surmised that Silver and his officer had been there so long without doing anything that Kobuk had become bored.

"I guess we should go in," Silver said.

"We could," Active said.

"Or?"

"Or we could call Dispatch on the radio, and get them to call Dolly on the telephone, and ask if Calvin would like to come out and talk to us."

Silver grimaced and said nothing.

"Seeing as how Dolly already knows we're here and all," Active said, twisting the knife a little because of the ladies' model thing.

Silver said, "Good idea," keyed the microphone in the Bronco, and gave the instructions to the dispatcher. A couple of minutes later, the radio crackled back to life. "Dolly says Calvin is having his morning coffee and you guys can come in and have some with him. She'll come to the door."

Active looked at Silver, who rolled his eyes and picked up the mike. "Roger."

Silver nodded toward the cop in the pickup. "Nathan, you know Alan Long here?"

Long was Inupiat, about the same age as Active, round faced and bucktoothed with a little too much enthusiasm. He was, Active recalled vaguely, an army veteran who had served with the military police and was mildly obnoxious. Active nodded and said, "Hey, Alan."

"Active," Alan said with a nod of his own.

Now Active remembered what it was that made Alan Long obnoxious. In a town where everyone who knew him even slightly called him "Nathan," Long called him "Active."

Active pulled his head and shoulders out of the Bronco and Silver drove it ahead far enough to park behind Long's pickup. The chief stepped out onto the late-winter hardpack, as did Long, and they gathered by the tailgate of the pickup.

Active saw curtain movement in a window and then Dolly Maiyumerak's eyes on them as he unsnapped the hammer strap of his holster and tucked it out of the way of the Smith &

Wesson. Silver eased his own pistol up an inch, then reseated it in the holster.

"Alan, you got your shotgun in the truck there?" Silver asked.

Long nodded, went to the passenger door of the pickup, and returned with a short-barreled pump.

"Buckshot?" Silver asked.

Long raised his eyebrows and said, "Double-aught." He worked the pump and a load snicked into the firing chamber. "I got your back, Chief."

Silver glanced furtively at Active with a grimace.

"Maybe he could go watch the rear door," Active said. "In that *kunnichuk*, three of us won't be any better than two."

"Good point," Silver said.

Long said, "Roger that, Chief," in a disappointed tone and trotted to a rear corner of the cottage, where he could see the back door and still have a little cover.

Silver looked at Active and grimaced again. "I gotta find that kid a woman. He watches too many videos."

Active grinned, said, "Roger that," and pointed at the sled hitched to Maiyumerak's snowmachine. The butt of a rifle stuck out of a scabbard lashed to a rail. "You think we're overengineering this?"

"Doesn't hurt to be careful," Silver said. His parka was unzipped and Active noticed for the first time the bulk of body armor under the police chief's shirt.

Active lifted his eyebrows in the universal expression for "I'm impressed," Silver shrugged, looking a little sheepish.

They walked into the *kunnichuk*, Active wondering if he should have worn a vest, too. Then he noticed a long-barreled shotgun leaning against a shadowed corner of the *kunnichuk* and relaxed slightly, though he said nothing to Silver.

A large chest-type freezer filled most of Dolly Maiyumerak's *kunnichuk*. The inner door to her house was left of the freezer, and there was room for only one person to stand between the freezer and the end wall of the *kunnichuk* to knock on the door.

"I could knock," Silver said. "I've got the vest."

Active shook his head, thinking of the shotgun in the corner and the rifle outside on the sled. "It's a trooper case," he said. "And Kevlar probably wouldn't stop a harpoon, anyway."

He stepped up, knocked, and stepped back, Silver standing behind and to his right in front of the freezer. Active didn't quite put his hand on the Smith & Wesson, but he did flip back his parka and hook both thumbs on his belt so that his right hand was near the pistol.

He heard Dolly's voice saying, "Look like they finally got up their nerves," then something unintelligible in a male voice, then steps coming toward them and then he couldn't help it, his fingers crept down over the grip of the Smith & Wesson as Dolly opened the door and glared out at them.

She took in the scene, shook her head, and swung the door wide open, disclosing Calvin in his underwear at a small and battered folding table, a coffee cup and cigarette before him. He took a puff and flashed his gap-toothed grin. "I'm just having a last smoke before you shoot me."

Trying not to be obvious, Active removed his hands from his belt and let his parka swing back into place over the Smith & Wesson. He heard a little stir from behind him as Silver did something similar.

"You could sit down," Dolly said.

They sat on folding chairs at the card table and she brought them coffee while Calvin smoked away and said nothing. He looked almost as if he were enjoying himself. "What about that other guy?" he said finally.

"What other guy?" Active said.

"The one that go around behind."

Silver shook his head. "Shit. Alan. I'll send him back." He stood up and headed for the door. Dolly hobbled to the single bed against the wall, sat down with her legs sticking straight out, and pulled a red thigh-length down parka across her lap. A wolf ruff was partly attached to the hood, and Dolly took up sewing it where she had presumably left off when they knocked.

Active, wondering if the ruff was really wolf, pulled out a notebook and looked at Calvin. "Your grandmother told you why we're here?"

"She say you think I kill Victor Solomon."

"Do you want a lawyer?"

"I never kill nobody and I never need no lawyer."

Silver returned from the *kunnichuk* and took his seat again as Active was asking Calvin what he had been doing the night Victor was killed. Calvin's sketch matched the accounts they had had from Dolly and Queenie. It matched right down to the two hours of *quiyuk* with Queenie of the headlights and bumper, which brought a smile to the lips of Dolly Maiyumerak, who was watching them from the bed.

"Your sled's empty," Active said.

Maiyumerak shrugged.

"Some people tell me you're a good hunter. But you didn't get any caribou."

"I never find the herd. That doesn't mean I'm bad hunter. Or that I kill anybody."

Active cocked his head at Maiyumerak. "Who else could it be? Someone got thrown out of Victor's meeting. Victor called someone *anaq* and threatened to throw him in a honey bucket. Who else would want to rob the museum and kill Victor?"

This brought a loud grunt of disgust from the bed, but only another gap-toothed grin from Calvin. "You want to know who do it?"

Nobody said anything, but Active lifted his eyebrows. Dolly Maiyumerak growled from the bed and rattled off something in machine-gun Inupiaq that went completely past Active. She was looking at Calvin, but Active thought she was watching him and Silver, too.

Calvin looked at her and said something soft in Inupiaq. The only word Active caught was *aana*. Dolly growled another unintelligible snatch of Inupiaq, and resumed work on the parka.

Calvin turned back to Silver and Active. "Uncle Frosty do it, that's what I think. I think Uncle Frosty's made cold by the universe and he break out of the museum, then he hang around and kill Victor Solomon because Victor want to put him in that display case for the *naluaqmiut* tourists to see." He nodded as if that explained everything.

Silver snorted. "Let's quit wasting time, Calvin. What would you say if I said we have a witness who saw your snowmachine at Victor's sheefish camp the night he was killed?"

"That's not—" Maiyumerak stopped talking and a slow grin dawned on his face. "You got that witness?"

"I didn't say that," Silver said. "I asked what you would say if I did say it."

Maiyumerak looked into his coffee cup. "If you said that to me, I would say somebody is full of *anaq*."

Silver, his hoary policeman's bluff called, flushed but said nothing.

"What was that about Uncle Frosty being cold?" Active said. "Is that—"

"It's just more of his bullshit," Silver said. "Superstition from the old days."

Calvin balanced his cigarette on the rim of his coffee cup. "You *naluaqmiut* are pretty smart. Invent snowmachines, rifles, outboard motor, cigarettes. Even *naluaqmiiyaaqs* like Nathan here, I guess. But maybe you don't know everything." He looked straight at Active.

Superstition or bullshit, it was the first piece of information, or misinformation, Calvin had volunteered. "I'd like to hear about it," Active said. "We *naluaqmiiyaaqs* have to learn all we can."

There was a loud growl now from Dolly on the bed and Calvin grinned again. It was impossible to tell if it signalled approval of Active's interest, or satisfaction at the bite from this fish, this gullible *naluaqmiiyaaq*.

"Sometimes if somebody die and they're not treated right, they don't go on to the next world," Calvin said. "They're made cold by the universe, that's what them old Eskimos call it. Their ears get so good, they can hear rabbits and foxes running in the brush. They can't feel the cold and their bodies get so light they can walk on top of the trees and jump across a river without getting wet."

Active watched Dolly as Calvin talked. Her eyes were on the ruff in her hands, but the hands weren't doing anything and her body language said she was listening closely to their conversation.

Calvin's hands floated up to illustrate the treetop walking and river jumping, and he uttered a long Inupiaq phrase, then nodded to himself. "Made cold by the universe is what they call it."

"And that's what happened to Uncle Frosty?"

Calvin nodded again.

"And now that he's killed Victor Solomon, now what?"

"Now maybe he'll lie down on tundra, die regular way, never bother anybody no more."

Active thought it over, watching as Dolly seemed to relax. Her polished old fingers pushed the awl through the ruff and she bent to study her seam.

Active stood up. "Chief Silver and I have to go talk in the *kunnichuk*," he said. He waved Silver toward the door as Dolly and Calvin exchanged puzzled looks.

CHAPTER SEVEN

"THIS FEEL RIGHT TO you?" Active asked when they were in the storm shed, with the door into the house closed.

Silver shrugged. "Pretty much, I guess. He and Dolly and Queenie all tell the same story about what he was doing Thursday night and Friday morning."

Active nodded. "Yeah, that part of it feels right. But— remember when Calvin started to talk about Uncle Frosty being made cold by the universe? Dolly yelled at him in Inupiaq, then he said something back and she calmed down, then he told us about Uncle Frosty walking on the treetops and killing Victor Solomon."

Silver nodded.

"You catch any of that? Their Inupiaq was too fast for me."

Silver squinted, thinking. "Not much of it. They were too fast for me, too. I think she was telling him not to play around, and he said not to worry, let us *pukuk* all we want, he can handle us."

"*Pukuk?*"

"Yeah, it means to poke around, get into everything. Like a little kid or a mouse or a weasel."

Active pursed his lips. "Let's split them up. You read Calvin his Miranda rights and haul him out. I'll stay here and talk to Dolly."

"We don't have enough to arrest him. The public defenders'll have him out in thirty minutes."

"You're not arresting him. You're just taking him out to your truck while I talk to Dolly."

Silver looked doubtful, then grinned and nodded. "It's your case, pal. Should I ask him what she said to him in there?"

Active thought it over. "No, let me question them both. Easier to compare stories that way."

Silver nodded and they went back into the house. Calvin was dressed now, in brown corduroy trousers and a faded green sweatshirt with a hood, zipper, and Nike swoosh. Dolly was still on the bed with her parka and ruff. Silver told Calvin to stand up and that he was being taken into custody in connection with the murder of Victor Solomon.

Dolly scooted off the bed and shuffled over to put a protective hand on Calvin's elbow. "He never kill nobody. You leave 'im alone."

"You need to back away from Calvin, Mrs. Maiyumerak," Active said. He stepped between them and suddenly Calvin was surrounded by the two officers.

"I tell you I never stick nobody with no harpoon," Calvin said as Silver reeled off the Miranda warning. "This is another violation of the Charter on the Rights of Indigenous Peoples."

Silver rolled his eyes and pulled a pair of handcuffs from his belt. "Am I going to need these?"

Calvin looked defiant for a moment, then frightened, then shook his head rapidly as he squinted no.

"Let's go then." Silver put his hand in the middle of Calvin's back and headed him toward the door. They passed into the *kunnichuk* and a moment later Active heard the outer door slam. He turned to Dolly Maiyumerak.

She had gone back to her bed, but she wasn't working on the parka. She sat on the edge, back rigid and straight, hands in her lap.

Active walked over and stood before her. "Your grandson could be in serious trouble, Mrs. Maiyumerak."

She pushed her lips out in a stubborn set but there was fright in her eyes. "He's good boy, just little bit crazy from dreaming about old days when there's no *naluaqmiut* around. He never kill nobody. He just take care of me, that's all he do. "

Active, feeling thoroughly ashamed now, sat down beside her. "You may have to go back to Ebrulik and stay with your son and his wife."

Dolly flinched. "I tell Calvin not to fool around with you guys. But he always think he's so smart. Now you're gonna put him in your jail and a-huh, a-huh . . ."

Active waited for the sobs to subside, then patted the old lady's shoulder. "Unless there's something that you could tell us that would help us find the real killer. If it's not your grandson."

Dolly put on the Eskimo mask again and Active let the inscrutability ride for a while. Then he made a show of standing up and zipping his parka. "Will you be all right here by yourself if your grandson is gone for a while? Could I take you someplace?"

The mask vanished and Dolly became a fearful old woman glaring at him out of red-rimmed black eyes. "Calvin tell me, 'Never say nothing, Aana.'"

Active sat beside her again. "Does Calvin want you to move back to Ebrulik?"

Dolly sighed, wiped her eyes on the hem of the red parka, and shot Active another fearful glance. "Somebody come to see Calvin, talk about somebody stealing Uncle Frosty from museum."

"You mean Jim Silver's men? The city police?"

"No, not them."

"Well, who?"

"You could ask Calvin."

"Maybe he won't tell us."

"Whyborn Sivula."

"Who?"

"Whyborn Sivula."

It was the oddest name Active had ever heard. He was sure it was the first time it had been uttered in his presence. "Whyborn Sivula came to see your grandson?"

Dolly lifted her eyebrows.

"Who's Whyborn Sivula?"

"Old man."

"From here?"

She lifted her eyebrows again.

"When was this?"

She was silent, thinking. "Wednesday afternoon, maybe."

Active counted back to Uncle Frosty's arrival and was about to say the burglary hadn't happened yet on Wednesday, when Dolly said, "No, Thursday. Whyborn come on Thursday. Thursday afternoon."

That fit. Uncle Frosty had disappeared from the museum Wednesday night or in the early hours of Thursday morning. The story was on Kay-Chuck by noon Thursday. "What did Whyborn say about the burglary?"

Dolly shrugged. "He go in *kunnichuk* with Calvin, like that Jim Silver now. I never hear what they say."

"Did Calvin tell you about it afterward?"

"He say Whyborn want to ask him did he take Uncle Frosty? He tell Whyborn he never do it, then Whyborn leave."

"Why was Whyborn interested in Uncle Frosty?"

"I don't know. My grandson never tell me anything else."

Active pulled out his notebook and wrote down Whyborn Sivula's name. "Thank you, Mrs. Maiyumerak."

She peered up at him, eyes narrowed in anxiety. "Will my grandson come back today? He never feed that Kobuk yet."

"I'll do what I can for him." The old lady looked like she knew she was being bullshitted, but she didn't say anything. She turned her gaze away, stripped dental floss out of a plastic box, threaded it into her awl, and resumed work on the red parka.

Active left the house and walked to Silver's Bronco. A frond of steam hovered over the tailpipe as the engine idled in the cold air. Calvin was slumped against the passenger door and appeared to be asleep. Silver was leaning against the headrest, but his eyes were open.

He grinned and lowered the window as Active approached. "So, you break the old lady, hotshot?"

Active let it pass and glanced at Calvin, now stirring. "Let's go over to the Suburban for a minute."

Silver reached over and shook Calvin's shoulder. "I'm going to go talk to Nathan. You don't touch anything while I'm gone, OK?"

Calvin shook his head and looked groggy. "What?"

"Just go back to sleep."

Calvin leaned his head against the passenger window and closed his eyes again.

"He was out in the cold all night," Silver said. "He'll be all right."

Silver turned off the Bronco and took the key. They walked across the street to the Suburban and climbed in. Active started it, switched on the blower, and put his fingers over a vent to see if the engine still had any heat to give. It did, a little, so he let it idle.

"You know a Whyborn Sivula?"

"Sure. Used to work at Chukchi Electric, but he's retired now, got some kind of little pension, I guess. Hunts, fishes, traps, still runs a whaling crew, too, I think. Why?"

"He came to see Calvin the day after the museum burglary and asked him if he did it."

"No shit."

"That's what Dolly says. His name ever come up in the burglary investigation? He on the tribal council, too?"

Silver shook his head. "Nope, we never crossed his trail once. What did Calvin tell him?"

"He said he didn't do it, according to Dolly. Any idea where we could find Whyborn?"

Silver looked thoughtful and scratched his scalp. "Seems like I heard he put out his whaling camp already."

"Can you tell me how to get there?"

"Sure, it's up by Cape Goodwin. You just cross the bay here to—"

"Not now, tell me later when we can look at a map. Right now, let's ask Calvin what they talked about."

"Wait a minute," Silver said. "There's something else. Dolly say anything about a kid named Lemuel Bass?"

"Who?"

"Lemuel Bass."

Active shook his head. "Why?"

"While you were in with Dolly, Dispatch called to let me know that Lemuel showed up at Harriman's store and tried to swap an amulet for some Pokémon cards. Old Tim Harriman had a property list I circulated from the burglary, so I guess he called Dispatch as soon as he saw this amulet."

"Our amulet?"

"Mammoth ivory with an owl's face."

"The kid say where he got it?"

"Don't think so. Apparently he took off while Harriman was calling us."

"Who is he?"

"He comes from a family that lives in a camp up around the

mouth of the Katonak," Silver said. "Dad's white, Mom's Eskimo, five or six kids up there, I've lost track, plus possibly an aunt, uncle, or cousin or two at any given moment. Lemuel's about eight now, I'd say."

"Calvin overhear the call?"

Silver wagged his head. "I went over to your Suburban and took it."

"Let's see what Calvin knows," Active said.

The two men left the Suburban and crossed to the Bronco. Silver started to open the driver's door. But Active, seeing Calvin still asleep on the other side, held up a hand.

He walked around to the passenger side, grasped the handle, and yanked open the door. With a surprised "*Arii!*" Calvin fell into Active's arms.

Active lifted Calvin to his feet and stood close, so that the dog trapper was pushed back against the Bronco. Active put his nose almost to Calvin's, catching a rank whiff of sleep breath. "What did you tell Whyborn Sivula about the burglary?"

Calvin wiped a patch of drool off his chin. "What? Who?"

"Whyborn Sivula. What did you tell him about the burglary?"

"I never—"

Active moved closer and put his hand to his hip. Silver had come around the Bronco and was now standing beside Active, so that Calvin was hemmed in.

"I never do it, that's what I tell him." Calvin talked fast, like he was worried about what Active might pull from his hip.

Active moved back a half-step, pulled a handkerchief from his hip pocket, and handed it to Calvin. "You missed a spot." He pointed to Calvin's chin.

Calvin took the handkerchief and cleaned up the drool. He wadded up the handkerchief and offered it to Active.

"Keep it," Active said. "What else did you tell him?"

"Nothing, I never—"

"What did he tell you?"

"Nothing, he just want to know—"

Active moved up a half-pace and Calvin jerked his head back, thumping against the window of the Bronco.

"He say it's Eskimo business from early days ago, maybe over now."

"What?"

Calvin frowned. "He say it's Eskimo business from early days ago, maybe over now."

"The burglary was Eskimo business from early days ago?"

"That's what he say."

"What did he mean?"

"I don't know. He never tell me."

"Did you ask him?"

Calvin lifted his eyebrows.

"And?"

"He never tell me. He just say again, it's old-time Eskimo business, I should forget about it."

Active stepped back, a full pace this time. "And he said maybe it's over now?"

Calvin lifted his eyes again.

"What do you think he meant?"

Calvin shrugged and squinted.

Silver spoke for the first time. "Did he say anything about Uncle Frosty being made cold by the universe and breaking out of the museum himself?"

Calvin looked away and didn't say anything.

Silver grinned. "So you were just bullshitting us when you said that?"

Calvin still didn't speak.

Active gave Silver a look and they both stepped back.

"How did Lemuel Bass get that thing from the burglary?" Active asked.

"Who? Is that one of Johnny Bass's kids from up at the Katonak?" Calvin swung his eyes from one officer to the other and back again. "What thing he take? He's pretty little to be a burglar, ah?" Calvin looked genuinely mystified.

"You can go back in now," Active said. "Your grandmother will be happy to see you."

Calvin's face brightened. "You mean I'm not arrest for killing Victor?"

Active shrugged. "Not yet anyway."

Calvin started for the house, but turned back after a few steps to look at them. "If you guys never think it was me anymore, then who you think did it?"

Both men shrugged.

Calvin revealed the gap in his teeth. "I still think maybe Uncle Frosty could do it himself." He looked at Active, then Silver. "That's old-time Eskimo business, ah?"

Calvin turned and started for the house again. Silver and Active looked at each other, and Silver said, "Shit."

Active lifted his eyebrows and nodded.

CHAPTER EIGHT

HARRIMAN'S TRADING POST FRONTED on Beach Street. It was a long, narrow, low-roofed building of weathered gray clapboard, sagging into the permafrost with age.

Its proprietor, Tim Harriman, was the last of the old-time white traders, Silver said as they walked up to the door and stooped to enter. "Wife's dead, kids in Anchorage and Seattle, no reason to be here except he's got no place to go," Silver said. "Missed too many planes, I guess."

Harriman proved to be a tiny man with white hair, patches of frosted crabgrass for eyebrows, and diamond bristles on his cheeks and chin. He wore a red flannel shirt, rust-colored Carhartt jeans with suspenders, and reading glasses on a cord around his neck. He reached over to a television behind the counter and turned off CNN as they came in.

The walls and shelves were a wild jumble of clothes, boots, fishing gear, tents, stoves, nuts, bolts, ivory carvings, Eskimo masks, baleen baskets, boom boxes, CDs, rifles, shotguns, ammunition, candy, pop, snacks, and a few staples that didn't need refrigeration. The place smelled of old things, dank earth, raw furs, seal oil, and dried fish—the Bush.

"Tim, you know Nathan Active with the troopers?"

Harriman put out a liver-spotted hand and nodded vigorously. "I do now, Jim. Pleasure to meet you, Trooper Active."

Active took his hand and said, "Mr. Harriman."

"Tim, call me Tim, everybody does." Harriman pulled open a drawer and laid the amulet on the counter, along with the picture Silver had circulated to Chukchi's merchants. "I reckon this is what you came for. Knew it the minute I saw it."

Active and Silver bent to study the object. It was a shiny brown oval about the size of a cookie. An owl's face was carved on the side Harriman had turned up. Just above that, a small hole was bored through the piece.

Active glanced at the picture and back at the amulet. "That's it, all right."

Silver nodded.

"Tell us about Lemuel Bass," Active said.

Harriman looked at Silver. "I thought you were working the museum burglary, Jim."

"You hear about Victor Solomon?"

Harriman nodded. "Killed at his sheefish camp with a harpoon is what they said on Kay-Chuck." He tapped the picture, which showed Uncle Frosty's harpoon as well as the amulet. "This harpoon?"

"Uh-huh," Silver said.

"That would explain why the troopers are interested, I guess." Harriman gave a satisfied chuckle. Active supposed an old man might feel that way, pleased and reassured, when he found his wits still worked.

"Did the boy say how he got the amulet?" Active asked.

Harriman shook his head. "He just rode up on his snowgo and came in and said he wanted to trade it for Pokémon cards."

The trader waved at a glass case of the cards on the countertop. "Damned rubbish I have to sell now. It used to be that everybody in town would come in for whatever they forgot to order on the summer barge. 'If you can't find it at Harriman's, you're better off without it.' That was my motto. But now, well, there's Arctic Mercantile and air freight and . . . shit, we might as well be living in Anchorage."

He stopped and shook his head. "You know how to tell if you're old, Trooper Active? It's when you start to find your past more interesting than your future."

"The past is the only thing you can trust," Active said. "It won't change on you."

Harriman stared at him and so did Silver.

"The only thing you can trust!" Harriman said. "I like this boy, Jim."

Silver shrugged. "He'll do, I guess."

"An eight-year-old driving a snowmachine?" Active asked. "There was no adult along?"

"Naw," Harriman said. "Lemuel's been driving by himself a couple years now. Smart little squirt. Guess that's why he took off when I told him I had to make a call, then I'd get him his Pokémon. Yelled, '*Arii!*' and tried to grab the amulet back, but I beat him to it." He gave the satisfied chuckle again.

"He comes in a lot?"

"Mostly in the summer," Harriman said. "See, the Basses live in a kind of camp on Lemuel's mom's Native allotment up by the mouth of the Katonak. Stay out there most of the year, except when Johnny brings 'em all into Chukchi for the summer. Then they live in Tent City out at the north end of the spit. Johnny does some stevedoring for Chukchi Lighterage and I think he runs a net in the commercial chum salmon fishery, too. That and the state Oil Dividend and welfare is about all they need to get by."

"Johnny Bass? That's Lemuel's father?"

Harriman nodded.

"And Lemuel buys a lot of Pokémon?" Active asked.

"He's kind of addicted, I guess. I don't know where he gets the money, but whenever he has any, he comes in for more

Pokémon. Sometimes he brings in stuff to trade, but I don't take it unless he's got a note from his mom saying it's not stolen."

"Did he have a note this time?"

"Nope, but I wouldn't have taken this amulet in trade regardless, because of Jim's picture." Harriman tapped it again.

Active dropped the amulet into a baggie and zipped it, just in case someone other than Tim Harriman and Lemuel Bass had left fingerprints on it. "What kind of snowmachine was he driving?"

Harriman wrinkled his brow in concentration and looked vacantly at a spot on the ceiling off to his right. "It was red and it was old," he said finally. "A Polaris, maybe."

"Thanks, Mr. Harriman," Active said.

Harriman nodded. "Let me know how it comes out, will you?"

Active started to leave, then turned back to the counter. "What exactly did Lemuel want?"

"Eh?" Harriman looked puzzled.

Active pointed at the Pokémon display on the counter.

"Ah." Harriman opened the case and took out a foil packet. "I believe this was the next addition to his collection."

"I'll take it." Active studied the packet. A grumpy-looking pale green dinosaur glared from the cover. He paid Harriman for the cards and pocketed them beside the amulet.

"What about this Johnny Bass?" Active asked when they reached the street. "It's not a local name, right?"

"Definitely nonlocal," Silver said. "An import from Oregon, I think it is. Basically trailer trash, as far as I can tell. Came up with the air force just before they shut down the old radar station, liked the country, and hung around when he got out. Married one of the Kimball girls and moved up onto her allotment."

"Ever been in trouble?"

Silver shrugged. "He's been investigated a couple times, but never busted."

"Investigated? For what?"

"Theft. Johnny, by reputation, is in the salvage business. Seems he finds a lot of abandoned stuff on the ice, along the trail, along the river. He salvages it and takes it back to camp, either uses it himself or sells it to someone who happens by and needs an ice auger, a couple of jerry jugs, a camp stove, whatever."

"And sometimes the stuff's not altogether abandoned?" Active asked.

"Supposedly," Silver said. "Twice he's been accused of pilfering stuff out of people's camps, that I know of. We city cops handled a complaint last summer when the Basses were living up at Tent City. Supposedly stole a boom box from one of his neighbors, but nobody saw him do it and we never found the boom box."

"You said it happened twice?"

"I don't know much about the other one. That one was a trooper case last wint—shit! I think it was Victor Solomon who made the complaint. Claimed Johnny snuck up in the night and stole some sheefish from his camp on the ice. Maybe he went back for another load this year and Victor caught him."

"Yeah," Active said. "And he just happened to be carrying the harpoon he had burgled out of the museum, with which he promptly stabbed Victor, and then left behind the self-same sheefish that were theoretically the object of the whole exercise."

Silver grimaced. "You're right, it makes no fucking sense whatever."

"Not a bit," Active said. "But we gotta talk to the guy. He ever been violent?"

Silver slapped himself on the forehead. "Oh, yeah, I forgot. The women's shelter tried to get us to charge him with knocking his wife around up in Tent City last summer. Then they both sobered up and she wouldn't sign a complaint. Same old shit. It makes you tired sometimes."

Active nodded. "So you up for a run out to his camp?"

Silver frowned. "I could send Alan Long. I gotta help burn down a house this afternoon."

Now it was Active's turn to frown.

"An old BIA* house," Silver explained. "The fire department is burning it so they can practice putting it out, and we gotta do crowd control, keep the kids from turning themselves into frankfurters."

"Does Alan know the way to Bass's camp?"

"I think so," Silver said. "He hunts rabbits up there sometimes. It's about four or five miles past Victor Solomon's sheefish camp. You can't miss it."

An hour later, Active was bouncing over the sea ice on the Ladies Model, following Alan Long's Ski-Doo north along the line of spruce saplings set into the snow as trail markers. Active looked for Victor Solomon's tent when they passed the spot, but saw no sign of it. That reminded him he had told Darvin Reed and Willie Samuels to bring in the dead man's camp. He made a mental note to get after them if it hadn't been delivered when he got back to the village.

A few miles farther on, Long stopped at a fork in the trail. Ahead, the route swung northeast to follow the shore of Chukchi Bay as it curved inland.

To their left, the Katonak trail wound off through a series of low, brushy islands marking the mouth of the river. Long pointed up the left bank, which started as flat tundra, then

*Bureau of Indian Affairs

rose to culminate in a hundred-foot cliff a mile or so upstream.

"Johnny's camp is in the woods this side of that cliff," Long said. "It's hard to spot from here but—there, Active, see that smoke?"

Active peered into the whiteness and thought perhaps he did see a wisp of gray rising from the spruce forest ahead. "Has Johnny Bass got dogs?"

Long nodded. "Lot's of 'em, last time I was by there."

Active grimaced. "No hope of a surprise visit, I guess. We might as well take the snowmachines in." He pulled the Smith & Wesson from its holster and dropped it into the pocket of his parka.

Long had a rifle slung across his back. He unslung it and checked the action, then laid it across the seat of his Ski-Doo and sat on it. He noticed Active staring. "It's how we do when we're caribou hunting," Long said. "Best place for a rifle if you have to get to it quick."

Active felt himself tightening, his armpits heating up under his parka.

"Look," he told Long. "We don't push this. We've got a murder suspect who presumably knows we're coming, probably a bunch of kids and their mother in there, maybe some in-laws—this has hostage crisis written all over it. First sign of trouble, we cool it and you go back to town for reinforcements, yes?"

"Unless we're being fired on," Long said.

Active nodded. "We defend ourselves, but we still back off if we can't talk Bass into surrendering."

They started the machines and followed the trail up the Katonak until a line of snowmachine tracks arced off to the left toward the smoke of Johnny Bass's camp. They gunned their engines, shot up the riverbank, and in another hundred yards found themselves in the middle of Bass's dog yard. On all sides, huskies erupted from their oil drums, shipping crates, and doghouses and set up the cacophony Active had expected, lunging at the two strangers till their chains jerked them up short.

Active backed off his throttle and motioned Long to come abreast as they eased slowly along the path through the dog yard toward what must be the Bass house. At first, it appeared to be a sprawling tent made from blue tarps, a metal stovepipe at the back sending up the feather of gray they had seen from the river. Two boys and a husky pup were building a snow fort when Active and Long came up, but they hustled inside when they spotted the two cops.

The tundra in front was littered with red, white, and blue Chevron fuel cans, an undetermined number of plastic jerry jugs, four round white propane tanks clustered in the snow, plastic cars and sleds and guns left out by Bass's kids, a cord or two of spruce firewood stacked against the wall of the blue-tarp house, an immense heap of beer cans, a Johnson outboard engine mostly buried in snow, and two snowmachines: one dead, up to its handlebars in snow with two rusted Chevron cans standing on the seat, the other an old red Polaris. A well-beaten path led to an outhouse squatting a few yards into the spruces.

Active and Long headed for the flap where the two boys had disappeared into the tent. Before they reached it, an Inupiat woman came out dressed in sweatpants and an old parka, a baby of a year or so perched on her right hip and sucking on what appeared to be a bottle of orange soda pop. The woman's hair was stringy and greasy, and approximately a third of her teeth were gone. She was about forty pounds overweight, had a bruise along her left cheekbone, and looked to be about forty years old, but it was hard to be sure. Maybe she was a used-up thirty. It seemed likely that marriage to Johnny Bass would accelerate the aging process in a woman.

She looked at the two men in their uniforms and frowned. "That Johnny never do it," she said, bathing them in beer breath.

"How do you know why we're here?" Active asked.

"I don't know anything," the woman said. "But whatever you're here about, Johnny never do it. He never do nothing."

"Then he can tell us himself. Will you ask him to come out?"

"He's not here. He's go out to check his snares with Billy and Gene."

Active peered around the camp. It could be true. The only dogsled in sight was mostly buried in snow and had no hitch on the front. It was hard to imagine life in camp without a functioning dogsled, so maybe Bass really was away. "You mind if we come in and look around, then?"

She frowned again. "I don't think Johnny would like it. You come back tomorrow, he'll be back then, all right."

Alan Long spoke up. "Well, if he never do nothing, then he won't mind if we come in, ah?" He pushed toward her and she stepped back a pace.

Active looked at Long, surprised by the mocking Village English. He looked back at the woman, who seemed a little frightened now. She shrugged, turned, and disappeared inside.

They followed her in. Once inside, Active saw the place wasn't really a tent. It was dirt-floored like a tent, carpeted intermittently with discarded snowmachine treads, wooden cargo pallets, and scraps of lumber. But the walls and ceiling were of plywood and studs, with pink insulation tacked and taped on. Presumably the blue tarps that covered the place were there to keep out the wind, rain, and snow, in lieu of more traditional coverings like shingles and siding.

They were in the kitchen, lit by watery light from a window in the back. A camp lantern, unlit, hung over a rickety dining table near a wood-fired cookstove. A six-pack of Budweiser stood on the table, one can pulled out of the plastic collar and opened.

The woman hovered nervously by the stove, brushing the stringy hair from her eyes and bouncing the baby on her hip. The baby itself regarded them with huge black eyes as it sucked on its bottle of pop, working on a set of teeth to match its mother's blackened stumps. Active realized he and Long had never gotten Mrs. Bass's first name, or introduced themselves. But now didn't seem the time for it.

Active looked around the dwelling. The other rooms, if they could be called that, were set off by flaps of dirty tent canvas or the all-purpose blue tarp. "We're going to look around, now," he told the woman. She nodded uncertainly.

He and Long took it room by room. One room turned out to be a metal shipping van somehow incorporated into the Bass warren. Inside, under a hissing camp lantern, were two boys, one reading a Superman comic, one asleep or feigning sleep in a dirty blue sleeping bag at the foot of a small bookcase loaded with boxes of Pokémon cards.

Shrieks could be heard issuing from another room. They looked in and found three little girls, stair-stepping upward in age from about three, Active guessed, fighting over Barbies. "*Arii*, you break off her head," one was saying as he stepped in They froze and glanced sideways with quick black frightened eyes at the two strangers, then looked back at their blonde-haired dolls, and were still frozen when the searchers moved on.

There was no sign of an adult male in any of the rooms. Active whispered to Long to go and chat with Mrs. Bass. Then he went back into the room with the two boys and squatted beside the sleeping bag. The husky pup they'd seen out front was curled up on the bag. It thumped its tail and smiled, dog-fashion. The boy with the comic smiled too, but uncertainly. He was five or six, Active thought.

"I'm Nathan," Active said, putting out his hand.

The boy shook the hand. "I'm Junior, and this is Siksrik here." He rubbed the husky's head.

Active fished around in his head for the meaning of *siksrik*. Finally it came to him. "He's like a ground squirrel? He digs holes all the time?"

Junior beamed and lifted his eyebrows.

"And who's this over here?" Active pointed at the sleeping bag.

"That's Lemuel."

"I thought so." Active poked at the figure in the sleeping bag. It didn't stir, so Active knew the sleep was fake. He poked it again. "Lemuel. You left something at Harriman's." Active pulled the amulet from his parka and crackled the plastic of the baggie.

There was no answer from the bag. Active pulled back the flap to reveal a pair of narrow, stubborn black eyes staring back at him. "I never leave nothing there," Lemuel Bass said. "I never go there." He looked everywhere but at the amulet and Active's eyes, then finally gave in and stared at the amulet.

"Never? Not even in the summer when you were living in Tent City?"

"Maybe couple times."

"You know that old *naluaqmiu* that runs it? Mr. Harriman?"

"Little bit maybe."

"He knows you pretty well. He says you come in for Pokémon a lot."

"Not that much."

"He wouldn't lie, would he?"

"I dunno."

"Well, he said you were in there this morning and you traded him this amulet for some Pokémon cards you wanted, but you left before he could give them to you." Active pulled the Pokémon cards with the dinosaur on the wrapper out of his pocket and showed them to Lemuel. The boy's eyes grew huge and he twitched as if he were about to snatch the cards into his sleeping bag.

"I brought them to you, all right, but I guess if that wasn't you at Harriman's, I'll have to take them back." Active returned the cards to his pocket. A soft "*Arii, that's Larvitar!*" escaped the bag.

"Maybe I was in there," Lemuel said. "That could be my cards, all right." A dirty brown hand emerged from the bag at the end of a skinny brown arm.

Active pulled the cards out again. "But I have to ask you something before I can give them to you."

The hand froze in midair. "Like what?"

"Like where did you get the amulet?"

"I think I find it somewhere."

"Where?"

"I dunno. I think I forget."

Active slipped the cards back into his parka and rose to his feet. There was another soft "*Arii!*" from the bag.

"Dad give it to me."

"Your father? When?"

"Yesterday maybe."

"Maybe?"

"Yesterday in the afternoon when he wake up."

"He slept till after noon?"

"Uh-huh. He's out late that night."

"What was he doing?"

"He never tell me. But he say he find this amulet and I can

have it if I never tell nobody about it." Lemuel started to snuffle. "Now he's going to be mad, maybe he'll burn my Pokémon like he always say."

"I'll ask him not to." Active handed the cards to the boy and left the room.

Alan Long and Mrs. Bass were talking about how the winter had been a little colder than usual, and whether that meant breakup would be late this year. "I sure hope it's not late," the woman was saying. "I like to move in to Tent City soon as we can, all right, go to bingo all time."

Active showed her the amulet. "Mrs. Bass, where did your husband get this?"

She bent and peered at the amulet with what looked like genuine, first-impression curiosity. "I dunno. I never see it before. How did you get it if it's Johnny's?"

"Lemuel tried to trade it at Harriman's this morning."

She opened her mouth to answer, but stopped and looked in the direction of the Katonak as the dog yard erupted. Over the uproar, they could just pick out the sound of a snowmachine climbing the bank from the river.

"That's Johnny," she said with an air of relief. "You should ask him about it yourself."

CHAPTER NINE

ACTIVE AND LONG STEPPED out the door as a white man with a huge potbelly and a bushy black beard shut down a snowmachine in front of the cabin. Johnny Bass, like his wife, seemed to be about forty, and had very few teeth in front. He had an ugly mullet haircut—short on the top and sides, long in the back—that was maybe a month overdue for a touch-up.

Two boys in their early teens rolled out of the sled behind him and stood staring at the two uniformed strangers, as did Johnny Bass. A rifle in a scabbard was lashed to a rail of the sled, but neither boy was near it, and Bass was in front of the snowmachine.

Bass glanced at his wife, hovering in the doorway, then his eyes swung between Active and Long and finally settled on Active. "Can I help you, officers?"

"Why don't you send the boys and Mrs. Bass inside and we can talk out here a little bit," Active said.

Bass shot a glance over his shoulder. "Billy, Gene, you take the rabbits on in so your mom can clean 'em. Lena, you keep everybody in the house for a while."

One of the boys grabbed a bulging gunnysack from the sled and disappeared into the cabin with his mother and brother.

Active and Long introduced themselves, then Active showed Bass the amulet. "Would you mind telling us where you got this?"

Bass peered at the charm, and shook his head. "It's not mine. I never seen it before."

Active gave a small, calibrated sigh and stared at Bass, waiting.

"Sorry I can't help you." Bass shrugged.

"Your son says you gave it to him yesterday afternoon. Would he lie about that?"

"I nev—wait a minute, let me take another look." Bass made a show of inspecting the amulet, then slapped himself on the side of the head with a mittened hand. "I musta been out 'n the cold too long. Come to think of it, I did give it to Lemuel. It's an old heirloom from my wife's family. She gave it to me when we first got married. Supposed to keep me safe on the trail, I guess, and it's worked pretty good all these years. So I just kinda decided it was time to pass it on to Lemuel."

Active shook his head. "Your wife told us she never saw it before. Would she lie about that?"

"Well, I thought it was her give it to me. I was dating a lot of those pretty Chukchi girls before I got married. Maybe it was one of them."

Long had eased around behind Bass during the conversation. Now he crowded up against Bass's shoulder and spoke loudly into his ear, almost shouting. "You're rapidly testing positive for bullshit here, Johnny."

Bass jumped and Active glanced at Long with a sneaking sense of admiration. Had he gotten the line from some video or cop show, or could it possibly be an original?

"Where were you night before last, Mr. Bass?" Active asked.

"I ain't answering no more questions," Bass said. "I want a lawyer."

"Then you're coming with us," Active said.

Long stepped behind Bass and handcuffed him as Active

began the litany: "You have the right to remain silent. Anything you say can and will be used against you in a court of law. . . ."

AT FIRST glance, Gail Boxrud looked as out of place in Chukchi as a palm tree or beach umbrella would have. Light gray eyes, fair skin, square, businesslike face, sandy hair done up in braids like a Swiss milkmaid.

Once you got away from the face, though, the public defender started to fit in. Red plaid shirt, Carhartt jeans, Sorels, a Carhartt jacket, a beaver hat with earflaps.

Just now, Boxrud was suffering a classic attack of public defender apoplexy in the office of Charlie Hughes, Chukchi's district attorney.

"Murder?" Boxrud said. "Don't be ridiculous! So he's out on the trail and he finds the amulet from your museum burglary. So what? That doesn't tie him to Victor Solomon's death."

Hughes smiled, his blue eyes twinkling in what Active suspected was appreciation of Boxrud's performance. On the other hand, Hughes's eyes always twinkled.

"Is that Johnny's story now?" Hughes turned to Active. "What is this, Nathan, version four, version five, what?"

"In that ballpark," Active said.

"Counselor, it is a fact," the district attorney said, "that your client has been lying to us from the moment he opened his mouth. It's also a fact that the harpoon used to kill Victor Solomon was taken in the same burglary with the amulet. I'd say he's tied to the murder. Nathan?"

Active nodded with a grin matching that of Hughes. He grinned partly so that their side would present a unified front to Boxrud, and partly because he was happy to be working the case from a nice warm office for a change, not out on the ice in the wind.

"So your theory is, Johnny robs the museum, waits a day, then goes out on the ice and stabs Victor with the harpoon, leaves it there, then goes home and gives Lemuel the amulet as, what, some kind of trophy?" Boxrud snorted. "Talk about your criminal mastermind."

"Well, counselor, let me bottom-line this for you. Long story short, this is the kind of case where, at the end of the day, we have to step up to the plate and think outside the box," Hughes said with another of his grins. "Which Nathan here has been doing a lot of. Nathan?"

Active stared at the prosecutor, momentarily stupefied by the chain of clichés. Where had Hughes come up with it, and what, in fact, was their theory of the case? "To start with, we know Johnny's a thief—"

"He's never been convicted!"

"Not here," Hughes interrupted. "But he did serve time for burglarizing a pawn shop in Grants Pass. We checked."

"I know, I saw the file," Boxrud said. "But that was Grants Pass and he was just trying to get his welding outfit back. This is Chukchi."

Active nodded. "It's a good story, anyway. But he is in fact a thief. So he burglarizes the museum, and, and . . ."

"And what?"

"Well, he knew how important Uncle Frosty was to Victor's plans for the museum, so maybe he figured he could sell Uncle Frosty back to Victor."

"You're saying he kidnapped a mummy and held him for ransom."

Active thought it over. It was starting to make sense now. "That's what I'm saying."

Boxrud shook her head. "Go ahead, I'm taking notes for my book on stupid Alaska cop tricks."

Hughes chuckled and Active pressed on. "So he takes Uncle Frosty from the museum." He paused, groping for the next chapter in the saga.

Hughes stepped in to fill the gap. "But he can't just—"

"Right," Active said. "He can't just haul Uncle Frosty up to Victor's front door and say, 'Make me an offer.'"

"No way," Hughes said.

"So he goes and hides him somewhere on the tundra," Active said. "Maybe somewhere around that camp of his. Then he takes the harpoon and the amulet over to Victor Solomon's sheefish camp to prove he's got Uncle Frosty."

"Right!" Hughes said. "And then—"

"And then he says, 'Make me an offer,'" Active said.

"But Victor—" Hughes said.

"Victor's not buying," Active said.

"He was a crusty old bastard, from everything I hear," Hughes said.

"Very crusty," Active said. "So Victor doesn't make an offer, he makes a threat. He says he's going to have Johnny locked up for robbing the museum and then he'll go out and find Uncle Frosty anyway."

"At which point—" Hughes said.

"At which point, Johnny is standing there with the harpoon in his hand, and he does what comes naturally."

Hughes and Active looked at each other in surprise and mutual admiration.

"I'm speechless," Boxrud said. "Dumbstruck. This is ridiculous."

Active stifled the impulse to point out the oxymoronic quality of a lawyer's being at a loss for words. Instead, he said, "It all fits."

"Like an old pair of mukluks," Hughes said. "End of story, case closed, it's a wrap, signed, sealed, and delivered. Your client is nailed, screwed, glued, and stapled. We go into court first thing Monday morning and you plead him guilty, yes?"

Boxrud actually was quiet now, looking thoughtful.

"You're thinking it's possible, right?" Hughes's grin was bigger than ever. "Believable, even. You're thinking, 'I've got a *naluaqmiut* client accused of killing an Inupiat elder and I have to take him before an Inupiat jury.' "

"I'm thinking I'll impanel a bunch of sensible old *aanas* and you guys will get laughed out of court."

"I'm thinking you're not so sure."

"I'm thinking I better talk to my client again."

"Fine," Hughes said. "If he's got something to say, bring him back with you. I'll call the jail and let them know."

Hughes made the call, then for twenty-five minutes he and Active talked about hockey, then about weather, then about Hughes's impending prosecution of an Ebrulik high-school teacher accused of bedding one of her students. Hughes hoped that, as rumored, the pair would marry before the case came to trial, thus saving the justice system much labor and expense.

"With all the trouble the school district has keeping teachers in the village schools, you'd think they'd encourage this sort of thing," Hughes was saying with a rueful wag of his head when his phone rang. He picked it up, listened for a moment, and said, "Send them up. We'll meet them in the small conference room."

Minutes later, Active and Hughes were facing Gail Boxrud and Johnny Bass over a table in a second-story room with fluorescent lights and a single window overlooking the houses along Beach Street and, beyond that, the ice of Chukchi Bay and the low sun swinging into the southwest sky as the afternoon wore on.

Bass was in handcuffs, a can of chew raising a circular bump in the front pocket of his orange jail coveralls. He had a Styrofoam cup in one hand.

"He didn't do it," Boxrud said.

"He did something," Active said. "Otherwise he wouldn't have had the amulet."

Bass started, then looked at Boxrud.

"He didn't rob the museum or kill Victor Solomon."

"So what's he got to say?" Hughes asked.

"Nothing," Boxrud said. "But if he did have anything to say, it would be that he found Victor dead in the sheefish camp, took a few of his possessions into protective custody, and left."

Active snorted and Hughes flipped a hand dismissively. "Protective custody," the prosecutor said. "Please."

"And he saw somebody out there."

Hughes's blue eyes narrowed and he cocked his head and said, "Who?" at the same time as Active.

Boxrud and Bass shook their heads.

"He doesn't know," Boxrud said.

"All right," Hughes said. "Let's hear the story. If it holds up, he won't be charged with anything to do with murder. Evidence tampering, maybe, but not murder or accessory to murder."

Boxrud and Bass bent their heads and whispered. Finally Boxrud looked up. "He'll plead guilty to misdemeanor theft if you don't ask for any jail time beyond what he's already served."

Hughes nodded. "But if his story doesn't hold up, everything he's said can and will be used against him. Etcetera, etcetera. And he stays in jail while we sort this out."

"I can't stay in jail." Bass spat a brown stream into the cup. "I've gotta get us some caribou."

"How long?" Boxrud asked.

Hughes looked at Active.

"A week," Active said.

Hughes nodded. "If we're not ready to charge him with murder in a week, we'll O.R. him on a theft charge."

"What's O.R.?" Bass asked.

"Own Recognizance," Boxrud said. "It means you get to go home if you promise to come back when they want you."

"Let's hear it," Hughes said.

Bass spat into the cup again and looked at Boxrud, who said, "Go ahead, it's OK."

"Yeah, I was out there that night," Bass said. "But I wasn't planning to rob Victor. I was coming down the trail from the Katonak toward where he had his camp and I saw there was lights, so I decided to drop in and see how was he doing."

"Lights?" Active said.

"Uh-huh," Bass said. "His tent was glowing like they do when there's a gas lantern burning inside, and there was a snowgo parked beside it with its light on, like it was running. I was still pretty far away but I could see that much."

"Uh-huh."

"Uh-huh. But when I turned off the main trail and headed toward Victor's camp, that snowgo started moving and headed back up toward the Katonak, kind of parallel to the trail in the direction I had come from, and then the light went out. I didn't think too much about it right then, but I guess whoever it was, he turned off his light when he saw me coming and stayed off the trail so as to get out of there without me being able to follow him."

"He headed toward the Katonak?" Active asked. "Not back toward Chukchi?"

Bass nodded. "That's what it looked like to me."

"But you didn't recognize him?"

"Well, no. I couldn't hardly see him."

"Wasn't there a full moon that night?"

Bass thought this over. " 'Bout three-quarters, I'd say, and it was pretty clear, I remember. Hadn't got all hazy yet like it did the next day."

"So what kind of snowmachine was it?" Active asked. "What was the driver wearing?"

Bass shrugged. "Couldn't tell much by moonlight."

"Could it have been Calvin Maiyumerak?"

Bass thought it over, then shook his head. "I don't think so. I think maybe he was old."

"Old? Why?"

"I don't know. Somethin' about how he carried himself, I guess."

"So you went on into the camp as this old guy drove off on his snowmachine?"

"Uh-huh. Victor was lying down there in his sheefish hole to where you couldn't hardly see him. Just that harpoon shaft sticking out above the ice and his feet up on the edge of the hole, that was about all you could see till you got right up on him."

Hughes looked disgusted. "Did you try to help him or did you just get right to work looting his camp?"

Bass looked offended. "'Course I tried to help him. I went down in the hole there, felt of his neck for a pulse, put my ear up to his nose see if he was breathing, but there was nothing. He was dead."

"It's hard to be sure sometimes," Active said.

Bass shook his head. "I've seen lots of dead things, and Victor Solomon was one of 'em."

"So you decided to rob his camp?"

"Well, I knew old Victor fairly good and he didn't have no family around to speak of. I didn't think he'd mind me using his stuff long as he didn't need it no more. So I took a couple things. I figured you cops would think whoever killed him took 'em."

"What things?" Hughes asked.

"Lessee. A jerry jug of snowmachine gas. His camp stove. And there was a can of Red Man on his cot there in the tent, so I took that. Matter of fact, this is it right here." He patted the round lump in his overall pocket.

Hughes exhaled noisily and shook his head. "Let's have it."

Bass looked at Boxrud, who nodded. "They want to check it for fingerprints."

Bass handed over the chewing tobacco, and Active put it in a baggie.

"What else?"

"Lessee, I think I took three of his sheefish, maybe four."

"But you left a bunch behind," Active said. "Nine, I think it was."

Bass nodded. "Well, I already had some I caught myself. Four was all I needed."

Active shook his head. "What else?"

Bass pondered, then spat again. Active noticed that he was able to do it without opening his jaws because of the gap in his teeth.

"I reckon that was it," Bass said. "Camp stove, Red Man, sheefish, uh-huh. That was it."

Now it was Boxrud who looked disgusted. "Johnny, the amulet."

Bass bared brown teeth in a grin. "Oh, yeah, the amulet. Shit."

"The amulet," Active said with a nod.

"Well, as I was rounding up his stuff, I kind of started to feel bad about old Victor lying out there by his sheefish hole. He seemed like a dead thing, but what if he wasn't? Like you said, Trooper Active, it's hard to be sure sometimes. So I went on out there to check him again, just in case. I felt of his pulse and there still wasn't any, I listened for his breathing and there wasn't any, then I kind of slapped him upside the head, like you would if somebody was asleep or maybe a little groggy. That's when it fell out."

"Fell out?"

"Yeah, that's when the amulet fell out of his mouth."

"It fell out of his mouth?" Active asked. He felt stupid, echoing Johnny Bass, but he couldn't help himself.

"CHRIST, WHAT a nut roll," Hughes said when they were alone again in his office. "What do you make of that business with the amulet?"

"In Victor's mouth, you mean? It's weird. Like some kind of ritual or something. What the hell is this about?"

Hughes nodded. "Yeah. And what about the old guy Johnny claims he saw leaving Victor's camp? Who could that be?"

Active ticked the known candidates off on his fingers. "Calvin Maiyumerak was supposedly with Queenie Buckland that night, and he's not old."

"And Sivula?"

"He's old but he wouldn't have any reason to be heading up the Katonak that I know of. Supposedly he's out in whaling camp, which is up the coast, not up the Katonak. And, if he did it, why would he go ask Calvin Maiyumerak about it?" Active paused and sighed. "Guess I'll be paying Whyborn Sivula a visit tomorrow."

Hughes nodded.

CHAPTER TEN

SILVER DROPPED HIS PARKA on a chair and walked to the map on his office wall. "It's too damn early to be up on a Sunday so listen close," he said. "I don't want to do this twice."

Active nodded. "I'm sorry but—"

Silver sighed wearily. "Yeah, I know, cases don't wait."

He turned to the map. "Anyway, here we are." He put a finger on the spot marking the village of Chukchi, then swept it over Chukchi Bay, an expanse of pale blue opening west into the Chukchi Sea.

"You just follow the snowgo trail—it's marked with spruce saplings—across the bay to this little spit of land here they call Tatuliq. It's only three miles." He tapped a tiny appendage dangling from the north shore of the bay. "People go there to hunt beluga and you'll see a lot of camps—tents, cabins, even a couple of sod huts from the early days. Stay on the beach and go past the camps. The trail's actually up on an old beach ridge a few yards back from the ocean. Up there, it's marked with permanent tripods made out of spruce poles—not the saplings they use out on the ice."

Silver ran his finger up the shoreline north of Tatuliq and looked at Active, eyebrows lifted in inquiry.

Active nodded. He had flown up the coast a few times on cases, but had never paid much attention to the geography.

Now he would have to travel it by snowmachine if he wanted to talk to Whyborn Sivula.

"About seven or eight miles past Tatuliq, the shoreline starts to swing west, out to sea, but the main trail goes straight on across the base of the cape—here—and continues north on up the coast. Don't follow it. You swing west with the coastline and keep that Ladies' Model of yours pointed right out toward Cape Goodwin."

Active grinned dourly, but nodded again as Silver touched the triangular peninsula representing the cape.

"After that, you'll have to wing it," Silver said. "The whaling camps are somewhere out here"—he gestured vaguely at the sea off the cape—"along the edge of the shorefast ice."

"Somewhere on the ice? That's it?"

Silver nodded. "There'll be a trail but it won't be marked. Look for a place where a bunch of snowgo tracks veer away from the beach out onto the ice and that should be it." The police chief grinned. "You'll know for sure when you hit the pressure ridges."

Active grimaced. He had seen pressure ridges from two thousand feet up. They looked like frozen surf. A jumble of blue-white slabs, like knife blades on edge, where storms and currents piled the pack ice onto the shoals off Cape Goodwin. What would the ridges be like up close? "You mean they go through that stuff with their whaling gear?"

Silver nodded again. "You want to catch a bowhead, you gotta get out where there's open leads. And that means getting past the shorefast ice to the edge of the lead. You'll see places where they've hacked through the ridges with axes and chainsaws."

"I guess there's no other way."

"Tough people," Silver said. "Anyway, once you get into the pressure ridges, there won't be much doubt about the trail. Generally speaking, at any given spot, there's only one way to go. Sometimes not even that." He grinned. "Sure your Ladies' Model is up to this, *naluaqmiiyaaq*? I could send one of my guys along as a guide."

Active shook his head and showed no flicker of response at being needled again about the purple Yamaha. "I'll be fine."

"Ah-hah." Silver paused, as if expecting more from Active. Finally he shook his head. "At least if we have to launch a Search and Rescue on you, the Ladies' Model will be easy to spot."

"So what happens when I get out to the ice edge?"

Silver shrugged. "Good question. When you get close, various trails will start to veer off to the different camps. Just pick one, and when you get to the camp, ask them how to find Whyborn Sivula's camp."

"Jesus," Active said. "There must be a better way."

Silver shrugged again. "Sure. Charter a helicopter, come booming into camp, scare off the whales, blow the tents around, piss everybody off. Yeah, that'll work. Cheap, too."

Active lifted his eyebrows in assent. "You know Whyborn much?"

"A little," Silver said. "Why?"

"I was thinking I might take the harpoon shaft and the amulet along, see how he reacts."

Silver's eyes opened wide. "Take your evidence out on the ice? You kidding?"

Active shrugged. "I'm going to send them to the state lab in Anchorage, but Carnaby already went over them for fingerprints and found nada, and I've got a ton of pictures."

"Carnaby struck out?"

Active nodded.

"Not surprising, I guess," Silver said. "Your guy probably would have been wearing gloves the whole time. From the cold, even if he wasn't thinking about fingerprints."

Active nodded again.

Silver looked at the map again. "One more thing you ought to know before you go, there's certain protocols on the ice."

"Protocols?"

"For one thing, don't take your snowmachine into camp. Too noisy, might scare the whales. You see a bunch of snowmachines parked back behind a pressure ridge, that's where you leave yours."

Active nodded.

"For another thing, if you got a red parka, don't wear it. A whale sees it, he'll think it's the blood of one of his own and bolt for Siberia."

"That it?"

"Well, yeah, except for the polar bears," Silver said. "They like to come in and hang around the whaling camps, see what they can scavenge. But just stay away from them and they won't bother you, usually. They're kind of an off-white yellowish color, so they're pretty hard to see against the snow and ice, but normally their eyes and nose show up pretty good if they get close. Two little black dots over a bigger one, you can't miss it."

Active nodded again, not sure if he was being ribbed. "Anything else? Do I need a visa to get out there?"

Silver smiled. "I know, I know. But, fact is, it's just not safe out there on the ice. Get a little too much wind from the west, or maybe a kink in the current, and the next thing you know the lead's closing and the pack's moving in and your camp's about to become a pressure ridge. Or you get a wind from the northeast, and all of a sudden the shorefast ice isn't fast anymore. Your whaling camp is on a floe headed for Siberia and liable to break up any minute."

He stopped and scratched his scalp. "My wife's father and kid brother got caught like that a few years ago. The kid, he got wet when the ice broke up under their camp during the night. You know how parents are. The old man took off his parka and put it over the boy. By the time it got light enough the next morning to come after them in the *umiaq*, he was already dead of hypothermia."

"The kid survived?"

"Barely," Silver said. "Anyway, watch yourself out there and don't be a smart-ass. It's serious business."

Active nodded and pulled his parka off Silver's office sofa, where he'd dropped it when they came in.

"Sure you don't want somebody along?"

Active shook his head. "No, really. I'll be careful. I'm looking forward to it."

Silver stared at him for a moment. "Look, take my dogsled. I'll throw in a tent, a sleeping bag, a stove, some other odds and ends. That way, if you get off the trail or maybe the weather comes up, you can hunker down behind a pressure ridge in some semblance of comfort till things straighten out. You got a rifle?"

"I can get a trooper rifle."

"Well, take it," Silver said.

Active nodded.

TWO HOURS and ten minutes later, he found the spot Silver had told him about, where the main trail left the shoreline, crossed the base of Cape Goodwin, and continued north. He could see maybe ten or twelve of the spruce tripods marking the main route. Past that, they were lost in the snow haze stirred up by the frigid west wind that had kicked in again overnight.

Active stopped the Yamaha, flipped up his goggles, and flexed his throttle thumb as he looked back at Silver's hickory dogsled. It was towing fine, all the bungee cords still in place, the blue tarp caked with snow thrown back by the snow-machine's drive track, but still covering the gear the police chief had lent him.

Active turned and studied the route ahead as the wind stiffened his face and brought tears to his eyes. The whalers' trail was a gray thread in the snow that ran west along the edge of a tall, crumbling bluff until it vanished in the haze. The beach beneath was a jumble of ice slabs driven onshore by the winter storms and now painted with snow by the wind. The result was a fantastic field of blue-and-white sculpture, with occasional patches of black where the ice had scraped up beach gravel as it hit the shore. Snow streamed off the crests like glowing smoke in the slanting light of the low Arctic sun.

He wondered for a moment how he would get down to the ice once he reached the cape, then decided not to worry about it. The whalers would know, and their trail led along the bluff.

He dropped his goggles back into place, flexed his thumb again, squeezed the throttle, and started along the trail. It wasn't marked by tripods or saplings, like the main trail. Nor was it as broad and deep as the heavily used winter thoroughfare that ran up and down the coast. But it was easy enough to follow across the treeless tundra, even when it veered away from the bluff to avoid the mouth of a gulch or find its way around a high spot.

Finally the trail came to a gulch and didn't veer. Instead it plunged through a fringe of snow-covered scrub willows to the bottom of the ravine and followed it to the beach. The trail threaded its way through the wrecked ice on the beach, then headed straight out into the rubble of the shorefast ice.

Active steered the Yamaha along the trail as it snaked through a natural notch between two slabs in the first pressure ridge, then across a pan of comparatively flat ice with a puddle of yellow-gray slush in the low spot, then toward a slot hacked in the next pressure ridge. The sled banged and fish-tailed behind him as he went up the slope and over the crest, then bucked and tried to overrun him on the downslope.

A mile farther on he crested a pressure ridge to find the downslope was a near-vertical cliff. He squeezed the brake lever as the Yamaha plunged down the incline, trying to keep the machine straight as the sled pushed at him from behind. The Yamaha jackknifed anyway and was sliding sideways when he leapt off. He landed on his left shoulder in an effort to protect the trooper Winchester slung across his back.

The Yamaha rolled, but the sled stayed upright. He heard a snap as the hitch parted. The Yamaha bounced into the air, hit the ice, and rolled again. The sled scooted down the incline on its own before pinning itself on a jagged chunk of ice at the bottom.

The Yamaha landed on its back at the bottom of the slope, engine screaming, drive tread flailing, the throttle handlebar buried in the snow. Active ran over and dug down into the snow and hit the kill switch. The Yamaha coughed to a stop.

He grabbed a ski with both hands and heaved, then yelped as the banged-up left shoulder objected. He tried again, letting the right shoulder do most of the work, and finally got the machine upright.

The windscreen was broken almost in half, the top piece flopping back over the handlebars, attached only by a couple of inches of Plexiglas at the right edge. He swore and tore it off and flung it into the snow.

He forced himself to calm down and look the machine over. Nothing broken but the windscreen and the hitch, as far as he could see. Maybe the right handlebar was bent a little, but probably not enough to hurt.

He pulled the rifle sling over his head and inspected the .270. No snow in the muzzle, the scope covers still held in place by their rubber bands. He slung it over his back again, registering another protest from his left shoulder.

Shaking his head, he trudged over to the sled. The load was still bungeed into place under its tarp. But one of the hickory slats at the front of the sled was splintered on the pinnacle of ice that had stopped it. He grabbed the sled and heaved it off the pinnacle.

Then he inspected the damaged slat. It was a goner, and Silver would be pissed, but it looked to Active like the sled would still carry its load. Probably the troopers would pay to fix the slat. He hoped.

The problem was how to make the hitchless Yamaha pull the sled. The tongue was a triangle of steel piping, about four feet from apex to base. The base was bolted onto the stanchions at the front of the sled.

At the apex, the tongue hitched to the Yamaha by a bolt through a hinged metal tab. The tab had sheared off the Yamaha and was still shackled to the tongue.

He pulled the sled over to the Yamaha with his right arm and ran through a mental list of the gear he had loaded back in Chukchi, some of it his, some borrowed from Silver. Camp stove, tent, gas, food box, sleeping bag, a thermos of tea, the harpoon handle that Vera Jackson had pulled from Victor Solomon's chest, now wrapped in two trash bags for its ride to Cape Goodwin. But no rope or wire on the list anywhere. He unbungeed the load, pulled back the blue tarp and checked, and was disappointed to find his memory was perfect.

True, Silver's tent probably included a few little ties and cords, but Active wasn't about to cut up the tent after breaking the man's dogsled. The kind of ties that came with a tent probably wouldn't be strong enough to pull a loaded sled through the pressure ridges anyway.

Active sighed, opened his parka, unzipped the fly of his snowmachine suit, and felt inside. Yep, he was wearing a belt. He pulled it out, threaded it through the apex of the tongue, then through the frame of the luggage rack at the back of the Yamaha, and buckled it.

He straightened up and studied it. It didn't look strong enough. He jerked the sled closer and looped the belt through the tongue and luggage rack again, then nodded in satisfaction. The double thickness of leather might work.

He rebungeed the tarp into place, climbed onto the Yamaha, released the kill switch, said a little please to the Great Perhaps, and hit the starter. The machine caught instantly and sounded right. He gave the throttle a gentle squeeze and moved off across the pan, twisting on the seat to check out his makeshift hitch. The sled was moving with the Yamaha. What more could he ask?

Active babied the rig across two more pressure ridges, then shut it off and coasted to a stop on the snow at a fork in the trail. One fork led straight ahead, over the next white pressure ridge. The other veered left and followed a kind of valley between the ridges. He was considering which way to go when a flicker of yellow-gray fifty yards up the valley caught his eye.

His gut lurched and felt hot and he stood up on the running boards and shrugged the rifle off his back and worked the bolt to put a shell into the firing chamber. He raised the Winchester to his eye, saw nothing, lowered it and flipped the scope covers off, raised it again.

At first he still saw nothing. Then an Inupiat woman stepped into view from behind an ice slab and lowered a sopping polar bear hide through a hole in the ice. A rope was tied to the polar bear's nose; several feet payed out, then the line went tight, vanishing behind the same ice slab that had concealed the woman. She must have been pulling the hide out of the hole when he had first noticed the flicker, he concluded.

He lowered the rifle and shrugged it onto his back before she could spot him pointing it at her. Evidently she hadn't heard him come up; perhaps it was because he was downwind of her.

He hit the starter button and let the Yamaha glide forward. She finally heard the engine and looked up, gave a little wave and then watched, hands on her hips, as he drove up and switched off the snowmachine. She was in her midfifties, he guessed, dark silver hair, glasses with round black frames, flowered parka with a big fur ruff, black snowmachine suit, Sorel boots.

They shook hands and introduced themselves. She was Rose Napana. Her husband, Charlie, she reported with some pride, had killed the polar bear two days earlier because it wouldn't quit hanging around their whaling camp.

The rope, Active now saw, was looped around an ice block a few yards from the hole. An old Polaris snowmachine with a dogsled behind was parked there, too.

Rose saw him eyeing the setup. She kicked the rope, stretched across the snow in front of her. "Them sea lice never finish yet," she said. "You want some tea?"

"Sea lice?"

Rose frowned and studied him. "You're that *naluaqmiiyaaq* trooper, ah?"

Active nodded.

"Sea lice are these little bugs, live in the water." Rose said it patiently and slowly like she was talking to a kindergartner. "They eat the meat and fat off the skin. Nice meal for them and I never have to scrape it. Good deal, ah?" She grinned. "But they're not done yet. One more day, maybe. Now you want some tea?"

He declined and asked if she knew the way to Whyborn Sivula's camp.

She lifted her eyebrows. "I'm going that way, you could *malik* on your snowgo."

He was deciding that "*malik*" must mean "follow" when Rose took a closer look at the Yamaha, then turned an admiring gaze on him. "*Yoi*, so pretty. I always want a purple snowgo myself. And electric start! Too bad you break your windshield."

From the ice she lifted a slab of snow that appeared to have been cut for the purpose and slid it into place over the polar-bear hole, to prevent blow-in and retard freezing, he supposed. Then she straddled her old Polaris, pulled the starter rope, and headed back up the trail toward the fork.

He steered his Yamaha in a wide, easy half circle to spare the leather hitch and followed her as she worked her way through the pressure ridges and out to the edge of the ice. There she stopped, and made a throat-cutting motion for him to do the same. He did, and flipped up his goggles.

The lead was a half-mile wide, Active estimated, a belt of indigo flecked with small white floes. The west wind was piling up small waves against the edge twenty feet from the front skis of his Yamaha. Wisps of sea smoke hurried across the water toward them.

Across the lead, he could see the ragged front of the pack ice, looking by some trick of perspective like a distant mountain range an ocean away.

"Whyborn is second camp that way," Rose said, pointing up the lead to the right. "You can't miss it. See you."

She pulled her starter rope and headed left down the lead.

Active followed the ice edge for a half-mile, then the trail pulled away from the water and skirted behind a rubble of pressure ridges where the ice edge swelled out to a kind of point. As he passed by, he saw several snowmachines parked behind the ridges, and a foot trail leading toward the water. The first camp, he surmised.

CHAPTER ELEVEN

FOUR-TENTHS OF A MILE farther on, Active found another gaggle of snowmachines behind the white slabs of a pressure ridge, another foot trail leading through the ridges toward the ice edge.

Active parked the Ladies' Model and debated what to take with him from the sled. Anything left behind might get pilfered, but he couldn't carry it all. He settled on the rifle, which he left strapped across his back, and the double-trash-bagged handle from Uncle Frosty's harpoon, which he pulled from under the blue tarp. He took off a mitten, reached into the inside pocket of his parka, and touched the baggie that contained Uncle Frosty's owl-faced amulet.

Then he picked his way through the pressure ridges to Whyborn Sivula's whaling camp.

A white wall tent like a tiny cabin squatted ten yards from the water, canvas rattling in the wind. A stovepipe poked out the top, sending up a thin tendril of gray smoke that left a sweet, oily smell in the air as it streaked away to the east. Slabs of white *muktuk* were stacked beside the tent. Active knew whalers hunted the little white beluga whales that often preceded the prized bowheads up the leads in the spring. The meat was good to eat, supposedly, and the *muktuk* made good fuel for the camp stove.

An *umiaq*, also white, crouched on snow blocks at the water line, a steel-barbed harpoon and a whaling gun like a giant's rifle pointing seaward from the bow. Inside were coils of rope and a huge white float.

The whalers had raised a windbreak of ice slabs near the *umiaq*. A half-dozen men lazed in the shadows behind it, drinking coffee, chatting idly, two of them playing cribbage with a pegboard made from a walrus tusk. Their card table was a blue-and-white plastic Igloo cooler.

Another man, with binoculars hanging from his neck, stood on the crest of the nearest big pressure ridge, looking out across the lead. Here it was choked with floes and slush, no longer the open expanse of indigo Active had seen when he and Rose first found the water. Perhaps as a result, the west wind, though still rising, created no waves here.

The lookout spotted Active and called out something in Inupiaq. Active thought he caught the word *naluaqmiiyaaq*.

In a moment, an Inupiaq in navy blue snowmachine pants and a brown down vest, but no parka or gloves, emerged from the tent and walked forward as Active covered the last few yards to the camp. The man blinked for a moment in the white light, then pulled mirror glasses from the vest and put them on.

Whyborn Sivula was slight and looked to be in his early sixties, his face a dark, polished brown with strong Mongol lines. He still had all his teeth, as far as Active could see, and the gray hair still had a little black in it.

But it was hard to be sure. He walked easily, like a man still with good knees and hips. So he could be in his early fifties.

Still, Inupiat men who spent much time out in the country weathered early to that deep and relatively wrinkle-free mahogany, Active had learned, and then seemed to stop aging for a while. So Whyborn Sivula could be in his early seventies.

Active pulled off his right mitten and put out his hand. "Mr. Sivula? I'm Nathan Active with the Alaska State Troopers."

Sivula shook hands, his eyes on the trash-bag-wrapped object at Active's side. "Everybody know who you are."

Active held up the harpoon. "Do you know why I'm here?"

Sivula said nothing.

"I talked to Calvin Maiyumerak."

Still nothing from the old whaler.

"Can I show you this?" Active raised the harpoon again.

"We could go inside, I guess."

Sivula led Active into the tent. Inside were two flat cargo sleds, covered now with caribou hides and sleeping bags to serve as benches and beds. Opposite the doorway, at the end of the alley between the cargo sleds, a homemade barrel stove muttered to itself. The sweet, greasy stench of burning *muktuk* was very strong. Something was bubbling in a pot on top of the stove. It smelled like beef stew. Or fish soup. Or both.

Sivula sat on one of the sleds and motioned for Active to use the other, and offered beluga stew from the stove. Active downed a bowlful, partly because it was local protocol, and partly because he was hungry and cold from the ride up the coast.

Then he turned his back to Sivula and laid the harpoon shaft, still wrapped in its trash bags, on the bright green sleeping bag that covered the other sled. Then he pulled the baggie from inside his parka and laid it beside the harpoon. He put the owl's face down, then slid out of the way and faced Sivula, whose eyes were riveted to the objects on the sleeping bag.

"Did you hear that Victor Solomon was killed?"

Sivula said nothing, eyes still on the green sleeping bag.

"He was killed with this harpoon." Active pointed at the exhibits on the sleeping bag. "And the killer left this amulet on the body."

Sivula still didn't speak, though Active thought he flinched slightly.

Active knew he was pushing it. Older Eskimos considered questions rude, particularly from a stranger. But today, there wasn't time for the proper formalities, and Sivula seemed hypnotized by the amulet and the shaft.

"These things were taken when Uncle Frosty was stolen from the museum," Active said.

Sivula definitely flinched now. "I don't know about that," he said.

Now Active was silent, holding eye contact until Sivula broke it. Active cleared his throat, looked at his feet. Still nothing. "I heard you went to Calvin Maiyumerak's house and asked him about the burglary." He looked not at Sivula, but forty-five degrees right of the mahogany face, at a rear corner of the tent.

Finally Sivula spoke. "He never tell me anything. Say he don't know anything about the burglary."

"Why did you want to know about the burglary?"

"I don't know." Active saw the mask sliding over Sivula's face, the one that meant a white person, or perhaps any authority figure, was asking too many questions.

"What do you know about the burglary?"

Sivula squinted and said nothing.

Active unwrapped the harpoon shaft, being careful not to touch it except on the ends, and also careful to expose the owl-face property mark for only a fraction of a second. Then he rolled the mark out of sight and looked at Sivula.

The whaler's body was rigid, his hands gripping his knees as if to keep from reaching across and grabbing the harpoon.

"These things here that were taken in the burglary and found on Victor Solomon's body, they have marks on them," Active said. He pulled the amulet out of its baggie and placed it on the sleeping bag, the owl's face still down. "My friend Jim Silver—you know Jim Silver, the *naluaqmiut* police chief?"

Sivula nodded, still rigid, his eyes never leaving the objects on the bed.

"Jim Silver said that, in the early days, the Inupiat put these marks on their equipment in case it got lost," Active said. "But he didn't know whose marks were on these things from the museum. Maybe an Inupiaq would know, someone who knows about the early days."

Sivula's eyes flicked to Active's, then back to the sleeping bag.

"Maybe you could help me," Active said. "Maybe you know the old marks."

Sivula squinted no again.

"So you can't help me?"

Another squint from Sivula.

Active sighed, then picked up the amulet, put it back in its baggie, and dropped it into the pocket inside his parka, not looking at Sivula. Then he rolled the harpoon shaft up in its trash bags and refastened the two miniature bungee cords holding the wrappings in place.

"Too bad," he said, finally looking into Sivula's face.

They stared at each other that way for a few moments. The tent rattled in the wind and the *muktuk* sputtered in the stove. Finally Sivula lifted his eyebrows. "Maybe I could take a look."

Active unwrapped the harpoon and amulet. "I'll show you, but you can't touch them. We have to send them to the crime lab in Anchorage to be analyzed." He turned both amulet and shaft so that Sivula saw the owls' faces simultaneously.

Sivula's face froze. "Saganiq!" he said. He slumped back onto his sled.

"What?"

"Saganiq. When I'm little kid, there's always these stories about this old *angatquq*, Saganiq. Very powerful, his *kikituq* spirit is *ukpik*—snowy owl." Sivula leaned across the alley between the sleds and pointed at the face of the amulet on Active's knee. "Saganiq is last old-time *angatquq* before Jesus comes to the Inupiat and we give up devil worship. There's so many stories about him. . . ."

His voice trailed off and he gazed at the amulet. "I'm never sure before Saganiq is real person, but now I guess so. Could I look at his *kikituq*?"

Active held the amulet over Sivula's knees. The whaler bent close and studied it for perhaps two minutes.

"So Uncle Frosty is Saganiq?" Active asked.

Sivula appeared to be thinking this over when the lookout from the pressure ridge thrust his head into the tent and said something in urgent Inupiaq. Sivula lifted his eyebrows and answered in Inupiaq, then stood and looked at Active. "I have to go outside now and look at ice. My boy, Franklin there, he say the pack ice is moving in on us now, maybe we have to pull our camp out."

"What does Saganiq have to do with Victor Solomon's killing?"

Sivula's face seemed to turn in on itself, looking back into the Inupiat past. "This is Eskimo business from early days ago, *naluaqmiiyaaq*," he said. "Best you leave it alone."

"But was Uncle Frosty Saganiq?"

Sivula's face veiled over in the Eskimo mask again as he pulled on a white parka and white mittens from beside him on the sled. "You should leave it alone, *naluaqmiiyaaq*," he said again. "All done now anyway."

He pushed through the tent flap and began speaking Inupiaq with Franklin just outside.

Active rewrapped the shaft and amulet and stepped out into the wind. It was faster now, the tent rattling more than before, the smoke from the *muktuk* smearing out a little flatter as it raced eastward and vanished in the pressure ridges. There was snow, too, just a few flakes whirling in the wind, but the taste of gun metal on Active's tongue meant more of it coming.

Whyborn and Franklin Sivula were trotting across the ice to the lookout point. Active peered out over the lead but was hard put to see any difference. It had been choked with floes and slush before, and it was now, though perhaps there was more ice and fewer patches of open water.

The real question was whether the pack ice was closing in on the camp. Active couldn't even guess. The loose ice was so dense, he couldn't tell where the lead ended and the pack began.

He turned to watch Whyborn and Franklin on the pressure ridge. Whyborn had the binoculars pointed across the lead. He swept them from left to right, then handed them to Franklin and charged down the slope and across the ice, shouting at his crew in a mixture of Inupiaq and English.

"Let's go, this lead is closing," Active heard him shout during one of the English passages.

Active watched as the whalers ran to the tent, spread back the door flaps and yanked the two cargo sleds out. One of them poured the water from the beluga stew into the stove to put out the fire, and in less time than he could have imagined, three men were lashing the *umiaq* onto one of the sleds, while three more piled the tent and camping gear onto the other.

Two other men hurried off down the ice trail and returned moments later on snowmachines.

Franklin Sivula stopped his work on the *umiaq* and looked at Active with a grin. "You better get out of here, man, no place for a *naluaqmiiyaaq*."

Active grinned back, and trotted down the trail through the pressure ridges to his Yamaha, hoping the hitch he had made from his belt would hold at least till he got Silver's sled back onto solid ground.

CHAPTER TWELVE

JIM SILVER SQUATTED BESIDE his dogsled and explored the shattered slat with a thumb and forefinger. But not for long, not in the cold wind whistling in from the west.

He grunted, straightened, put his glove back on, and looked at Active. "Don't worry, Nathan. I think my brother-in-law can probably patch it up pretty cheap. Screw on a little section of hickory from underneath, be good as new. Won't even show hardly. Carnaby will barely notice it on your reimbursement claim."

"Sorry, man," Active said.

"Ah, forget it. That kind of stuff happens on the trail. Goes with."

"Well, thanks," Active said. "Look, I need to tell you what Whyborn Sivula told me, or didn't, and then I need to look through the Smithsonian paperwork on Uncle Frosty. I've been chasing around so hard on this—"

"You need to sit down and think about it a while?"

Active nodded and they started up the stairs into the Public Safety Building, Active talking as they went. Whyborn Sivula had told him so little that he was able to tell it all to Silver before they reached the police chief's office on the third floor.

"Saganiq, huh?" Silver tossed his parka on the sofa, dropped into the chair behind his desk, and waved Active into a seat in front. "Maybe I've heard the name, maybe not. Doesn't ring any bells, at any rate. Now that they're all good Christians, the Inupiat don't like to talk about their old *angatquqs*."

The police chief opened a file drawer beside his left knee and pulled out two green hanging folders, each containing a half-dozen or so manila files. He dropped them on the edge of the desk in front of Active.

"You troopers may as well take custody of them," he said. "Victor Solomon's murder case obviously takes precedence over my little burglary, and I think solving one solves the other, eh?"

Active nodded and picked up one of the green folders. "A lot of reading here. Guess I better get at it." He picked up the other folder and stood.

Silver shrugged. "I could give you the 101 course on it. I browsed the files pretty good when I was trying to come up with a list of what was in Uncle Frosty's crate so I could figure out what was taken in the burglary."

Active laid the folders back on Silver's desk and dropped into the chair, then pulled out a notebook and pen. "So?"

"So." Silver said. "It's 1920. The federal government is trying to make sure the navy has enough oil if there's another war. They set up this system of what they called the Naval Petroleum Reserves."

"Like the one—"

Silver nodded. "Yep, like the one up on the Arctic Slope. They were scattered all around the country. The most famous one was Teapot Dome in Wyoming, which figured in one of your standard big-bucks Washington scandals of the time, but, yes, we got our own. The National Petroleum Reserve-Alaska, created in 1923. They never found much oil there, but BP and Exxon are still looking."

"Fascinating," Active said. "And?"

"And you're wondering what this has to do with Uncle Frosty?"

Active nodded. "Somewhat."

"And I have the answer," Silver said with a smile. "Before you can have a petroleum reserve, you gotta send out surveyors and geologists to take a first guess at where the oil is, right? So in 1920, this party from the U. S. Geological Survey wanders across the Arctic Slope all summer. It's called the Henderson party after the geologist in charge, guy named Joseph Henderson. The Henderson Bay oil field on the Arctic Slope is named after him."

Active nodded.

"Pretty soon, it's mid-August," Silver continued. "Starting to frost, Henderson is wrapping things up, getting ready to beat it down to the coast and catch the last boat out before freezeup. The party is up in this big saddle that leads right through the crest of the Brooks Range from the Arctic Slope into the Chukchi Basin."

Silver stood and put his finger on the spot on the map behind his desk. "Place called Shaman Pass."

Active stiffened in his chair and stared at the chief. "Shaman Pass. What—of course."

Silver's eyes widened. "Shit. They must have named it that because of what Henderson found up there. I bet I heard it on Kay-Chuck a hundred times since this Uncle Frosty thing came up, but I never made the connection before."

Active walked to the map and stared at the spot above Silver's index finger. Shaman Pass lay about a hundred and fifty miles north of Chukchi. The north side of it drained into the Colville River, which emptied into the Arctic Ocean a couple of hundred miles east of Barrow. The south side of the pass drained into the Katonak River, which wound through the Brooks Range past Johnny Bass's camp to empty into Chukchi Bay a few miles from the office where Active stood at that moment. Most of the features in the area bore Inupiaq names he didn't recognize.

But there was one exception. Active traced his finger along

the route of the stream that ran south out of the pass and emptied into the Katonak. "And this is the Angatquq River, I see."

Silver said, "Shit" again and shook his head.

Active turned back to the map and ran his finger up the Angatquq River to the summit. "And this is where they found Uncle Frosty? Shaman Pass?"

Silver nodded, looking a little grumpy at having his story foreshortened. "Basically, yeah. Henderson is camped out up in the pass and they find this cave in the rocks. And in the cave is Uncle Frosty. The surveyors and geologists get pretty excited thinking maybe they've got a mummy from way back, some kind of anthropological treasure. So they take Uncle Frosty down to the coast with them, ship him back to Washington, turn him over to the Smithsonian."

"And was he from way back?"

Silver shook his head. "Nah, the anthropologists at the Smithsonian weren't excited at all. They apparently concluded he'd only been there twenty or thirty years. So they preserved him and put him in the basement and there he stayed till Victor Solomon had him brought to Chukchi."

Active was silent, thinking it over. "You ever been up there, to Shaman Pass?"

"Couple times. Once on a snowmachine trip over to Caribou Creek when my father-in-law was still alive, and once when I landed up there with Cowboy Decker on a Search and Rescue. Actually, it was just a search. We never found the plane, but Cowboy thought he saw some debris up a little side creek, so we landed." Silver shuddered. "Bad place. Hungry country."

"Why?"

Silver wagged his head. "It's the main vent through the Brooks Range in that part of the country, so it's windy as hell.

Blows so hard up there it's actually been known to kill caribou, according to the old-timers around here. Plus, there's a hell of a gorge just below the summit that can be a bitch to get past if you're on a snowmachine. And then there's the *inuksuks*."

"*Inuksuks?*"

"Yeah, the little stone men the old-time Eskimos used to build. I guess they were trail markers or something. Every now and again you'll be up some little valley around Shaman Pass there and you'll get this creepy feeling something's watching you. And when you look around, there's an *inuksuk* sitting up on the hillside above you. Seems stupid to say it, but it's kinda creepy."

Active walked back to his chair. "Why'd the Smithsonian think Uncle Frosty was from Chukchi?"

Silver shrugged. "Don't know. All the file says is, based on Henderson's journal, that's what they concluded. So when the Indian Graves Act got passed, the Smithsonian did its inventory, found Uncle Frosty in the basement, and wrote the Chukchi tribal council did they want him."

"And Henderson's records? They're in these files here?" Active tapped the folders on Silver's desk.

Silver shook his head. "Nah. I guess they're still at the Smithsonian. Or the U. S. Geological Survey. Or somewhere."

THE CLOSEST "somewhere" turned out to be the University of Alaska Geophysical Institute in Fairbanks. Active discovered this after two hours of fruitless telephone calls and Internet searches that Sunday afternoon, and twenty minutes of productive telephoning the following morning.

As a helpful librarian named Bruce Marion at the geophysical institute explained, the original records of the Henderson party were in the national archives in Washington, D.C., but the institute in Fairbanks had long ago obtained a complete copy so as to get Henderson's geological data on the Arctic Slope.

When Active asked Marion to mail him a copy, there was a pause. "As I recall, that file runs about two thousand pages, mostly geological field data," Marion said. "Are you sure? I could—"

"All I really need is Henderson's journal," Active said. "How big is that?"

"Hang on a moment, let me check something," Marion said.

The librarian laid down the phone and Active listened to the sound of computer keys clacking above the background hiss of the long-distance circuit and thought about that morning's bullet dream, a repeat of the one two days ago. The assailant with the knife that maybe wasn't a knife, the useless gun. He started a little and shook his head to clear his mind when Marion came back on.

"Thought so," the librarian said. "Do you have Internet access out there in—where is it?"

"Chukchi," Active said. "You mean Henderson's records are online? I couldn't find them with any of the search engines."

"Not all of his records. Just his journal and a bibliography of the rest."

"But why—"

"It's in a section of our holdings that's public but not publicized, if that makes any sense."

"Not really," Active said.

"We don't think our computers could handle the load if we opened all of our archives up to the search engines and we started getting hits from all over the world," Marion said. "You're a state employee, do I have to tell you about the budget situation?"

Active grunted in acknowledgment.

"So we can't afford to upgrade our computers, either. As a result, the Henderson material is in what we call our Gray Archives—not indexed, but accessible if you know the Internet code. I'll give it to you, just don't put it on the Google search engine, OK?"

Active grunted again and copied down the string of letters, numbers, dots, slashes, and tildes, then read it back to Marion.

Marion said he had it right, so Active said thanks and goodbye and turned to the computer beside his desk.

He started Internet Explorer, typed in the address Marion had furnished, and watched the little globe spin in the corner of the screen. He sent up a prayer to the cybergods that Bruce Marion's elderly Internet servers wouldn't be too busy on a Monday morning to open the Henderson archives.

They weren't. In less than a minute, Active had a menu onscreen that offered two items: "Journal of Joseph Henderson, USGS, May–August 1920," and "Bibliography, Henderson Party, 1920."

Active clicked on the journal and soon had a menu breaking the journal down by week, from May 18, 1920, through August 28. He clicked on the first week in August and began reading.

Each of Henderson's entries was a succinct record of what they had found during the day, where they had camped, the weather, where they planned to go the next day. The geologist was all business except when it came to the four Eskimos he had hired in Barrow.

Their main job was to guide the expedition to the long-known natural oil seeps that had given rise to the idea of an Arctic Slope reserve in the first place. They also helped with camp chores and transportation, and brought in fresh meat whenever the party encountered the caribou herds that summered on the Arctic coastal plain. Henderson identified only one of the Barrow Inupiat by name—Iqlavik, who seemed to be the senior hand among the four.

The party had discovered Uncle Frosty on the morning of Monday, August 16, according to Henderson's entry that night. One of his geologists had come across a little cave while chipping rock samples from an outcropping near their camp in Shaman Pass. The geologist had crawled in to see if the walls of the cave looked any different from the rock on the face of the outcropping, only to put his hand on a fur-wrapped bundle that turned out to be Uncle Frosty. After that, Henderson wrote:

> We removed the remains from the cave and made a cursory examination. The furs crumbled away to reveal the body of an ancient Eskimo male, apparently preserved by the dry, cold climate of this region, who had been killed by a harpoon thrust to the chest, perhaps for ritualistic reasons, as we found an amulet of an owl's face between his teeth.
>
> I directed that he and his effects be wrapped in canvas so that we could transport him to civilization for analysis by competent anthropologists.
>
> This discovery, and my decision to retrieve the remains, unsettled two of our Eskimos, who said the mummy would bring us bad luck, as they supposed him to be an old shaman from the Chukchi Basin long rumored to have been killed here, which event gave this spot its name, Shaman Pass.
>
> But Iqlavik, the great skeptic, came to my rescue as usual. He scoffed at this, saying he had never heard of such a rumor and, anyway, it was obvious this old shaman, if that's what he was, couldn't cause bad luck to anyone or

he would have prevented his own murder by afflicting his would-be assassin with some very bad luck indeed. Moreover, Iqlavik said reprovingly, now that they and all other Barrow Eskimos had accepted Jesus as their savior and given up devil worship, no old shaman, dead or alive, could cause trouble in any case, and, even if he could, why not let the white men take him away with them, as it would certainly be harder for him to cause trouble for anyone in Barrow if he were thousands of miles away in Washington, where all the white men lived.

This led to a furious discussion in the Eskimo language that I could not follow, but it ended with Iqlavik informing me the remains could be brought out as long as I agreed that the two reluctant ones could place a crucifix inside the canvas wrappings and that neither of them should be required to handle the remains in any way.

Once this was settled, I asked what they knew about the old shaman's murder. There was little to go on here, as the two of them who had passed along the rumor had heard it only on a visit to Chukchi, never in Barrow, and had not bothered to collect many details as they had never put much stock in it before now. He was probably killed "early days ago," before the "nahlogmes," or whites, came into the country, they thought.

Active surfed through the journal to its end, but found only one other reference to Uncle Frosty. The entry merely noted that Henderson had taken the remains aboard a government revenue cutter at the mouth of the Colville River and crated them up for shipment to Washington.

Active began saving Henderson's journal to his hard drive. Why and how had the same owl-faced amulet found in Uncle Frosty's mouth by Joseph Henderson's party almost eight

decades ago ended up in Victor Solomon's mouth? Why and
how had the same harpoon Henderson had found in Uncle
Frosty's chest wound up in Victor Solomon's chest?

Active dug into the folders he had gotten from Silver and
flipped through the pictures of Uncle Frosty. Finally he
stopped at a close-up of the mummy's face. Some of the flesh
was gone, but it was possible to see that the mouth was locked
open. Perhaps it was from rigor mortis setting in as the body
had cooled in Shaman Pass. Or perhaps it was Uncle Frosty's
final scream. Active shook his head. Maybe so, maybe no, but
what was the connection to Victor Solomon's death?

If any.

CHAPTER THIRTEEN

ST. MARK'S CATHOLIC CHURCH was a weathered gray two-story building with a rectory and parish offices on the ground floor, a chapel with a small steeple above, and a snow-covered gravel parking lot in front.

Active parked the Suburban with its tail to the wind to conserve heat in the engine, then walked to the rectory door and knocked. He waited as the west wind whistled past, pushing shredded snow across the parking lot. An Inupiat woman of about thirty came out, her eyes reddened and wet. She looked at him, pulled up the hood of her parka, and brushed past in silence.

Father Sebastian James followed her out and watched from the doorstep as she mounted a red four-wheeler, yanked the starter rope, and drove off into the wind. "Some problems the Lord solves right away and some take a while," the priest said, putting out his hand. "Good to see you again, Nathan."

James was a thirtyish Inupiaq, narrow faced and serious, with round steel-rimmed glasses that gave him an ascetic look. The only sign of his profession today was the collar. He came from a village upriver, and had gone to Notre Dame, Active had heard.

They knew each other slightly, but Active, as an agnostic,

could never decide what to call the priest. "Father" seemed overformal and insincere, while "Sebastian" might be too familiar and perhaps even insulting with the collar in place. "Mr. James" was unthinkable.

"Good to see you, too," Active said.

James smiled like he had gotten a joke, and led Active through a living room, then a kitchen that smelled of seal oil, and into a small study. It was walled with books and two diplomas proving the Notre Dame story was true. A copier stood in one corner, next to a computer and printer on a wheeled work stand.

"Victor's death was a terrible shock," James said, seating himself behind a heavy desk of scarred blond wood. "And now . . . you said on the phone he was killed by an old-fashioned whaler's harpoon?"

Active nodded. "That's the conclusion I expect when the autopsy's done."

James shook his head. "Any idea when that will be? We can't conduct our funeral service until the body comes back from Anchorage. He was our deacon, you know."

"By the end of the week, I hope."

"Can I offer you some coffee? Tea? Pilot bread?" James waved a hand toward the kitchen.

Active declined, then was silent, thinking how to get into it.

"Problems with the investigation?"

Active sighed. "It is a bit of a tangle at the moment. Do you have any idea who would want to kill Victor Solomon, or why? Any gossip from your parishioners?"

The priest shrugged. "Lots of talk, lots of dismay, of course, but no real information. Victor lived alone, had no immediate family. No one knew him very well. He could be difficult."

"I've heard," Active said. "Even to the point of seeming almost unchristian at times?"

"The Lord's igloo is very large," James said with another smile. "Plenty of dried fish and seal oil even for a grouchy, lonely old hunter." The priest was silent for a moment. Then, "But this harpoon?"

"Yes?"

"Did you say on the phone it was Uncle Frosty's?"

"Yes, it was taken in the museum burglary, and it's really almost our only lead. But I can't see where it points us."

"Eh?"

"It seems to have belonged to an old *angatquq* who was murdered long ago in Shaman Pass. Ever hear any stories about something like that?"

The priest shook his head. "Don't think so. But, of course, the elders who might remember superstitious talk from the old days wouldn't discuss it with a priest. Even an Eskimo priest."

"Apparently his name, Uncle Frosty's name, was Saganiq."

"Sorry, that doesn't ring any bells eith—" James put a hand over his eyes, then removed it and gazed for several seconds at a spot a foot above Active's head. "Saganiq? Wait, now, where have I seen—I know I—"

He snapped his fingers, turned his chair, and looked at the cemetery outside his window. He stood up and said, "Come with me."

James led Active back through the kitchen and out a rear door. He paused a moment near the first headstone, then made his way along a central pathway past the rows of grave markers, looking at them as he went. Finally he stopped and pointed at a granite headstone two graves in from the path. "Look at that," he said.

The face of the stone was plastered with blown snow. Active pulled a glove from his pocket and slapped it clear. It read:

Matthew Solomon
"Saganiq"
1860(?)–1918

"Saganiq is buried here? He didn't die in Shaman Pass?"

James nodded in satisfaction, hunching his shoulders against the wind. He had come out without a coat. "I knew I'd seen that name somewhere around the church."

Active was lost in thought for a moment. "Maybe it's not the same guy. Saganiq—"

"Have you noticed the surname?" James was giving him a quizzical look.

Active looked at the stone again and blurted out: "Jesus, his English name was Solomon?" He realized what he had said. "Excuse me, I . . . I . . . "

James waved a hand and grinned. "Jesus has heard worse, I'm sure."

"But if Saganiq was Matthew Solomon, then he was—"

James nodded again. "Victor Solomon's relative, almost certainly. I could look it up in the church records."

"Thanks," Active said. He glanced around at the other graves nearby. They had wooden markers, not stones. Evidently Saganiq had been a wealthy and important man by the time he was buried as Matthew Solomon. Then Active noticed that most of Saganiq's neighbors in the cemetery had died the same year as the shaman. "What happened in 1918?"

James had already started for the church. He turned, shivering, and looked at the grave markers from that year. "The Spanish influenza," he said. "A third of the people in this town died in nine days, I've heard. In Brevig Mission, down by Nome, seventy-two of eighty died in five days."

"Another western import," Active said.

James smiled his "I-get-it" smile, but said nothing. He turned and led the way back into his study. There, he walked to one of the bookshelves lining the wall, ran his fingers along the spines, and brought to his desk a big green volume labeled "1917–20."

He flipped through the pages until he found the one he wanted, then spread the book open on his desk. "Here's Father Hanlon's entry on Matthew Solomon's death . . . let's see, he left one son, Walter Solomon, um, age eighteen when Matthew died."

The priest took off his glasses and tapped them on the open page with a thoughtful look. "Yes, I remember Victor saying his father was named Walter. So Matthew would have been Victor's grandfather."

"And Victor? He never had any kids?"

James put his glasses back on. "Two, but they died when they were little. His wife, too. They're all out back there, in the cemetery."

"What happened?"

The priest looked depressed. "There was a house fire while Victor was out hunting, or so I've been told. This was long before my time, but I gather his wife had a drinking problem whenever Victor wasn't around to keep her under control. Somehow the kids set the place on fire while she was passed out."

"You hear a lot of stories like that around here," Active said.

"Uh-huh," James said. "Too many."

"Yet you retain your faith?"

James said, "Uh-huh" again, and didn't elaborate. He

seemed to have become fascinated by the 1917–20 record book.

Finally Active broke the silence. "This Father Hanlon who was here when Matthew Solomon died. Did he bring Matthew into the church?"

James looked up. "In all probability. He founded this mission in 1901, and served here till, um, 1923, I think it was."

"Would his records show when Matthew Solomon was converted?"

"They should, but you'll have to do a hand search to find it." The priest smiled his joke smile. "The records are strictly chronological. No subject headings, no cross-tabs, no nothing. This was before Yahoo and Google."

"Mind if I give it a shot?"

"No problem." James stood up and pointed at the shelf where he had gotten the 1917–20 volume. "Have at it. I've got to make a house call. Just let yourself out if you finish before I get back."

Active nodded his thanks. James said, "Feel free to copy anything you find," and left the study.

Active photocopied the entry about Matthew Solomon's death from Spanish flu, then searched the pages preceding it for an entry on his conversion.

No luck, so he replaced the volume on the shelf and studied the neighboring volumes. There were only two earlier volumes in the series. One was dated 1901–1910, the other 1911–1916. Apparently, Hanlon hadn't had much to record for the first few years of his ministry in Chukchi, then things had gotten busy.

Active opened the first volume and flipped through it, scanning Hanlon's neat clerical hand for any reference to Saganiq, Solomon, shaman, or *angatquq*. As of the close of

1910, Saganiq was still outside Jesus's big igloo, as far as Active could tell from Hanlon's records.

He opened the second volume and found the entry almost immediately. Saganiq had entered the igloo on February 3, 1911:

> The Eskimo Saganiq came to me today and asked to be received into the church. He admitted that he had been a great sinner, an *angatquq*, had practiced witchcraft and done many other sinful things, though he swore it was not true, as rumored, that he had murdered the false prophet Natchiq. Indeed, after Natchiq's disappearance in the mountains, had not Saganiq taken in Natchiq's widow as his third wife until her death in childbirth soon after? At any rate, Saganiq said, he had now given up his old and sinful ways, including polygamy, had embraced the white man's god, and was ready to follow the teachings of the church with his one and only surviving wife. So I took his confession and brought him into our church, giving him his Christian name, Matthew Solomon. And thus did the Lord save the last of the Chukchi devil-doctors, the only other remaining adherent of this barbaric practice having hung himself last spring.

Active walked to the copier and laid the entry facedown on the glass. His original theory had just risen from the dead. Except it was more complicated now. Saganiq wasn't the victim from Shaman Pass. He wasn't Uncle Frosty. He was in all probability Uncle Frosty's killer.

As Active pushed the button to copy the entry, he lectured himself on the perils of tunnel vision in the law enforcement business. The harpoon found in Uncle Frosty wouldn't have

belonged to Uncle Frosty. Of course not. It would have belonged
to his killer. Saganiq.

Why had he not seen it before? Because he had gotten it
into his head from the start that the harpoon had belonged to
Uncle Frosty. In fact, he remembered Jim Silver saying exactly
that over Victor Solomon's body at the sheefish camp. "It's
Uncle Frosty's harpoon," Silver had said.

And he, Nathan Active, professionally trained Alaska State
Trooper, had not once reexamined the assumption.

He shook his head and tried to focus on the case instead of
his own stupidity. Why had Saganiq killed Natchiq, if that
really was Uncle Frosty's name? And why had Saganiq left
behind something so valuable as a harpoon, representing as it
did countless hours of hand labor in a primitive society. And
why would an *angatquq* like Saganiq leave behind his amulet?

But most of all, why would someone go to the trouble of
stealing Uncle Frosty—Natchiq—from the museum, along
with Saganiq's amulet and harpoon, and then spearing Victor
Solomon with it?

Active had just reached the end of the 1911–16 volume
without finding any other references to Matthew Solomon or
Natchiq when Sebastian James returned from his house call.
"Come up with anything?" the priest asked.

Active showed him Father Hanlon's account of Saganiq
joining the church. "You ever hear of this Natchiq?"

The priest studied the photocopy and shook his head.

"He would presumably be Uncle Frosty, assuming we take
Saganiq's denial of killing him for what it's probably worth,"
Active said.

James nodded. "Presumably."

"If this Saganiq really was an *angatquq* and a killer, how did
he end up in the church?"

James chuckled. "I think Father Hanlon's entry speaks for

itself. Saganiq's conversion signaled the end of the devil-doctors."

"You really think that? The *angatquqs* were in league with the devil? Weren't they just the traditional version of a priest? Wouldn't you have been one yourself, in those days?"

James looked into himself as though he had never considered the question. "I hope not," he said at length. "By the time the *naluaqmiuts* showed up, the *angatquqs* were as corrupt as a priesthood can be. Some tried to do good, the female ones in particular, but too many of the male *angatquqs* used their power over our people for the usual perks: wealth, women, privilege. So when the white man brought in Christianity along with his rifles and his medicines, we Inupiat were ready for the Word. The power of the *angatquqs*, like much of the rest of our culture, crumbled away like hoarfrost." James paused in thought for a moment. "Except the *angatquqs*, I think, deserved it."

"So Saganiq was just joining the winning team?"

James nodded. "A conversion of convenience, I'm sure. I'm just surprised it took him so long. By 1911, the battle was long over. He must have been a stubborn man."

Active started to speak, but James raised a hand.

"Actually, perhaps I'm being a little unfair to the *angatquqs* and to the Inupiat who watched the white man arrive. Do you know much about the history of this area just before contact, Nathan?"

Active shook his head. "Very little, I guess. The Yankee whalers showed up in the late eighteen hundreds?"

James nodded. "And they came at a bad time for the Inupiat. According to the anthropologists, there was an amazing famine in the Chukchi basin around that time, starvation on a biblical scale. For two years in a row, everything vanished—no caribou, no whales, no fish, no birds, no berries. Or almost none. When it was over, the population of this area was ten percent of what it had been before."

"Ninety percent mortality? That's, that's . . ."

"Died, or moved away in search of food," James said. "The survivors who described it for anthropologists in the 1930s and 1940s told of starvation, cannibalism."

"I had no idea," Active said. "I knew life was hard back then, but I guess I assumed the land always provided enough to get by."

"Not always," James said. "So when the *naluaqmiuts* showed up, the Inupiat were a chastened people. Nothing they or their *angatquqs* could do had been able to bring back the fish or game, and then the white man steams over the horizon with plenty to eat, new technology, and a new religion. Or maybe the new religion was part of the technology." James smiled, a thin, wry smile. "Whatever it was the *naluaqmiut* had, it seemed to work, so we bought the whole package."

"Including the liquor that killed Victor Solomon's family."

"That, too," James said. "That, too." The priest studied him for a moment, then, "And you?"

"Me?"

"How are things with you? I look at your face and . . ." James shrugged.

"I'm fine. Police work carries its share of stress, of course." Active shrugged back, trying to make it look nonchalant.

James smiled. "It's all right. The Lord doesn't mind if you take comfort from Nelda Qivits. It's where you end up he cares about, not the path you take."

Active stared, speechless. How many others knew about his visits to the little cabin near the hospital?

Outside the church, he paused in thought for a long moment, then headed the Suburban north up Second Street. Nelda's place was six houses south of the hospital. As he knocked, he wondered again why she was the only person he could discuss the bullet dream with. All he knew was, it had something to do with questions and advice.

The one time he had tried to discuss it with Lucy, there had been a barrage of questions, a shower of advice. How long had he been having the dream? How often? Who was the person holding the gun? Was it her? Did he want to get counseling? Maybe he should take some time off work. Go visit his adoptive parents in Anchorage and stay in his old room for a while.

He had frozen in the spotlight of her love, the blaze of her anxiety, and then she had told Martha, his birth mother, about it, and he had had to repeat the ordeal the next time he went to Martha's house for Sunday dinner. He was even less able to discuss the dream with Martha Active Johnson, the most terrifying woman on earth, and she had ended up as hurt, frustrated, and scared as Lucy.

Still, their unanimous recommendation of counseling didn't seem like such a bad idea. Except he didn't want it on his record. No cop in his right mind wanted anything in his personnel records about mental problems. Nothing that would make the brass think he was cracking up, or might in the future.

Then, not long after the first bullet dream, Active had been sent to a village on the Isignaq River to bring in a man named Grover Weldon on his third domestic-violence arrest in a year. Unlike the other two times, this time the wife beater drew a newly hired magistrate who happened to be a middle-aged no-bullshit Inupiat woman named Charlene Plunkett. Zinc-haired Charlene Plunkett had taken one look at Grover Weldon, said he was sick inside, and ordered him to see a tribal doctor named Nelda Qivits. That was—what—six, seven months ago? And Grover had stayed out of trouble, as far as Active knew.

Anyway, "sick inside." That had resonated. And the next time Active had a bullet dream, he found himself knocking on Nelda Qivits's door. The thing was, Nelda rarely asked a question about the bullet dream or offered advice. She never reacted to anything he said about the dream, but somehow it worked. She would chatter away like any old *aana*, swapping idle gossip till he found himself talking about what was on his mind. Afterward, he felt better and the dream didn't come for a while.

Now, however, he had had it twice in three days, so here he was at Nelda's door again. She opened it finally, stared into his eyes for a long time, and said, "Come on in, *naluaqmiiyaaq*, I'll make sourdock tea. Good thing you came, look like." She switched off the TV and hobbled into her tiny kitchen.

He followed her in and watched from the dining table as she filled a saucepan with water, threw in some of the sourdock root reputed among the *aanas* to cure almost anything, and turned on the heat. The bitter smell of the stuff filled the room as she came to the table and sat across from him. "You had that dream again, ah?"

He nodded. "Two days ago and again this morning, the same each time. And I'm thinking about it more when I'm awake."

He told her about the figure coming through the door with the knife or whatever it was, about his own fruitless efforts to shoot the assailant.

"Maybe it wasn't a knife this time?"

"Maybe not. I couldn't tell."

"Harpoon maybe," she said. "Tea's ready."

Active thought it over while she went to the stove, filled two cups, and returned. That sounded right, a harpoon. So right that he got nervous thinking about it, felt his breathing accelerate. But was it memory, or suggestion?

"It could have been a harpoon," he said. "And I think he

stabbed me this time. Except the phone rang right at that moment and Lucy poked me with the antenna. So I don't know."

"Same harpoon kill old Victor, maybe."

He looked into the old lady's headlight glasses, a new wave of shocked recognition washing over him. And then, before he could work out the feeling any further, he found himself telling her what he knew of the story, how in some way Victor Solomon's murder seemed to be connected to Uncle Frosty, who seemed to be a false prophet named Natchiq.

She nodded and looked into her cup, which was empty. "Seem like I hear a little bit about Natchiq when I'm young girl, but I can't remember it now."

He lifted his eyebrows.

"You'll find out for yourself, ah?"

"Except I'm too late for Victor Solomon."

Nelda studied his eyes some more. "No problem with *quiyuk*, ah?" She gathered the cups and went to the stove for a refill, once again giving him time to think things over.

Active tensed up at this question. It was one of the few questions Nelda would ask him, and she asked it every time. And it was the one question he wished she wouldn't ask.

Not that it wasn't logical. You didn't need to be Sigmund Freud to see the implications of the bullet dream. So far, there was no problem with *quiyuk* between him and Lucy, at least not much. It was just that he was afraid that thinking about the possibility of a problem, and talking about the possibility, would, in fact, bring on the problem, so he was starting to avoid *quiyuk*, which Lucy was starting to figure out. Now he wished Nelda would just shut up about it. But how to say that to a seventy-something *aana*?

What he said to her was, "I don't know. Maybe."

She cackled. "Well, you sharpen up your harpoon, try it out on that Lucy girl's *muktuk*, ah?" She raised her cup and drank the sourdock tea, eyes huge and bright and merry through the headlight glasses.

Not for the first time, he found himself rendered speechless by Nelda's earthiness. He tried not to be surprised by anything that came out of an *aana*'s mouth, but Nelda always found a way.

By the time he thanked her and got out onto the street again, though, he was grinning a little. He supposed Inupiaq had as many metaphors and euphemisms for sex as English did, and this was no doubt another one. Or maybe Nelda had coined it on the spot. But—harpooning the *muktuk*? He laughed out loud.

That was the way it was with what Nelda said. First, you were shocked. Then it was funny. Eventually, though, you had to face the fact that it actually meant something.

CHAPTER FOURTEEN

HE FOUND LUCY AT the Dispatch console in the public safety building, highlighting passages in an accounting text. She wore white Levi's and a white sweater today, and looked dazzling as usual.

"Got a minute?"

She didn't look up. Today's bullet dream had come just before dawn, leading to another fight before breakfast.

"Still mad, huh?"

Finally she raised her gaze from the book. "Still shutting me out?"

"I'd let you in if I could. But I . . ."

She closed the textbook and looked him in the eye. "But?"

"I can't explain it. Someday, maybe I'll get my mind around it and be able to talk about it. But not now."

"Except with Nelda Qivits."

He sighed. "I'm sorry."

"But not sorry enough to talk about it."

"Not sorry enough to apologize again, that's for damned sure." His voice was louder than he'd intended, and the words were out before he could stop them. "You've had two or three apologies already and that's all you get for one bullet dream. The only question is, are you go—" He finally forced his mouth shut, shocked by his own rage and his self-indulgence in letting it out. And by the crushed look on her face.

"Now I really am sorry," he said. "That was completely out of line."

She turned away and touched her eyes, then faced him again with a shrug. "Maybe someday."

"I'm trying, I really am."

"I know that, somewhere inside, I think. I'll try, too."

He glanced around and, seeing no one near, kissed her quickly, picking up a slight taste of salt from compressed and unresponsive lips.

"Thank you," she said with a stiff nod. "How did we get started down that road again, anyway?"

"I don't know," he said. "It certainly wasn't what I came to talk about."

"Which was?"

It took him a moment to recall. "Did you ever hear any stories about a couple of old *angatquqs* named Natchiq and Saganiq?"

She thought for moment, then shook her head. "Don't think so. You want me to ask Aana Pauline?"

He nodded and she slipped on her headset, then punched in her grandmother's number on the Dispatch console. He listened as she asked Pauline Generous about the two shamans.

Finally Lucy slipped the headset off one ear and looked at him. "She says she's heard the names a couple of times from some of the old people around here, but doesn't really know much about them."

Lucy concentrated on her headset for a few seconds, then looked at him again. "She was raised in the Nome area and they never talked about Saganiq and Natchiq down there. And Pauline never got back up here to Chukchi till she was a grown woman, so she wasn't around when the people who knew them might have still been alive. But she's on her way to the Senior Center, so she said maybe she'll ask around over there."

Lucy thanked her grandmother and disconnected the call. "Maybe your mother would know somebody who knows about them. Working at the school like that, she meets the elders when they come in for Inupiat culture classes."

Active stared at her for a moment. Usually Lucy and his mother were immovable rivals. Neither would ever suggest he spend time in the other's company, not ordinarily. Perhaps the bullet dream had brought them together. An alliance of the excluded.

"Thanks," he said. "I'll give it a try."

He scanned the area again, then leaned over for another kiss. This time her lips were soft and full, seeming hungry for his, and her tongue flicked briefly against his own. She returned her attention to the accounting text with the tiniest of smiles as he said goodbye and headed for the door in a state of mild agitation.

MARTHA ACTIVE JOHNSON WAS sliding a tray along the serving line at the Chukchi High School cafeteria when he found her. "Got a minute?"

She beamed. "For you, sweetie? Always! Get a tray and we'll eat in my office, ah?"

As he pulled a tray from the stack at the end of the counter, he marveled again at his birth mother's youthfulness. Instinct told him a grown man should have a mother who looked a little gray, a little pudgy, like Carmen, his adoptive mother in Anchorage.

Not Martha. Martha had been only fifteen when he was

born and was just now moving into her midforties. But she didn't look even that. No sign of middle-age fat, black hair still glossy, smooth-faced except for the laugh lines around her mouth and sparkling black eyes.

They loaded up with meat loaf, mashed potatoes, green beans, applesauce in tiny plastic cups, and half-pints of milk in cardboard pyramids, then he followed her through the halls to her office. TEACHER AIDE COORDINATOR, a sign said on the door. Another one, in multicolored letters, said, GO HUSKIETTES! STATE 2A!

She put her tray on her desk blotter and cleared a space on the opposite side for him. He put down his tray, pulled up an ugly orange plastic chair, and applied himself to the meal. The food tasted better than he expected, especially the green beans. Maybe cafeterias had changed since his school days. Or maybe Chukchi High just treated its students better than Bartlett High in Anchorage had.

Martha speared a chunk of meat loaf with her fork, rolled it in the mashed potatoes, and popped it into her mouth. She grinned as she swallowed. "You came to tell me how much you miss me and what a great mom I am, ah?"

Active grinned back. "I'm moderately fond of you and you're an adequate mother, up to a point."

"*Arii!*" she said. "A woman who doesn't want a broken heart should never have any kids. Just dogs." She sucked some milk from her carton. "So, what you want? Did your washer at the bachelor cabin break again?"

"No, no, it's not laundry this time, *Aaka*. It's work."

Her eyes turned serious. "Oh. You never find out who kill old Victor Solomon yet, ah? I thought it was that crazy Calvin Maiyumerak."

He shook his head. "Probably not. But that's what I came about."

"You think it was one of our students?" She looked alarmed.

He waved a hand in dismissal. "No, no, of course not. But I need to know about a couple of old-time *angatquqs*, Natchiq and Saganiq. Did you ever hear of them?"

She was silent a few moments, frowning. "Seem like—yes, I think your grandfather talk about them sometimes when I'm little girl."

"Jacob knows about them?"

"Seem like it, all right. But what do they have to do with Victor getting killed?"

"I don't know yet. But apparently Victor was the grandson of one of them, Saganiq. What did Jacob say about them?"

She frowned again, then shrugged in frustration. "I can't remember. In them days, I didn't want to hear any Eskimo stuff. I was ashamed to be Eskimo. I wanted to be white."

The conversation was taking an alarming turn toward the confessional. "Do you think he still remembers those old stories?" Active said. "I could go visit him at the Senior Center."

"Probably," Martha said. "His mind is still pretty sharp, at least about the old days. He just forgot his English after his stroke is all."

"I know. I'll need someone to translate. I can't keep up with his Inupiaq."

She misted up. "I can't translate for you. He won't see me."

"Why not?"

"I don't like to say."

"*Aaka*, I need to know this."

She wiped her eyes with a corner of the napkin from the cafeteria tray. "It's because of you, partly. And Leroy."

Leroy Johnson was Martha's husband, Active's stepfather, technically speaking, and the father of Active's teenage half-brother, Sonny.

"Leroy and me? Why?"

"Your *Ataata* Jacob never like *naluaqmiuts*, Nathan. He think they ruin our country up here with their airplanes and booze and welfare. So he's mad when I give you away to Ed and Carmen, because they're white, then he's mad again when I marry Leroy, because Leroy's white. Finally he just stop talking to me. Won't look at me if I go in there or anything."

He should have known this, he realized, but somehow he hadn't. He had seen Jacob Active a couple of times when his adoptive parents took him to Chukchi in largely unsuccessful efforts to keep him in touch with his roots. And he had visited the old man twice since being posted to Chukchi two years earlier. The visits were awkward and ceremonial, because of the language barrier raised by his grandfather's stroke.

And Martha had always hovered in the background during these visits. He had never seen the two exchange as much as a word, in English or Inupiaq.

"Did he stop talking to you around the time he had his stroke, by any chance?"

"Yeah, I guess. But—"

"The same time he forgot how to speak English?"

She nodded.

"Well, maybe it's just the stroke that makes him act this way. A stroke can change an old person."

His mother looked doubtful as she toyed with a piece of meat loaf. "I don't know. He was pretty mad about it, even before the stroke."

There was a long silence. Then Martha applied the napkin to her eyes again and looked at him. "Sometimes I'm afraid you're kind of like him, how you're always mad at me about adopting you out."

Active now found himself misting up. She was so isolated.

Disowned by her father, her mother long dead, and blessed with him for a son, a son who couldn't forgive her, couldn't help her convince herself she had done the right thing in signing him over to Ed and Carmen. He rubbed his brow and sighed. How did she manage to remain so happy so much of the time? "I'm not mad, *Aaka*. It's just that I, well—"

"I knew I was too young and wild to take care of you and you turned out all right, ah?"

"I know you did your best." He leaned forward and touched her hand.

Her eyes narrowed and she studied his face. "You're still having that dream, ah?"

He wrinkled his nose in the Inupiat squint of dismay and negation, and said nothing.

She sighed and dropped the napkin on her plate. "Anyway, I know you need a translator if you will talk to your *ataata*. How about that Lucy girl? Doesn't she translate for the court sometimes?"

Active nodded, masking his surprise. Now Martha was suggesting he spend time with Lucy. They must both be terribly worried about him.

ACTIVE RETURNED to the public safety building and found Lucy still in the Dispatch booth. "You know my grandfather?" he asked.

"Little bit," Lucy said. "When I was a girl, he'd come to school for Inupiat culture class and tell Eskimo stories or talk about whaling or sealing or how to keep alive on the ice. Why?"

"Martha says he knows about Natchiq and Saganiq. But I can't keep up with his Inupiaq. She suggested you could translate for me."

"Martha said that?" Lucy looked as surprised as he had been.

He lifted his eyebrows and said, "I know."

Lucy frowned. "Jacob doesn't speak English? He used to speak it pretty well, at least Village English, when he came to our classes. Otherwise most of the kids couldn't have understood half of what he said."

"He forgot his English when he had his stroke. That's what Martha says."

"Sure, I guess I can do it," Lucy said. "Give me a minute to find somebody to take over here." She turned and was saying,"Daphne, could you . . ." as she vanished through the door at the back of the Dispatch booth.

She returned with her parka and they started out as Lucy's replacement, an Inupiat girl who looked like a teenager, slid into the chair at the Dispatch console.

"This could be awkward," Active said as he steered the Suburban toward the Senior Citizens' Cultural Center, which lay on the shore of the lagoon behind the village. The west wind that had closed the lead and driven the whalers off the ice the day before was still rolling in, driving wisps and eddies of snow before it, whipping clothes on the lines in backyards, and hunching the shoulders of the few walkers on the streets.

"Why's that?" Lucy asked.

"Jacob doesn't like my mother and I don't think he likes me, either. I bet he hasn't said more than twenty words to me all the times I've seen him."

Lucy stared at him. "What's the problem?"

"I only found out today when I asked Martha to translate. Apparently he's got a thing against the *naluaqmiuts* for generally ruining life for the Inupiat, and against Martha for getting involved with so many of them."

"Like Ed and Carmen."

"And Leroy. And maybe me, too, because I grew up with white people."

Lucy clucked her tongue sympathetically. "Old people."

"Some old people," he said

She snapped her fingers. "You know who Jacob does like?"

"Who?"

"My grandmother."

"Pauline?"

"Yep. She talks about him all the time when she comes back from visiting people at the center. There's even talk . . ."

"What talk?"

"I've heard she and Jacob had something going after his wife died."

"She won't discuss it?"

"Not really," Lucy said. "She just kind of grins if I try to ask."

"Well, that's not like Pauline."

"I know. She's so earthy. Usually sex, grocery shopping, and the weather are all the same to her. I think the difference is, this might have been while my grandfather was still alive."

"No."

"Yes." Lucy was grinning now.

"Your grandmother and my grandfather."

"Hey, it's a small town with long, dark winters. If it wasn't for the tepee creeping, everybody would go crazy."

"This is Eskimo country."

"All right, igloo creeping."

"Wait a minute, we're not cousins or something, are we?"

She laughed. "No, no, this was when Jacob and Pauline were both in their fifties. Long after my dad was born."

"Well, thank God for that."

She laughed again. "Anyway, I think Pauline would probably help us. Her English isn't good enough for her to be a real translator, but she can bail me out if I get stuck with the Inupiaq. And I think she'll charm old Jacob right out of his . . . well, right out of whatever he knows about your old *angatquqs*."

CHAPTER FIFTEEN

ACTIVE PARKED THE SUBURBAN at the senior center. Like nearly every other building in Chukchi, it boasted T1-11 siding and a shingle roof. A gaggle of four-wheelers and snowmachines were parked in front, along with two pickups and a rusted-out yellow Subaru.

The center was a three-spoked wheel with no rim. Each spoke was a wing where the elders had their bedrooms. The cafeteria, TV room, and administrative offices filled the hub.

Active checked in at the office and they found Pauline in a game of snerts with three other old ladies in the light pullover parkas called *kuspuks*.

"Hi, Aana," Lucy said to Pauline, nodding to the other women at the table.

Pauline looked up from her cards through her big cataract glasses, smiled, and returned Lucy's greeting. "And it's good to see you too, Nathan," she said. "You guys come over sometime, I'll make some fish-head soup."

"I'd like that," Active said. "How about the second Tuesday of next week?"

Pauline grinned and shook her head, looking to Lucy for sympathy. "Same old Nathan, ah? So bossy."

"Did you ask anybody about Saganiq and Natchiq?" Lucy asked.

"I asked these ladies here, but they don't know anything. That right, Annie? June? Bessie?"

The snerts players nodded in unison, looking mildly crestfallen at their failure to be of help.

"Well, Nathan thinks his grandfather Jacob might know something. You want to help me translate?"

Pauline beamed and glanced down the hall leading, Active knew, to his grandfather's room. Then she caught herself and looked serious. "Maybe Nathan will give me a ride to bingo tonight in his trooper truck, ah?"

It was Pauline Generous's usual price for any favor he asked. He sighed in resignation. "With the flashers on," he said.

"And the siren."

He shook his head and masked a grin. "And the siren."

"OK, I'll help then." She excused herself from the snerts game and they made their way down the hall to Jacob Active's room.

Active saw through the half-open door that his grandfather lay sleeping on top of the bedcovers in the afternoon sun, Kay-Chuck playing softly from a little radio on a stand beside the bed.

Jacob Active had creased brown skin stretched tight over his cheekbones and a shock of silver hair that stood straight out from his head like dandelion fuzz. He wore a hearing aid in his left ear. Its lobe was missing, taken by frostbite on the trail long ago, according to Martha. The right side of his face drooped from the stroke, and a silver thread of saliva trailed from that corner of his mouth. Beside the radio on the nightstand lay a pair of cataract glasses as big and thick as Pauline's.

Nathan sensed Pauline beside him, and moved so that she could look in. Her face softened. "You want me to wake him up?"

Active nodded and the old woman walked to the bed, took a Kleenex from a box on the nightstand, and wiped the sleeper's chin. Then she touched his arm. "Jacob," she said. "Jacob, it's Pauline."

Jacob stirred and blinked, looking lost and confused. Pauline handed him the glasses. He put them on and peered about. "Ah, Pauline," he said. Then came a few phrases of Inupiaq in the whispery old-man's voice.

Pauline answered in Inupiaq, then stepped aside to show him who was with her. The old man smiled at Lucy and glanced briefly at Nathan, then away.

"I'm going to tell him why we're here, then Lucy can talk to him," Pauline said with a look at Nathan. She spoke again in Inupiaq. Nathan heard his own name, then Lucy's, Victor Solomon's, Saganiq's, and Natchiq's.

Jacob was silent for some time after Pauline finished, then he squinted and rattled off a burst of Inupiaq.

Pauline spoke again. Nathan heard his own name again, and the Inupiaq word for grandson. Then Pauline leaned over and spoke into Jacob's hearing aid, so that only she and Jacob knew what she said.

Finally the old man raised his eyebrows and said, "*Ee*," the Inupiaq word for yes.

Pauline rearranged his pillows and helped him sit up against the headboard, then turned. "He'll do it, but he wants some tea. I could bring it while you guys get started, ah?"

She left the room. Lucy pulled a chair up to Jacob's bed and took a seat. Nathan pulled up a chair, but a little farther off, and took out his notebook.

Jacob spoke in Inupiaq for a few seconds, then looked at Nathan.

"He says how is your mother and is she still with that white man?" Lucy translated.

"Tell him she's fine, and, yes, she's still married to Leroy, and she still loves her father."

Lucy made the translation. Jacob frowned and looked away from them for a moment, then spoke in Inupiaq.

"He says he loves her too, and he's sorry that some things can't be helped when you get too old. But he does want to help you in your trooper work, so he will tell you what he can remember about Saganiq and Natchiq. He finds that he can't remember what happened this morning, but things from his youth are as clear as if they happened yesterday. Still, he's not sure he can remember all that he heard when he was a boy. But he will do his best."

Active nodded. "That's all I ask, Ataata." He thought Jacob smiled slightly at the Inupiaq word, but it was impossible to be sure.

The old man spoke again through Lucy, Nathan interrupting with questions only when he couldn't help himself. The account was halting at first, but picked up speed and assurance as it went on. It was as if one memory led to another, like the links in a chain.

"You want to know about Saganiq and Natchiq, ah? My dad and the other people his age used to speak of them often when I was a boy. I think my dad knew both of them a little bit, maybe. Maybe when he was a boy he saw Natchiq sometimes. And that Saganiq, maybe he still lived around here until just before I was born.

"Anyway, my dad and those other people, they said Natchiq came from way up on the Isignaq River, around that place we call Rough Creek today. Nobody lives there any more, but, used to be, if you would go up there and look around in the willows, you could see the old pits where those people had their houses. One time I went up there with my dad and we walked around and dug down into a couple of pits to see what we could find. Dad, he dug up this old broken ax made out of jade, and he says, 'Maybe Natchiq used this to chop a tree, ah?' I don't know if you can still do that today, since the whites made their national park up there.

"Anyway, Natchiq came from up there around Rough Creek. There was just him and one sister, but I guess she died when she was little, because I never heard anything about her. So he grew up mostly by himself, just him and his mother up there on Rough Creek.

"When he was little, he would always help her out and he learned lots of things from her, like how to make a sod house or set snares for rabbit and ptarmigan, that kind of thing. What people needed to know to stay alive in those days."

"What about his father?" Nathan asked. Lucy translated the question, and Jacob frowned in concentration for a moment.

"That's a funny thing, those old stories never said anything about Natchiq's father. Maybe his father died when he was little, or maybe his father left his mother for some reason. I never heard. The stories only tell about his mother, and how he always helped her out and learned things from her.

"But he also learned things himself just by watching and listening, and pretty soon he was the best hunter around that place. He could catch any kind of game. If it was squirrel or caribou or bear, didn't matter, Natchiq could catch it. Or maybe the game gave itself to him because of who he was. That's what some people thought.

"His magic or whatever it was started one day when he was out checking his snares. He came to a nice place by the river, so he sat down to rest on a piece of driftwood. Pretty soon he heard a little bird chirping. Then he listened close and he heard that it was chirping in Eskimo and it was saying, 'Father and son, father and son.' And then he went home saying it to himself. 'Father and son, father and son.'

"After that, he went back to that spot whenever he could, because he always felt real peaceful and calm whenever he heard that little bird chirping, 'Father and son, father and son.' Then after a while, the little bird added to what he was chirping. He starts to say, 'Father and son, the source of intelligence. Father and son, the source of intelligence.'

"Now Natchiq was getting home later and later every time and his mother was starting to worry. She asked him why he was so late, and he said he was just tending his snares, because that little bird never said, 'Tell about me.'

"So Natchiq was going around saying to himself what the bird said—'Father and son, the source of intelligence. Father and son, the source of intelligence'—and he went to his resting spot to hear the bird whenever he could."

"What did he mean by that, 'the source of intelligence'?" Nathan asked.

"Nobody ever really knew except Natchiq. Sometimes he called it his father. His father in the sky."

"It sounds like the *naluaqmiut* God."

"That was what a lot of people thought later on when the whites finally come into our country and started to talk about Jesus and everything. They thought Natchiq's source of intelligence was God. But at that time when Natchiq was still alive, the Eskimos had never heard of God yet or seen any white people, and Natchiq never explained anything about his father in the sky."

Jacob looked confused, and there was a hurried conference in Inupiaq. Then Lucy turned to Nathan. "He can't remember where we were. Wasn't he just telling us how Natchiq's mother was starting to worry because he came home so late?"

Nathan nodded. Jacob picked up the story and Lucy continued translating.

"Sometimes Natchiq wouldn't come home at night at all,

and his mother got more and more worried. She kept asking, 'Why are you gone so long? What do you do?'

"Suddenly he decided it was time to tell his mother, so he said he'd been listening to a little bird and he told her what it said: 'Father and son, the source of intelligence.'

"When she asked him where it was, this source of intelligence, he said it was somewhere up above, but he felt so much reverence, he didn't even dare look up to see.

"Now his mother was worried more than ever. She asked him, 'Are you turning into an *angatquq*?'

"He told her not to worry, he wasn't turning into anything. He was just listening and learning. He told her, 'I know something is helping us, and that the little bird calls from somewhere. But I don't know the source.'

"After that, his mother started to calm down for some reason, and never worried anymore. 'I'm almost an *aana* now,' she told herself, 'but I never heard of the source of intelligence before.'

"One day Natchiq told his mother that his source of intelligence was saying it was better if he married a certain girl. He went off hunting to the north with some other men and when he came back, there was this girl in their camp who came to visit his mother. He asked her to eat with them and then after they ate, they were building a new sod hut when Natchiq put his head down and thought for a long time. When he looked up again, he said he'd been in a peaceful place, in contact with his source of intelligence. 'It is better if I marry this girl,' he said then, and that was how he got married.

"So he lived up there around Rough Creek with his mother and his wife and they had a happy, peaceful life, because he was a good hunter, and he had his source of intelligence in the sky."

"And Natchiq said he was not an *angatquq*?"

Lucy started to translate, but Jacob raised his eyebrows and spoke first, apparently having figured Nathan's question out for himself. Lucy waited till he finished, then delivered the response.

"He says Natchiq was not an *angatquq*. He hated the *angatquqs*."

There was a tap at the door. Lucy opened it and Pauline came in, followed by an aide in a light green uniform carrying a tray with tea and a stack of pilot bread on it. The aide set it across Jacob's lap and he helped himself with gusto remarkable in an eighty-two-year-old, Active thought. Pauline sat at the foot of the bed, one hand on his ankle, and watched as he ate.

When the pilot bread was gone, Jacob took a sip of tea, nodded at Lucy, and picked up the tale again.

"See, before Natchiq came along, the *angatquqs* ran everything. A few of them were good. They tried to help the people when life was hard. But most *angatquqs* used their power to take whatever they wanted—food, women, boats, furs, fishing nets, anything.

"They controlled everything by taboos. If your daughter got sick, it meant you broke some kind of taboo, even if you didn't know it was taboo. Like if you ate caribou with your left hand instead of your right hand, maybe that was a taboo. But only the *angatquqs* would know. So if somebody in your family got sick, then you had to go to the *angatquq*. He would talk to his spirits, find what taboo you broke, and tell you what to do about it. Maybe you couldn't eat any berries for a year, or any *masru*—"

Here Lucy broke into a brief discussion with Pauline, at the end of which Lucy explained—in English—that she hadn't been able to think of the English term for the plant known as *masru*. But, with Pauline's help, she now believed the white man called it the Eskimo potato.

At the sound of this term, Jacob's face brightened

momentarily and he raised his eyebrows, repeating the phrase in English. "Eskimo potato, *ee*, Eskimo potato." Then he resumed the story, and Lucy resumed translating.

"Maybe you can't eat any Eskimo potato for one year. And you have to pay the *angatquq* or your daughter still don't get well."

"The *angatquqs* got paid?" Nathan asked.

"Oh, yes, that was how they got rich. Sometimes an *angatquq* would be the richest man in the village, and he would have three or four wives maybe.

"A lot of the taboos had to do with women. Like when a young girl became a woman, people in those days thought she was unclean. So she had to live in a hut by herself, maybe for a year. There would be a bucket of water out front, but no one could drink from it but her.

"It was the same way if a woman was having a baby. She couldn't be around other people. She had to go out in a hut or snowhouse by herself and have the baby all alone. No one was allowed to help or go around her for a few days. If she had a hard time, maybe she or the baby would die.

"Some taboos, maybe they were just to have fun with your kids. Like if the northern lights were out, you couldn't whistle or they would come down and cut off your head, that was one taboo. But even today, a lot of old people still won't whistle if the northern lights are out.

"A lot of other taboos had to do with food. Like how you couldn't cut caribou skin during fishing season or you would die. Or if you ate beluga whale the same time you ate berries or anything else from the ground, you would die. Or during the dark of the moon, you had to put ashes on your food, or you would die unless you got an *angatquq* to help you."

"The people let the *angatquqs* do this?" Nathan asked. "They believed what the *angatquqs* said?

"The people in those days never really believed anything.

They just had fear. Their whole life was based on fear. They never had anybody to teach them any different till Natchiq came along."

There was a tap at the door and everyone paused. The aide returned, now bearing a tiny paper cup with a tablet in it. "Time for his blood-pressure medicine," she said.

She spoke to Jacob in Inupiaq, and he obediently downed the tablet, chasing it with the last of his tea. He raised the teacup and spoke to her, and she lifted her eyebrows and took it away with her.

Jacob noticed the pill cup in his hand and gave it to Lucy, who dropped it into the waste can beside his bed. Then he looked at Nathan and began speaking.

"Pretty soon, word started to spread about Natchiq, because everywhere he went, he would talk about his source of intelligence and he would act different from other people. When he put up his tent, he would put down willow branches for his bed, instead of spreading his furs on the ground. And he took baths and kept himself clean, like we do now, which people never did in those days.

"And always he carried a long pole with him, and he would put it up outside his tent wherever he camped. Every seventh day, he would put a strip of sealskin on top of that pole, and he wouldn't do any work. He would just play a drum and look like he was thinking, maybe in a trance or something.

"People laughed at him when he did that. They would say, 'You're just lazy, that's why you don't work.' And Natchiq would say he was only doing what his father in the sky told him.

"Then they would ask, 'What did he tell you?' and that's when Natchiq would start to talk against the taboos. He would tell the people they didn't have to live in fear, and he would break all the taboos.

"Like the taboo about a young girl having to live alone when she first became a woman, he broke that taboo. He came to this camp up on the Katonak River where there were people living, and there was a young girl off in a sod house by herself. He went there and he drank from the water bucket in front of her house, and everybody thought he would die. But the next morning, he was alive like anyone, and people started to wonder about the taboo. When he got down to Chukchi, he did the same thing again. And he told the people that the old taboo about women having their babies all alone was wrong too, and pretty soon it would go away like all the other taboos.

"He kept breaking all kinds of taboos. When he came down to Chukchi, he went across to that place Tatuliq where everybody hunts beluga. Everybody was afraid to eat beluga at the same time as berries or any other food that came from the ground because of the taboo. So Natchiq, he went and picked some wild rhubarb and cooked it in his tent. While it was cooking, he went along the beach asking people for a piece of beluga blubber to eat with the rhubarb. People were so scared by this, a lot of them went in their tents and wouldn't even talk to him. But finally someone gave him some blubber and he took it back to his tent and ate it with his rhubarb and nothing happened. Never got sick; the next day he was healthy and strong as any of them. After that, a lot of people started eating beluga with any other food, just like we do now.

"Any other taboo, he would break it whenever he could and tell people they didn't have to be afraid. He said, 'If we don't believe in the taboos, then they don't have any power over us.'"

Jacob stopped talking. Lucy queried him in Inupiaq, but he waved her off and motioned Pauline over. He spoke into her ear in Inupiaq and she responded, "*Arigaa*."

Then she eased him off the bed and helped him hobble into the bathroom.

Nathan and Lucy watched this without a word.

Finally, Lucy broke the silence. "Aren't they beautiful together? I just hope—" Apparently having thought better of whatever was to come next, she kept it to herself, and neither of them said anything more until Jacob was back on his bed.

He spoke in Inupiaq to Lucy, who turned and looked at Nathan. "He says where was he before he went to the bathroom?"

"He was talking about how Natchiq broke all the taboos."

Lucy translated this. Jacob lifted his eyebrows and said, "Ah-ha."

"BESIDES BREAKING the taboos, Natchiq always made prophecies, too. He said a new kind of people, white people, would come into the country and then everything would change for the Inupiat."

"Nobody had heard of white people in those days?" Nathan asked.

"Maybe a few people had heard of white-man ships passing by the coast, or maybe when Siberian people came over to trade, maybe they talked about seeing white people, but there weren't any around Chukchi and nobody here had ever seen any. This was right before all the whalers came into our country with their ships, I think.

"Anyway, Natchiq said everything would be different for the Eskimos when all the whites come. People would wear different clothes, eat different food. Some Eskimos would be made rich and some would be made poor.

"He predicted there would be thin pieces of birch bark that people could write on. He said boats powered by fire would ride in the sky. 'This is what some of you will travel in someday,' he told them, 'a boat powered by fire.'

"And he said there would be boats that could go up the river without anybody poling or without people and dogs on the banks pulling them up by ropes.

"A lot of people didn't believe him. 'That will never happen,' they said. 'You're going crazy, that's why you talk like this.'

"But Natchiq just said it was what his source of intelligence told him, and he kept doing whatever he wanted. Another thing he predicted was that the newcomers, the whites, would find something of great value to them up by where the Walker River runs into the Isignaq. A big city would grow up there, that was what he said, with lights that stretched to the mountains on both sides of the Isignaq.

"Later on, after Natchiq was gone and his predictions started coming true, like about all the white people coming into the country and the boats that could run by their own power, some of the Eskimos that still remembered him started to think he wasn't crazy after all. They thought maybe he could be right about the whites finding something they want at Walker River, too. So they moved up there and started Walker Village, thinking they would get rich when the whites finally made their strike. Maybe they still think that, ah?"

Jacob looked Nathan's way as Lucy translated this. Nathan gave the nod that seemed to be called for, and Jacob continued.

"Ah-hah. But the rest of what Natchiq said about Walker was not so good. He said that after it became a big city, there would be two winters together and no summer in between, with snow up to the treetops. Then, when breakup came, the flood would reach all the way to the shoulders of the mountains and a great big whale would surface on the river, right where Walker used to be. Then there would be a day that was split in half."

"What did he mean by that?" Nathan asked. "The end of the world?"

"He never explained it. When people would ask him, he would just look sad and not say anything. Maybe he was sad because his father in the sky didn't explain it to him, or maybe he did know what was coming next, but it was too sad to tell."

There was another break as the aide returned with Jacob's teacup, refilled. Then he continued.

"Of course when people started to listen to Natchiq about the taboos, the *angatquqs* got worried. They said, 'Don't believe anything Natchiq says—he's crazy.'

"But Natchiq answered that he was more powerful than the *angatquqs*, because their power came from the earth but his power came from his father above.

"At that time there were lots of *angatquqs* around Chukchi and the biggest one was Saganiq. He and the other *angatquqs* tried to find some way to kill Natchiq. In those days, *angatquqs* could do what they call—"

Lucy interrupted the proceedings with an apologetic look at Nathan. "I don't know how to translate what he's saying—it's a new word to me. I have to talk to Pauline."

She turned to her grandmother, still perched on the foot of the bed and now sipping from Jacob's teacup. Inupiaq flew back and forth between Jacob and the two women for a few moments, and then Pauline said, "He mean soul travel."

Lucy nodded in recognition, smiling. Then she continued the translation.

"Those old *angatquqs* could do soul travel. Their spirits would leave their bodies and fly around, sometimes they would even run into each other and have big fights on these trips. At least, that's what people thought, in those days.

"So Saganiq decided to use soul travel to find Natchiq's soul and kill him. He went out flying and pretty soon he came to

Natchiq. Natchiq was sitting on his chair and all around him was this bright glow. Saganiq tried to attack his soul, but the glow just got brighter and then Natchiq's chair started to rise upward. Saganiq tried to attack again, but the glow got even brighter and Natchiq's chair rose even more. Pretty soon, the glow was so bright that Saganiq couldn't even look at it, and he knew he couldn't kill Natchiq that way.

"When Saganiq come back to his body, there was Natchiq waiting, and he said, 'The one of the earth has tricked you. He is weak, not strong. Only my father in the sky is strong.'

"But Saganiq wouldn't give up. Him and two other *angatquqs*, they put a spell on some food to poison it and they gave it to Natchiq. But when Natchiq ate it, nothing happened. He just laughed and said, 'Even the poison you make doesn't hurt me. I eat it up. I could swallow you up if I wanted to.'

"Now Saganiq was really mad and he said, 'I think something might block the passage if you tried.' And he pulled out his *kikituq*, this amulet of a snowy owl that he always carried in his clothes, and he waved it in Natchiq's face. Natchiq just laughed again and said, 'I could swallow that, too.' He tried to take it, but Saganiq put it back in his clothes and he walked away.

"Not long after that, Natchiq was out hunting one day, and he caught a baby snowy owl that got lost from its parents. He brought it back, made a cage for it out of willow branches, and he kept it that way. He tamed that owl and he named it Saganiq and whenever anybody would come around, he would show them that tame owl named Saganiq sitting in its cage. Until finally one day, Natchiq killed that owl and ate it, to show people that Saganiq and the old-time *angatquqs* didn't have any power anymore."

Nathan shivered, and interrupted despite himself. "He ate Saganiq's *kikituq*?"

"Ah-hah, Natchiq cooked it and ate it and everybody thought he would die for sure that time. But he didn't die, he stayed as strong as ever. And after that hardly anybody would listen to Saganiq or the other *angatquqs*. The people didn't worry so much about taboos, either. Our people finally started to have a happier life. They did it themselves, even without the whites and their Christianity.

"Well, the *angatquqs* didn't have their power anymore, and Natchiq started to think it was time to go north, to tell the people up there what his father in the sky said about the taboos and the *angatquqs* and what would come in the future. So one day when it was just starting to be spring, like now, Natchiq told the people he was going to what we call Barrow now, where there was also lots of *angatquqs*, then maybe Canada. Him and his wife, they took off up the trail and they never came back."

"What became of them?" Nathan asked.

"I guess nobody ever found out for sure, or at least I never heard. Some people thought Natchiq made it through the mountains to Barrow, and then went to Canada. Some people thought Saganiq's *kikituq* flew up there and killed Natchiq's soul somewhere in the mountains, but maybe his wife made it back to Chukchi, only she was so weak by then she died, too. This was right about the time the *naluaqmiut* missionaries started to come in, and they told people not to talk about anything to do with *angatquqs* if they wanted to go to heaven. So everything after that kind of got lost from not being talked about, even though lots of people had memories of what happened with Natchiq before the missionaries came."

Nathan was silent for a time, digesting his grandfather's story. Fascinating enough, and probably with elements of truth. But what did it have to do with Victor Solomon's murder?

"What family was Natchiq from?" he asked. "Are his relatives still around today?"

Lucy translated this, and Jacob squinted a no, then spoke in Inupiaq.

"Like I say before, he come from up on the Isignaq River, and nobody lives at that place now. If he's connected to any family around here, I never heard about it. Maybe his people moved into some of the villages upriver and got new names from the *naluaqmiut* and they don't even know they're related to him. Or maybe his line died out if he died on the trail. His story is all broken up and now nobody knows who he was."

"I think someone knows," Nathan said. Jacob looked at him sharply and he realized the old man had understood at least the gist of what he had said.

"Who?" his grandfather said in English.

"Did you ever hear Whyborn Sivula talk about Natchiq or Saganiq?"

Lucy translated, but Jacob seemed to figure it out before she finished and spoke rapidly in Inupiaq to her.

"He says he never heard anything like that, and why do you think Whyborn would know who Natchiq was?" Lucy translated.

"Tell him I'm going to talk to Whyborn and find out the rest of the story, and then I'll come back and tell it to him."

Jacob smiled and lifted his eyebrows and said, *"Arigaa."* Then he laid his head against the pillows and closed his eyes.

CHAPTER SIXTEEN

ACTIVE PARKED THE SUBURBAN on Fifth Street in front of House 419, the number he had gotten from Dispatch and written in his notebook. The house was small and old, the paint on the T1-11 weathered to a pale rose that might have once been red. The structure roosted three feet in the air on wooden posts set into the ground. It was a common construction technique in Chukchi, employed to prevent buildings from thawing the permafrost below and being swallowed by it.

The posts seemed to have worked pretty well in the case of House 419, except at the northwest corner. There, the house had a pronounced sag.

Whyborn Sivula and his son, Franklin, the lookout from the whaling camp, were at work on the low corner as Active came up. They had a big jackscrew under a beam and Franklin was cranking as Whyborn sighted along the floor line to see if the corner was coming up to level. A few pieces of scrap lumber were stacked on a snowdrift nearby.

Active rolled down his window and watched for a couple of minutes as the corner lifted slowly off the post, the house timbers groaning. The two Sivulas ignored him, along with the wind ripping in from the west. He waited a couple minutes more.

"Mr. Sivula. Could you tell me about Natchiq?"

Active watched for Sivula's reaction, but there was none. The whaler bent down, picked up a section of two-by-six from the scrap pile, and slid it into the gap between the corner and the post. There was still some space left, but not enough for another slab of wood. "Franklin, you could jack it up a little more, then put in one more piece, ah?"

Franklin looked to be in his late thirties. He was squat and muscular, with a square face, heavy features, and short, bristling black hair. He frowned at the corner, sighted down the floor line and turned to Whyborn. "It's good now. Might be too high if I jack it up any more."

"It's OK if it's a little high," Whyborn said. "When summer come, that post will sink again and our house will be level. Then it'll sink some more and we'll jack it up some more next winter."

"*Arii*, this permafrost." Franklin grinned and resumed cranking the jack with a big monkey wrench.

Whyborn turned and finally acknowledged Active's presence. "Only *natchiq* I know is seal, Trooper Active. *Natchiq*, that's what us Eskimos call seal."

Active realized now why the word had seemed familiar when he read it in Father Hanlon's journal. "I know that, but this Natchiq is Uncle Frosty, Mr. Sivula."

Sivula turned sharp black eyes on Active and studied him for a moment. "You know about Natchiq?"

"I know he was killed by Saganiq long ago and somehow that led to Victor Solomon's death. And I think you know the connection."

Sivula looked west into the wind and studied the snow-covered ice of Chukchi Bay. Finally, he said, "You come in, have some tea, maybe we'll talk."

Active climbed down from the Suburban and followed him into the house, to sit at a little table in the kitchen while

Sivula heated water on an electric range. When the kettle whistled, Sivula brought two cups with teabags to the table and poured in steaming water. He dipped two spoons of sugar into his own cup and pushed the bowl toward Active, who shook his head and took a sip of tea.

"Victor Solomon is my friend since we're boys," Sivula began. "So I'm sorry he's kill."

Active nodded. "Can you tell me who did it?"

"Don't know," Sivula said.

"I thought Victor was your friend."

"Maybe I know who took Uncle Frosty from the museum. But I never think that's who kill Victor."

"Doesn't it have to be the same person?"

Sivula tilted his head and studied Active. The house was silent, except for a sudden groan from the timbers as Franklin jacked up the sagging corner. "I don't think so. But like I tell you in my camp at Cape Goodwin, it's old-time Eskimo business, done now anyway."

Active shook his head. "Not till whoever killed Victor is caught and punished."

"This man I know, he's old like me, maybe not around too much longer. Maybe if I tell you story, then you'll know you don't need to put him in jail? You're Eskimo too, ah?"

"I'll listen," Active said.

Sivula shrugged and looked into his teacup. "If I never tell his story, then maybe you don't find him."

"Some of the old people in town will know about Natchiq and Saganiq." Active stood up and zipped his parka. "My grandfather Jacob Active told me some of it and there must be someone who knows the rest. I'll—"

"You'll find him, ah?" The black eyes measured Active from the depths of the mahogany face.

"Me or some other trooper. We'll do whatever it takes."

Sivula looked into himself for a long time. "Then maybe I could tell you something," he said finally. "See what you think."

He drank from his cup and looked at Active, who sat down and pulled out a notebook and pen.

"Maybe better if you never write. Just listen."

Active nodded and put the notebook back in his pocket.

"Me and Victor Solomon, we're both born here, same age. We play together as boys, *pukuk* so much them old *aanas* always yell at us, try hit us with their walking sticks." Sivula's cheeks creased and he chuckled at the memory. "We're good boys, but you know we're full of . . . "

As Sivula groped for the word, Active realized he didn't know it, either. "Full of life," he suggested.

Sivula lifted his eyebrows and grinned. "Ah-hah, that right. Life. We're good boys, but we're full of life. When we get bigger, we hunt and fish together as young men, but not so much after Victor's family is killed in that fire. Seem like he's mad all the time, always want to be alone."

Active noticed for the first time the quality of Sivula's voice. It was low and rich, almost hypnotic.

"Anyways, there's always stories around town, how Victor's grandfather, Saganiq, was big-time shaman early days ago. But Victor will never talk about it. Couple times when I try ask him, he just tell me some things it's better not to talk about."

Sivula paused, as Active had learned was the custom with Inupiat storytellers, particularly old ones. It was also customary not to interrupt, to let the story unfold as it would, but he decided to take a chance. "Did you ever ask Victor's father about it?"

Sivula shook his head. "He's already almost old man when Victor's born, die when Victor and me are still pretty little."

Active nodded and sipped at his tea.

"So when I'm pretty grown up, I go in army, learn to be diesel mechanic. After that, I live in Nome long time, I'm traveling mechanic for Alaska Rural Power Co-op. You know about that?"

Active nodded.

"Ah-hah," Sivula said. "This one time, they send me to Caribou Creek to help put in new generator at their power plant up there. You ever go to Caribou Creek, Trooper Active?"

Active shook his head. "But I've seen pictures. It's east of here, in the Brooks Range?"

Sivula lifted his eyebrows. "Ah-hah. Funny place for Eskimos, all right, way up in the mountains like that. No seal, no *muktuk*, not so much fish." He shook his head. "They get lots of caribou maybe. But me, I'm a saltwater Eskimo."

"I guess it's what they're used to," Active said.

"I guess." Sivula shrugged. "Anyways, I'm up there at Caribou Creek couple weeks maybe. Caribou Creek have this power-plant operator that I work with on this new generator they're getting. One day, somebody tell me he's from Chukchi family so I ask him about it and he say, yes, his father's from Chukchi, move up to Caribou Creek before he's born, marry woman from there."

Sivula paused again. Active ventured another interruption. "When was this?"

Sivula frowned in concentration. "He never say when his father move to Caribou Creek." He shrugged. "Way back, I guess."

"No, I meant you. When was it that you went to Caribou Creek and met this man?"

"Ah, when I go? Maybe twenty-five years ago, all right. Maybe thirty."

"What was his name, anyway?"

Sivula stared into his teacup. "That was long time ago. I think I can't remember his name anymore."

Active let the silence ride for a while, hoping Sivula would rethink the lie, then decided to let it go. "Did he say why his father moved up there?"

Sivula pondered for a moment, then shook his head. "He never tell me, no."

Active nodded and Sivula picked up the story again.

"When job's over, generator's all running OK, he ask me to go hunting with him, up in Shaman Pass." Sivula raised his hands, as if to draw a map in the air, then paused and looked at Active. "Or maybe it was that other big pass up there, Howard Pass, where we went," he said, looking away. "Hard to remember now that I'm old."

Active sipped his tea and waited out this second lie.

"Anyway," Sivula said finally, "this guy have a Native allotment on a little creek up there. He got an old sod hut and a wall tent he leave up all the time, like any camp before everybody start making cabins. Except I see there's *inuksuk* on little hill behind the camp. You know about *inuksuk*?"

"A little bit. They were trail markers, scarecrows?"

Sivula lifted his eyebrows. "Ah-hah. Them old-time Eskimos always build them, but nobody do it today. Sometimes they build whole line of *inuksuks* for when they catch caribou. Them caribou think they're real men, get scared and run into lake or wherever them Eskimos chase 'em. Or sometimes, they build 'em on the trail, show which way to go. Have hole in the head, you look through, that's way to go. Or sometimes, they got nothing to do in camp, they just build them for fun. You see, Trooper Active?"

Active nodded.

"Ah-hah," Sivula said. "Well, this guy got an *inuksuk* at his camp, all right. I never see *inuksuk* since I'm little, so I jokes. I ask him, does it send him a telegram when it see caribous in the pass? He just grin little bit, say his father—"

Sivula paused, listening. Active heard the outer door to the *kunnichuk* slam, then the inner door open to admit Franklin. "I think that corner is good now, Dad. It's couple inches high, like you say."

Sivula's son went out again, and the old man pointed across the room to the corner in question. "Our house never sag till two, maybe three years ago. Then that one post start sinking, after all this time. You think that global warming they talk about is melting our permafrost?"

Active shrugged. "I don't know. Maybe."

Sivula picked up his cup, noticed it was empty except for the tea bag, and poured in some more water. "What I'm saying before?"

Active backtracked to before Franklin had come in. "About the man's father and the *inuksuk*."

"Ah-hah, that right," Sivula said. "He say his family put it in when they first make their camp, and then we don't talk about it anymore. Next day, we hunt along one of them rivers that run into the pass from the side. He seem kinda slow to me, always look at the country real careful, but I think that's just his way. Anyway, the hunting is pretty good, we get seven caribous. He keep four, I bring three back to Chukchi with me on the plane."

Sivula smiled at the thought and stopped talking. Active wondered if that was the story, in its entirety. He often failed to get the point of Inupiat stories, he had discovered. Sometimes, he thought this was because he was dense, or because the cultural gap opened by his years in Anchorage was too wide to be closed. Other times, he thought maybe Inupiat stories just had no point in the white sense of the word. Maybe they were just stories and this one was over. But Sivula shook his head and looked serious again and picked up the thread.

"So we load the caribous on our sleds and tie 'em down and we're ready to go back to his camp, but then I notice he's walk back to a cliff along the river. This is springtime, pretty warm, long days, and this cliff get lots of sun, so it's mostly thawed out. He start pulling rocks out and pretty soon I see he's making another *inuksuk*, right there in that little valley."

Active sipped at his tea, wishing there were some polite way to say to Whyborn Sivula, "Cut to the chase." But he knew it was impossible. Old men told their stories at their own pace everywhere, he supposed. Certainly, old Inupiat men did so.

"So I ask him about it. He look at me real serious, and then he tell me, he think his grandfather's body is up there in the pass somewhere and he always try to find it when he's hunting or trapping there. After he go up and down one of the side creeks, he always build *inuksuk*, so he'll know he already searched it. I guess that's why he look that little valley over so good when we're in it."

Sivula paused and sipped some tea. He noticed that Active's cup was empty, and picked up the kettle with a questioning look. Active covered the cup with a hand. Sivula set the kettle down again.

"Anyway, I ask him what he mean about his grandfather, he just say it don't matter and I know he don't want to tell me."

Sivula paused again and Active, interested to the point of impatience now, even rudeness, said, "And you think—"

Sivula held up his hand. "After that he's real quiet, all the time we're back at the camp, cut up them caribous, eat dinner. After dinner, he smoke his pipe for a while, then he just start talking without me saying anything. He say his grandfather is old-time Eskimo prophet name Natchiq. Natchiq try to fight the *angatquqs*, so this big-time *angatquq* name Saganiq kill him up there and hide his body somewhere, that's what this guy's father tell him. So his father and him, they always look for Natchiq's body when they're up in the pass. That's why his family build that camp up there. They think they'll find old Natchiq somewhere around there, maybe see if he's really kill by Saganiq, then they'll put his body out on the tundra the old-time way."

Sivula looked at Active. "You ever can't decide what to say next, Trooper Active?"

"Sure, sometimes," Active said, puzzled. "I think it happens to everybody."

"Ah-hah," Sivula said. "Well, that's what happen to me when this man say he think Saganiq kill his grandfather. He stop to smoke his pipe and I try think if I should tell him that Saganiq's grandson is my friend Victor Solomon in Chukchi."

"Ah," Active said. "I see the problem."

"But then he start talking again before I can say anything. He ask me if I think he's crazy, to look for his grandfather up there in the pass. I don't want to say nothing, so I just tell him, maybe them foxes and ravens already get Natchiq's body long time ago. He tell me that would be good, because it's old Inupiat way, but his father always say he think Saganiq hide Natchiq somehow, so it's like he'll be in cage or something."

Sivula paused, then started to speak, then shook his head. "After that, he say he don't want to talk about his grandfather anymore. He ask me if I want to play a little cribbage. He turn on Kay-Chuck on this battery radio he have up there and pull out this caribou horn that he's drill holes in and we play cribbage all night with some old nails for pegs."

Sivula paused again, so Active dropped in a question. "Did you tell your friend Victor about it when you got back to Chukchi?"

Sivula nodded. "Little bit. I say I run into this guy in Caribou Creek who say his grandfather was some old guy named Natchiq, then I watch what Victor will do. Victor never say nothing. He just look at me and raise his eyebrows. Then he grin."

"And did you see the man again?"

"Couple times, all right. Once at Alaska Federation of Natives convention in Anchorage, and once at class for power-plant mechanics in Nome." Sivula shrugged. "But he never tell me any more about his grandfather, and I never tell him I know Saganiq's grandson. I never forget what he tell me that night in his sod hut, though."

Another pause, possibly terminal. "So that's why you went to see Calvin?"

"Ah-hah," Sivula said. "When I hear Uncle Frosty is found in Shaman Pass, I always think maybe he's Natchiq. Then, when he's robbed from museum, I think probably Calvin do it, because of how he always make trouble. But Calvin say he never take Uncle Frosty, so I start to think maybe this guy hear about it on Kay-Chuck like me, come down to get his grandfather from museum, take him away and put his body out on tundra old-time way."

Active was silent for a time, thinking over the story.

"That day when I came to your camp at Cape Goodwin?"

Sivula lifted his eyebrows. "When we have to get off the ice. Probably we're out there too early, but for a saltwater Eskimo it's hard to stay in town when them bowheads start coming up the leads. When this storm is over, maybe they will open up again."

Active nodded. "You looked at the harpoon and the amulet and you knew they were Saganiq's. Was it from the property marks?"

Sivula sighed, almost inaudibly. "That man in the pass, he tell me snowy owl is Saganiq's *kikituq* spirit."

"So when you saw the owl carved on the harpoon and amulet—"

"That is when I know for sure those things belong to Saganiq and that Uncle Frosty must be Natchiq, just like that man tell me," Sivula said.

"And that's when you knew he killed Victor Solomon?"

Sivula dropped his eyes. "I never think he kill anybody. I think he steal Natchiq from the museum all right, but he never kill Victor Solomon."

Active said nothing, until Sivula continued.

"Because if he got away with Natchiq from the museum, why did he come back next day and kill Victor Solomon? He got what he wanted already."

Active stared at the cover of his notebook for several seconds. Sivula had a point, the same point Gail Boxrud had made trying to get Johnny Bass off the hook. "But only the killer would have the harpoon and amulet."

Sivula turned his measuring gaze on Active again. "I think this guy take Natchiq and then head back into the mountains to put him out on the tundra, like his family always want, but first he throw away the harpoon and amulet on the trail because they're Saganiq's, maybe unlucky for anybody in that family. Then somebody come along and find them on the trail, go kill Victor Solomon with the harpoon and leave the amulet there, too."

Active pursed his lips and gazed back at Sivula. "The person who just happens to find the harpoon and amulet also just happens to want to kill Victor Solomon? Too much coincidence."

Sivula shrugged. "There might be somebody like that."

Active sensed Sivula was trying to nudge him toward Calvin Maiyumerak, without having to name the name. "Still too much coincidence. We troopers don't believe in coincidence."

"So you think this man I'm telling you about did it?" Sivula asked.

Active said nothing, but lifted his eyebrows.

"Even if he did, it's over now," Sivula said. "Old-time Eskimo business, all done. Nobody else will be kill. Maybe you don't need to bother him, ah?"

"You still don't remember his name?"

Sivula was silent, examining the depths of his teacup again.

"Do you know that *naluaqmiut* Bush pilot, Cowboy Decker?"

"Ah-hah," Sivula said. "Fly for Lienhofer Aviation. I ride with him sometimes."

"Could you tell him how to get to this man's camp in Shaman Pass?"

Sivula rubbed his chin and looked into the far distance. "I tell you already, I'm not sure where it was. Shaman Pass, Howard Pass, I dunno. Like I say, it's long time ago. Hard to remember, now that I'm old."

Suddenly his face crinkled in a grin and he chuckled. "Maybe this guy never find Natchiq because he look in wrong pass all his life? Pretty funny, ah?"

Then the bland, impassive contours of the Eskimo mask dropped over his face.

AN HOUR later, Active was in Carnaby's office, finishing his briefing and pitching a trip to Shaman Pass.

"But wait a minute," the trooper commander said. "Whyborn

never actually named the guy? Then how do you know he's this Robert Keller—"

"Robert Kelly."

"This guy Robert Kelly? Tell me that part again?"

"I called the village public safety officer in Caribou Creek, said we needed the name of an older man, used to run the power-plant up there, supposedly comes from an old Chukchi family, had a camp in Shaman Pass, or maybe Howard Pass."

"And he—"

"Took him about two seconds to come up with the name. 'Oh, sure,' he says. 'That's old Robert Kelly.'"

"And the camp? How do we know where it is?"

"That part was harder. The VPSO calls his wife on the CB, she calls her aunt, whose brother-in-law—"

"Christ, never mind. Anyway, somebody somewhere in the Caribou Creek gene pool has actually been to the place?"

Active nodded. "Uh-huh. South side of Shaman Pass, edge of the mountains, between two creeks. Moose Creek and Ptarmigan Creek, they think."

"They think?" Carnaby stared in disbelief. "That's it? This guy Robert Kelly, if he is the same guy, tells Whyborn Sivula a story in caribou camp thirty years ago and that's your big lead? And now some people in Caribou Creek think they know where the camp is and you want to hire Cowboy Decker and fly all the way up there—how far is it, anyway?"

"About one seventy five, Cowboy says. I had him call the guy in Caribou Creek who knows where it is."

"Let's see." Carnaby grabbed a pencil, pushed Active's travel authorization off the desk blotter, and scratched out numbers. "A Super Cub on skis will make, what, about ninety miles an hour?"

Active shrugged and nodded.

"So you got roughly two hours up and two hours back, maybe an hour in the pass looking for this camp, which may not even be there anymore, and figuring out a landing spot if you do find it—"

"Cowboy says he kind of knows the area, all right."

"Has he actually ever been to this camp? Seen it?"

Active shook his head.

Carnaby snorted. "Trust me, Nathan, it won't go according to plan. This is the Bush. Let's just say five hours for the round trip. What's Cowboy's Super Cub go for these days? Still two-fifty an hour?"

Active sighed. "It's three hundred now."

Carnaby threw down his pencil. "There you are, then. Fifteen hundred dollars to cruise up for a chat with this Robert Kelly, if he's even there."

"He is," Active said. "Our guy in Caribou Creek said he's been out at camp for a couple weeks. I guess he spends most of his time there, now that he's retired from the power plant. His wife passed on a few years ago, and his girls live in Barrow and Point Hope."

"Well, at least you've done some homework." Carnaby studied the fifteen-hundred-dollar price underlined and circled on his blotter. "But suppose he is there. Suppose he even has Uncle Frosty on display out front. How do you tie him to Victor Solomon's murder?"

"Well—"

"According to what Whyborn told you, Robert's one mission in life is to get Uncle Frosty or Natchiq or whatever you call him hidden somewhere in Shaman Pass so the ravens and wolves and foxes can do their work in the old-time Inupiat way, correct?"

"Yes, but—"

" 'Yes, but' my butt! There's going to be no sign of Uncle Frosty up there and Robert Kelly's not going to have any idea what you're talking about and you're going to come back with not a shred of evidence, nothing but a fifteen-hundred-dollar hole in our travel budget. What, are you guys taking your rifles? Is this just a caribou hunt on the state nickel?" He pushed the travel authorization back across the blotter to Active.

Active couldn't help grinning.

"What?"

"I don't own a rifle," Active said.

Carnaby shook his head, but appeared to calm down.

"You want to listen now?"

Carnaby shrugged, but put on a somewhat less baleful expression.

"I think there's a good chance Kelly won't have had a chance yet to hide Uncle Frosty—"

"And why—"

Active held up a hand. "—because of this storm. Cowboy says judging from what we've been getting down here the past few days, the pass is probably getting sixty-, seventy-knot winds, blowing snow, visibility maybe fifty feet, maybe less."

"But if this Robert Kelly spends all his time out in the country anyway maybe he could—"

"Cowboy says not," Active said. "Not in that kind of weather. Not in that pass."

"I don't know," Carnaby said. "There's something about this that still doesn't feel right. Let's say it is Robert Kelly. He steals Uncle Frosty from the museum Wednesday night, maybe the wee hours of Thursday morning, right?"

Active nodded.

"Why would he wait till Thursday night, Friday morning, to

kill Victor Solomon? Twenty-four hours later. What was he doing for a whole day?"

"I don't know," Active said, uneasy that Carnaby had put his finger on the same soft spot as everyone else. "But Robert Kelly's all we've got. If we don't go talk to him, the case is basically dead, as far as I can see." He pushed the travel authorization across to Carnaby again.

"I still like Calvin Maiyumerak for this," Carnaby said. "Maybe we should sweat him a little more."

Active shrugged. "We tried. He's unsweatable, unless something turns up to shake his alibi with Queenie Buckland."

"How about Johnny Bass? He doesn't even have an alibi."

"He's pure sleaze, but I got the feeling he was telling the truth. For once in his life."

Carnaby sighed. "What about this past weekend? You canvass old Victor's neighbors?"

Active nodded. "Silver's people did. Nobody saw nada. I went through his house, too. More nada."

Carnaby frowned at the travel authorization, making no move toward his pen.

"I don't know," Active said. "Maybe I should take somebody with me. This Kelly, if he's our guy, already killed somebody. This could be dangerous. Maybe I should get a bigger plane, take Dickie Nelson along for backup."

Carnaby's frown deepened to a glare of pure suspicion.

"Cowboy says the only other plane that can get in up there is probably the Lienhofer Beaver . . ."

Carnaby reached for his pen.

". . . which goes for eight-fifty an hour."

Carnaby signed the authorization and handed it to Active. "You're like a goddamn toothache."

"Just doing my job." Active folded the authorization and put it in an inside pocket.

"But seriously," Carnaby said. "I am a little nervous sending just one guy on this."

"Goes with," Active said.

Carnaby nodded. "Uh-huh. But be careful. Wear a vest, take one of our rifles, use whatever cover you can find up there. You guys going up this afternoon?"

Active shook his head. "The storm's starting to peter out, all right, but Cowboy doesn't think there's any point trying to get in up there before morning."

"So it's first light?"

"Yup," Active said. "The dawn patrol."

CHAPTER SEVENTEEN

IT WAS JUST AFTER six-thirty the next morning when Active stopped the Ladies' Model beside the right wingtip of the red-and-white Lienhofer Super Cub. The plane was parked on the sea in front of Chukchi, roped down with two metal anchors frozen into the ice, and facing into what felt like about thirty miles an hour of west wind. The plane's nose was draped in a blue insulated engine cover, oil stained on the underside. Occasionally a gust rocked the kitelike craft, yanking the tie-downs tight.

Next to the plane's left wing stood an avgas barrel with a hand pump on top. Next to that stood a snowmachine and sled that Active recognized as belonging to Cowboy Decker. Low dunes of snow trailed downwind from the gas barrel, from the tail of the plane, and from each of its skis.

The clamshell half-doors on the side of the cockpit popped open—one flipped up and one down—and Cowboy climbed out of the front seat, a cigarette between his yellowish teeth and a baseball cap on his head. Like Active, he wore white rubber army-surplus bunny boots and a snowmachine suit. Unlike Active, he wasn't wearing a parka, but Active saw one thrown over the backseat. Cowboy did have a knit headband around his ears. Huge nylon-covered mittens dangled at his sides on a cord looped over his shoulders. He wore steel-framed glasses, which Active had discovered was somewhat unusual in the Arctic. Most of the bespectacled used plastic frames, because they didn't pick up the cold as much. Metal frames, he had heard, would freeze your ears.

"Morning, Cowboy," Active said.

Cowboy nodded. "Nathan." The pilot cut his eyes toward the Yamaha. "Nice snowmachine."

Active studied the pilot's expression to see if there was going to be a remark about the color, but Cowboy only said, "What happened to your windshield?"

This gave Active an excuse to tell about his crash on the way to Whyborn Sivula's whaling camp, which in the recounting became much more a near-death experience than it had been in reality.

The pilot held an aviation chart in his hand, which was clad in the light wool glove people wore under their mittens if the cold was more than mildly serious. After acting appropriately impressed by Active's snowmachine accident, Cowboy signaled they should turn their backs to the wind, and they sheltered the map with their bodies as they studied it. To the east, the way they were facing, a dull orange glow on the horizon showed where the sun was just coming up over the rolling tundra behind the village.

The pilot jabbed a gloved forefinger down on the map. "The guy in Caribou Creek says Robert Kelly's camp is around in here."

Active bent his head to study the spot. He saw a circle marked in pen south and west of the summit of Shaman Pass. It was in an area of pothole tundra lakes between two streams that emptied into the Angatquq River, which drained the south side of the pass.

"Think you can find it?" Active asked. "That's a pretty big circle."

Cowboy shrugged. "I can go to the spot, sure. Can I find the camp? Probably, but it may take a while. The guy says it's in a stand of willows on a little creek that isn't on the map. I gotta admit, though—I've been through the pass a few times and I never saw a camp in there."

"You want to go or not?"

"It's the state's nickel," Cowboy said. "I get paid whether we find it or we don't."

Active turned and looked north, the way they would go to reach Shaman Pass. The foothills of the Brooks Range barely showed through the snow haze and the morning dusk that had not yet been cut away by the rising sun. The wind bit his face and brought tears to his eyes. It was five below, Kay-Chuck had said while he was shaving, windchill minus forty-five. Tiny streams of snow flowed over his boots like smoke. Beneath the rushing of the wind he heard a faint hiss as the snow scraped over the ice, the snowdrifts, the fabric skin of the Super Cub. "What about this wind?"

"Now who doesn't want to go?"

"I mean, what's it going to be like up in the pass? Will we get in?"

Cowboy looked north now. "I think," he said. "It's still easing off and sometimes it'll calm down inland before it will here on the coast, though the weather service is saying we may be about to get another one of these blows. Only way is go look." He shrugged again.

Active said, "Let's go, then."

Cowboy pointed at his dogsled, where two rectangular metal cans rested in a wooden crate. "You fill those up from the gas barrel while I preflight her."

"We can't make it on your tanks?"

"Just barely, especially if we spend much time looking for this guy Kelly's camp." Cowboy flicked his cigarette into the air. The wind carried it out of sight. "Throw in an extra ten gallons, and you don't have to worry about it."

While Active figured out how to work the pump on the avgas barrel, Cowboy pulled the engine cover off and stuffed it through a door in the fuselage behind the cockpit. Then he pulled a little heater out of the engine compartment, snuffed it, and put it behind the Super Cub's passenger seat. Finally, he checked the engine oil and the fuel level in the two wing tanks, then turned to Active, who was just topping off the second can of avgas. "You about done?" Cowboy shouted.

Active nodded and carried the cans to the side of the plane. Cowboy stowed them behind the passenger seat, shrugged into his parka, and climbed into the front seat.

Active looked at the ropes still attached to the wings, then at Cowboy. "Aren't you going to untie it?"

Cowboy, busy at the controls, didn't turn his head. He just yelled. "Too much wind. She's liable to blow away. I'll get her cranked up and hold her in place with the engine, then you untie her and jump in."

"What? No! Is that safe?"

"You want to go or not?"

Active shook his head in resignation and trudged around the tail of the plane to the left wing as the propeller turned and the engine began to cough. By the time he reached the attachment point at midwing, the engine was running steadily. He flipped off his mittens and let them dangle beside him on their cord as he loosened the knot and pulled the end of the rope through an eyebolt fastened to the wing strut. His wool undergloves weren't much protection. His fingers were stinging by the time he finished with the right tie-down and crawled into the passenger seat behind Cowboy. He fastened his seat belt and shoulder harness, feeling huge and clumsy in his parka with the Kevlar vest under his shirt and the Smith & Wesson poking him from its holster on his belt. He slipped on a headset for the intercom, pulled his parka hood over the headset, and put his mittens back on.

Cowboy's voice crackled in his ears. "You ready back there?"

"Yep," he lied.

The engine revved up but the plane didn't move. Cowboy throttled back, then revved it up again. It still didn't move.

"Shit," the pilot said through the intercom. He throttled the engine back to idle. "The skis are froze in. You get out and take hold of the right wing strut there and rock her till she breaks loose. I'll hold her to a crawl till you get back in."

Active looked at the wing strut in question, the frozen-in skis on either side of the cockpit, and the back of Cowboy's parka. He thought of many things he could and probably should say. But what he said was, "OK."

He slipped off the headset, unharnessed himself, opened the doors, and crawled out of the plane into the blast of propwash. He walked over and put his right shoulder under the wing strut and heaved. The plane rocked, but the skis didn't budge. The landing gear seemed to be spring-loaded somehow, which made sense for a plane that had to bounce down on gravel bars and snow-covered tundra. In any event, the plane and the skis appeared to be capable of quasi-independent motion, and the skis stayed on the snow however hard he rocked the wings.

He glared over at Cowboy, who gave him a grinning thumbs-up and hit the throttle. The engine roared, Active rocked the wings again, and finally the right ski broke free. The plane tried to pivot left, but Cowboy caught it with the rudder and then the other ski came loose.

Cowboy throttled back as the Super Cub began to crawl forward. Active ran to the cockpit door and got his upper half inside, then wriggled the rest of himself in. Cowboy shut the doors and let the crawl continue as Active rebuckled the safety harness.

Finally Active yelled, "Ready" over the intercom. Cowboy hit the throttle and the skis rattled across the drifts that covered the ice of Chukchi Bay. A gust caught them and the right wing started to lift. Cowboy sawed at the controls and then they were flying. "You see now why us Bush pilots get the big bucks?"

At first Active couldn't speak. "You should pay me," he croaked when his breathing slowed. "I'm doing all the work."

"Goes with," Cowboy said.

Visibility improved as they climbed out of the surface haze kicked up by the wind. The ice of the Chukchi Sea stretched away to the west, the wind pulling long ribbons of snow toward the village. To the north, they could see over the Sulana Hills into the frozen valley of the Katonak River, which crawled like a white snake toward the heart of the Brooks Range.

Lazy tendrils of snow curled off the crests of the Sulana Hills. "Shit," Cowboy said through the headphones. "Gonna be bumpy. Your seat belt fastened real tight?"

"Now who doesn't want to go?" Active asked.

"Not me," Cowboy said.

Active was pondering Cowboy's response when the first jolt of turbulence hit them. The gas cans clanked behind Active and he shot straight up until his shoulder harness arrested his flight, at the same moment his head collided with the steel tubing in the ceiling of the cockpit. His parka hood was up, so it didn't hurt much.

But it was embarrassing. He wondered if Cowboy had noticed. He jerked his seat belt an inch tighter, and cinched down the shoulder harness until he felt like a hunchback.

"Now is your seat belt fastened real tight?" Decker asked. Then he snickered.

Active settled down to suffer, thankful that he had at least been blessed with a stomach immune to airsickness.

Once they had jolted their way across the Sulana Hills and entered the broad lower valley of the Katonak, the turbulence subsided. Active loosened the seat belt and shoulder harness and relaxed a little.

Cowboy came on the headphones with a scratch of static. "So this Robert Kelly guy. You really think he killed Victor Solomon with a harpoon?"

Active debated how much to tell Cowboy. Since it was police business, the pilot should in theory be told nothing at all, except that the troopers needed to question Robert Kelly in connection with an investigation. Robert Kelly might be dangerous, however, in which case there should in fact be a discussion about how to minimize Cowboy's exposure to that danger. And if Robert Kelly wasn't dangerous—well, then this long, cold, bumpy plane ride was a waste of fifteen hundred taxpayer dollars. Just like Carnaby had said.

"Could be," Active said finally. "That's why I want to talk to him."

"What if he harpoons you, too?"

"I'm wearing body armor. The harpoon'll bounce off."

"Uh-huh," Cowboy said. "And what about me?"

"Let's just find his camp and take it from there. If it doesn't look safe, we'll land a mile or two away and you can wait for me while I go in on snowshoes."

Cowboy was silent for a few minutes as the Super Cub chugged over the tundra, creeks and pothole lakes of the Katonak Flats. "OK, but I'm keeping my finger on the starter button. Anybody comes my way and it's not you, I'm outta there."

Cowboy was silent for a few minutes, then said, "And then what?"

"What do you mean?"

"What if you don't come back?"

"Fly back to Chukchi and tell Carnaby," Active said. "He'll figure out something."

"Sounds like an unsafe operation to me."

"Goes with," Active said.

"What's your theory on luck, Nathan?" Cowboy asked after a pause.

"Well, the more the better."

"No, seriously. You think you're born with a set amount, like a quota, and when you use it up, that's it, you're a goner? Or are some people just born lucky and they stay lucky till they get old and die of boredom?"

"I never thought about it," Active said. "I don't know about the quota idea, though."

Cowboy paused again. "Yeah, me neither. But I wonder sometimes."

"Wonder what?"

"Where that saying came from. You know, 'His luck ran out.'"

"I see your point."

Cowboy nodded. "That's why I don't like it when somebody says I'm lucky. What if I've used up my last allotment and the next time I get in a tight spot I'm not gonna make it out?"

Active didn't reply for a while. "What are you saying?" he asked finally. "Are we in a tight spot now?"

He saw the pilot hunch forward and peer up the valley toward Shaman Pass.

"Not yet," Cowboy said. "Not that I know of."

Active shook his head. This must be Cowboy's version of the bullet dream. He wondered if the pilot had his own version of Nelda Qivits.

As they ascended the Katonak, the valley narrowed, the Brooks Range closing in on both sides. The peaks were buried in the clouds. Lower down, long pennons of snow waved from knife-edged white ridges.

The turbulence hit them again, the gas cans clanging against each other behind Active's seat, the Super Cub rattling in a dozen unidentifiable places. Active tightened his shoulder harness and seat belt, and tasted salt blood from his cheek when a sudden hammer blow from beneath slammed his teeth together. After that, he kept them clenched, hoping that Cowboy would growl through the intercom that enough was enough and turn the plane around.

Cowboy didn't say anything. Finally Active unclenched his teeth to ask if the clouds were low enough to close them out of the pass.

"Nah," Cowboy said. "These clouds are three thousand feet, maybe four. The pass is only a couple thousand."

They pounded on up the Katonak for another twenty minutes, then Cowboy banked the Super Cub left and pointed the nose up a white furrow that meandered away through the tundra to the north. "The Angatquq River," Cowboy said.

Active was about to say something in acknowledgment when a boil of turbulence rolled the Super Cub into a vertical bank and he found himself staring straight down at the willow-fringed bed of the Angatquq. Cowboy said, "Shit!" over the intercom and got busy with the controls.

When the wings were level again, Active peered up the slowly rising terrain into the white reaches ahead. Shaman Pass, it appeared, was a broad, low saddle, white and rumpled in winter's grip. From this distance, there was no sign of the gorge below the summit that Jim Silver had mentioned.

To their right, low hills stretched away to the east. To the left, high mountains marched off to the west. If he remembered

Cowboy's map properly, Robert Kelly's camp lay at the foot of those mountains on the left side of the pass.

"Looks like you're going to get your money's worth," Cowboy said through the intercom.

Active, studying the route ahead, didn't try to figure out Cowboy's point. "What?"

"We're going to get into the pass."

"Yeah, I guess we are," Active said.

CHAPTER EIGHTEEN

WITH THE WIND STILL on their tail and the terrain rising in front, the Super Cub jolted toward the pass at what seemed an ever-increasing speed. Under the wings, wind-whipped willows in the bed of the Angatquq blurred, sharpened, and blurred again as clouds of snow swirled over them. Away from the creek, the occasional stunted black spruce on the tundra bowed before the gale. Active thought of Jim Silver's yarn of the winds in Shaman Pass killing caribou.

"How much wind you think we're getting here?" he asked.

"I don't know," Cowboy growled back through the intercom. "Forty, fifty, maybe."

"Can you land in this?"

"If we can find a sheltered spot," Cowboy said.

Active waited for more, but the headphones were silent. He concluded that was all Cowboy wanted to say about it.

They continued their leaflike rush upriver until they passed a big creek coming in from the left. Cowboy held up the map, looked from it to the terrain below and back again, then heeled the plane over and followed the creek upstream. Cowboy's voice crackled over the intercom. "This is Moose Creek. Somewhere between here and the next big one, Ptarmigan Creek, is where the camp supposedly is. Right up against the foot of the mountains on some little creek too small to get on the map."

Cowboy flew upstream until Moose Creek climbed into the mountains through a narrow gate in the rocks. There, the pilot turned the plane right and skirted the base of the mountains. Four or five miles ahead, Active could see the trace of what must be Ptarmigan Creek threading down into the Angatquq.

They were over rising terrain now, crossing a low ridge that separated the watersheds of Moose and Ptarmigan creeks, a churning blanket of snow sweeping over it. The wind was on their tail again, hurrying them across the folded tundra at what seemed twice the normal speed of a Super Cub.

They crested the ridge and immediately spotted a tiny creek running along its base towards the Angatquq. It was, they could see now, the only stream in the chunk of country between Moose and Ptarmigan creeks.

"This has gotta be it, huh?" Cowboy sounded a little nervous through the headset.

"Seems like," Active said. "You see anything?"

"Not between here and the Angatquq," Cowboy said. "If this is it, Robert Kelly's camp must be back up the canyon a ways."

By now, the wind had swept them past the creek and they couldn't see into the canyon that ushered the creek out of the mountains. Cowboy made a wide, looping turn over the low ground toward the Angatquq, then swung back in to the base of the mountains perhaps a mile downwind from the mouth of the canyon.

Now they were headed almost straight into the gale, moving over the ground so slowly that Active thought he could get out and walk. Here, close to the hills, the turbulence was a continuous, relentless jolting, the Super Cub banging and clanging as if it would come apart.

Cowboy skirted the base of the mountains, and throttled back as they approached the mouth of the canyon where Robert

Kelly's camp should be. Cowboy lowered his wing flaps and their ground speed dropped near zero as the plane jolted past the canyon mouth. Then they stopped entirely, the Super Cub hovering raggedly in the gale sweeping over the tundra. Active marveled at this, that Cowboy should be able to suspend a plane in midair. Not for the first time, he puzzled over the two Cowboys: on the ground, a hollow blowhard in a baseball cap, in the air, a wizard in a headset and mirror sunglasses.

Cowboy saw it first. "Look at that!" he shouted through the headset. "That second bend up there, right bank, back in the brush."

Active peered through the snow haze, saw the outline of a cabin in wind-whipped willows, a snowmachine, and dogsled—he felt the plane rolling, for an instant saw the left wing pointing straight down at the creek bed, sensed Cowboy fighting for control, heard the pilot shout, "Aw, fuck me Jesus!" and suddenly they were several hundred yards down the creek from the mouth of the canyon, the camp now out of sight.

"My God," Active said into his headset after Cowboy restored some stability to the plane. "What was that?"

"Hell of a blast coming out of that canyon," Cowboy said. "Some kind of venturi effect, I expect."

Active had no idea what a venturi effect was, but this didn't seem the time for a lesson. "Can we go back for another look?"

"You kidding?"

"Well, we came all this way."

"Fuck," Cowboy said. "Well, maybe if we come in higher."

The pilot made a wide, climbing turn over the white lowlands, and brought the plane up to the canyon mouth again, but five hundred feet higher than before. They still caught a blast from the canyon, but it was less now, and Cowboy was more prepared.

From the higher angle, they could see better into the camp in the willows. "You see anything that looks like a sod hut?" Active asked.

"Nope," Cowboy said.

"Well, Whyborn said it was a sod hut. Could this be the wrong camp?"

Just then, a man emerged from the cabin, looked up at the Super Cub, hurried to a mound in the snow a few yards away, and vanished into it.

"There's your sod hut," Cowboy said.

Active grunted assent and kept his eyes on the entrance. As they drifted past the mouth of the canyon and started to lose the view, Active saw the man come out of the hut with a bright blue man-size bundle in his arms and drop it into the dogsled.

"Look at that!" Active felt the heat rising in his stomach, even his groin, that meant he somehow had crossed that line past which there were no ifs or whys, only hows. "He's taking off! Get me down there!"

Cowboy started another of his wide turns over the lowlands. "No way," he said. "We were hovering back there."

"And?"

"And that means the wind speed is higher than the takeoff speed of this airplane. There's no way to land. We'll just get blown over backward."

Active studied the tundra whirling past beneath them as Cowboy brought the plane around and lined up for another pass by the canyon mouth. Up ahead, the gusts swept a cascade of snow over the rounded ridge that had at first hidden Robert Kelly's creek from them. Between gusts, the surface of the ridge looked sculpted and smooth, except for a few tufts of dwarf willow sticking through. "Can you hover over that ridge?" Active asked.

Active saw Cowboy's head turn as he studied the surface.

"Yeah," the pilot said. "Probably, for a few seconds at least. So what?"

"So go hover. I'll just step out onto the snow."

"No fucking way. I'm not explaining to Carnaby how you, how I . . ." Cowboy stopped talking and cleared his throat and Active thought the pilot was feeling that heat in his stomach, too.

"Fuck, it might work," Cowboy said. "I've heard of people skydiving out of a Super Cub. But what are you going to do till I can get back in here?"

"I'll just take Mr. Kelly into custody and we'll wait in his cabin."

"That easy, huh?"

"One bad guy, one trooper. That's how we do it."

"You're the fucking cowboy here," Cowboy said. "You know that?"

Active didn't say anything, but he smiled to himself a little.

Cowboy turned the Super Cub slightly, aiming at a little saddle on the crest of the ridge. "Just remember," he said through the headset. "You're going to be stepping out into fifty, sixty miles an hour of wind. First thing you do, drop down flat till you get your bearings and figure out if you can walk in it or not."

The pilot popped open the clamshell doors. A hurricane roared into the cockpit. Active slipped off his headset, unbuckled his seat belt and shoulder harness, and zipped up his parka, then braced himself against the ceiling as the Super Cub jolted toward the drop zone.

Cowboy descended slowly. Finally they were over the saddle, the skis maybe three feet off the striated, wind-packed snow. Cowboy gave a thumbs-up. Active grasped the door frame and pulled himself into the opening. He put one foot in the metal stirrup below the door, gathered himself, and jumped.

As he jumped, a gust caught the plane and heaved it upward. By the time his foot left the step, the skis were a dozen feet off the snow, not three, but it was too late. As he fell, he felt the wind take him and then he was cartwheeling over the lip of the ridge and down the cliff.

He fetched up in a clump of willows in the bed of Robert Kelly's creek, snow in his mouth and eyes, snow down his neck where the parka hood had flipped back in the fall. His left shoulder, still sore from the snowmachine crash on the ice, now was angry to have been banged again and complaining that someone was trying to pry it apart with a hot, jagged, rusty crowbar.

As Active's breathing slowed, he became aware of the sound of a snowmachine engine, just discernible under the moan of the wind sweeping over the cliff above him. He struggled to his feet in the willows, drawing fresh protests from the left shoulder as he flipped off his mittens and groped for the Smith & Wesson on his belt. His fingers found the holster, unsnapped and empty. Frantically, he pawed through the snow around him until his wool undergloves contacted the cold, hard steel of the grip.

As he came out of the willows, he saw a black Arctic Cat headed his way, dogsled in tow, the driver's attention focused downslope, where Cowboy was making another circle in the Super Cub and heading back toward the mouth of the canyon.

Active realized the driver hadn't seen him yet. He waved his right arm until finally the man on the snowmachine looked his way. The driver spotted the Smith & Wesson still in Active's hand and hit the throttle.

The snowmachine roared ahead and Active lined the sights up on the engine compartment. Maybe a couple of lucky shots would disable the machine. Then he realized the driver was not just accelerating, but also swerving—toward him.

Active shifted his aim to the driver and fired twice before the snowmachine hit him. He went down on his back, lost the pistol again, felt a front ski pass over the left half of his body, then the cleated rubber drive track, then the dogsled. He felt a jerk on his left arm, felt more pain from his left shoulder than he could have imagined, and realized his hand was caught in the frame of the sled. He plowed through the snow and rocks and willows a few yards before he could work his hand out of the rope webbing that held the sled's wooden stanchions to the runner.

As he lay facedown in the snow, waiting for the agony in his left shoulder to subside so that he could stand up, he was dimly aware that the snowmachine was slowing, perhaps turning—was the driver coming back to finish him off?

The blaze in his shoulder wasn't subsiding at all. It was getting hotter and hotter. Waves of fire radiated from the joint, sweeping through his stomach—the nausea!—through his head, so warm and relaxed in his head now, the shoulder barely even noticeable, what had been the problem with it anyway?

CHAPTER NINETEEN

SOMEONE WAS COMING THROUGH the door of the cabin as Active swam back up to consciousness. He didn't know how he knew where he was, but he did, so being in the cabin was all right.

But the figure in the doorway wasn't all right, because he was the driver of the snowmachine and he had something in his hand—a rifle or a harpoon, it was difficult to tell. Active remembered clearly that he should be afraid of the driver, though not why.

So Active went for his gun, which, if he remembered right, was on his belt. Then he discovered he couldn't get his right hand up to the gun. He jerked and jerked but his arm wouldn't move and pain shot through his left shoulder like a fire snake was crawling into the joint. He heard himself grunting, "Unhh, unhh, unhh," and that was when he realized this was another version of the bullet dream.

The driver must have stabbed him in the shoulder, the latest innovation in the bullet dream. Usually, Active would wake up just before the bad guy got him. He would pull his gun and try to fire, but the bullet would dribble out the end of the barrel with a little "pop" and fall to the floor. He would try again, squeezing the trigger as hard as he could, jerking it convulsively like someone being electrocuted or having an orgasm, but still the bullets would just pop out of the muzzle and fall to the floor. The bad guy would laugh and raise his gun and—and then Active would wake up and the bullet dream would be over.

But not this time. This time the bullet dream kept going. The bad guy had stabbed him in the shoulder with his rifle, which made no sense unless the rifle had a bayonet on it. Did it? He tried to see through the gloom of the cabin—was there a blood-smeared bayonet on the snowmachine driver's rifle? Could the driver have shot him? He hadn't heard a shot but maybe the rifle had a silencer on it? He raised his head again to peer—

And then the bullet dream was over and he was awake.

He was in a cabin and it was the cabin from the dream. He was on the floor, and he was bound—that part of it had been real. He couldn't move his arms or his feet.

Another thing that was real was the blaze in his left shoulder. It was like someone had poured a cup of avgas into the joint, then tossed in a match. It seemed familiar, somehow.

Hockey, that was it. A hockey game at the University of Alaska Fairbanks. Two skaters from the other team had forced him into the sideboard. Somehow in the melee, his arm was caught, twisted. He had clutched the arm, fainted, and been carried off the ice.

When he woke up, a doctor told him he had dislocated his shoulder and passed out from the shock. "No problem, as long as we fix it right away," the doctor said as he gave Active a shot of Demerol. Then he had laid Active on the floor, put his foot in Active's armpit, and yanked. Even through the Demerol fog, Active thought he felt the pop as the ball slipped back into the socket, and that was that.

What had the doctor called it? Relocated? No, reduced, that was it, reduced. He had reduced the dislocated shoulder.

The shoulder was sore as hell for a while and Active wore

a sling that was strapped to his chest to immobilize the arm. He had skipped several weeks of the season, gotten well, and forgotten about it. Until now. Now it was all coming back to him.

He shifted on the floor, trying and failing to find a position that hurt less. He did find out what his hands were bound with: duct tape. So were his feet, and they seemed to be tied to the wall with a piece of green nylon camp cord. Another piece of it lashed his hands to his belt, which probably explained why he hadn't been able to move his arm in the bullet dream.

There was a groan from across the cabin and he became aware of a metal cot against the opposite wall, with someone on it, facing the wall, his back to Active.

That realization and the pain in his shoulder cleared away more of the fog. Now he remembered jumping—no, falling—out of Cowboy Decker's Super Cub, falling because of the gust that tossed the plane upward just as he was stepping off. He remembered being blown over the bluff and tumbling down the side, landing in the willows, the snowmachine coming at him, firing at the driver, being hit. . . .

So that had to be the driver, presumably Robert Kelly, up there on the cot, groaning. Robert Kelly must have dragged him back into the cabin, trussed him on the floor like this, then lain down for a nap. But that made no sense. Robert Kelly was trying to get away with Natchiq's remains in the blue tarp. Why would he take time to do all that? Was this still the bullet dream after all?

Active peered around the cabin. It was a standard Bush camp. Plywood and two-by-four construction; windows on the front and sides; white foam-block insulation on the walls and ceiling; snowshoes, animal traps, and other gear hanging from nails pounded into the studs. An oil heater muttering in a corner, a Coleman cookstove on a plywood counter, two

Coleman lanterns, unlit, hanging from the beams overhead, just the one cot for sleeping, a battery-powered radio on a wall shelf beside the cot. Apparently Robert Kelly didn't have company very often.

A beat-up wooden table stood in the middle of the cabin, between him and Robert Kelly's cot. In fact, he had to look under the table, between its legs, to see Robert Kelly's back. Now he tried to look up and over the edge of the table to see what was on top. A roll of duct tape, a can of Prince Albert pipe tobacco, a bottle of something that looked medicinal, a wad of white rags with red-brown stains.

Of course. He must have hit Kelly when he fired the Smith & Wesson out there in the willows. The bottle was probably iodine and those stains on the rags were blood. Kelly hadn't laid down for a nap before taking off. He was wounded. Maybe dying.

But evidently he had dragged Nathan Active into the cabin and tied him up on the floor before collapsing. Why? Why not leave him out in the willows to freeze to death? In fact, if you're the killer of Victor Solomon and you're trying to get away, why not finish off the trooper who had just dropped out of the sky and shot you?

Active shook his head. It was too much to think about, with his shoulder hurting like it did. The question was, what now? He was tied up, but given some time he could do something about that. Bend at the waist, draw up his knees, and he could get his hands on the tape at his feet. A few minutes, and he could have them undone. His hands would still be taped, but at least he would be mobile, maybe find something to cut his hands loose. His left arm was useless, but his right one still worked and of course Kelly was wounded and weak, if Active had this figured out right.

Active rolled onto his right side, curled his legs and waist to push his hands toward the tape at his feet. The fire snake writhed in his shoulder and he had to stop, relax, and close his eyes until the pain subsided a little.

When his pulse was close to normal again, he took a deep breath and lunged at his feet, like a fat man trying to prove he can still touch his toes. The fire snake took over his entire being, his body was one big dislocated shoulder. A scream tried to boil up from somewhere. Active clamped his jaws down on it and held it to a grunt. But that big happy bubble of warmth blossomed in his brain, and he felt himself sliding off into shock again.

THIS TIME there was no bullet dream. Active just woke up and opened his eyes, prodded back to consciousness by the pain in his shoulder, completely clearheaded at last. The snowmachine driver sat on the edge of the cot, an old .30-30 carbine across his knees, a pipe between his teeth. He wore insulated pants with suspenders, a plaid wool shirt, unbuttoned, and caribou mukluks. A heavy parka with a green corduroy cover lay on the cot beside him. Active thought he glimpsed a gleam of silver inside the wool shirt, but couldn't place it.

"Don't try to get away," the driver said. He jacked a shell into the firing chamber of the carbine. "I should shoot you."

"I won't," Active said. He relaxed, eased his body straight again. The blaze in his shoulder died down a little.

He studied the driver. Narrow face, somewhat egg-shaped, with leathery, supple-looking mahogany skin, same quality of vigorous but unguessable age as Whyborn Sivula. A slightly beaked nose; silver hair, eyebrows, and mustache; silver bristles on his cheeks and chin. A half-healed cut over his brow.

And calm, resigned eyes.

"You're Robert Kelly," Active said.

The driver lifted his eyebrows. "*Ee.*" The calm eyes were still on Active. "What your name?"

"Nathan Active. I'm an Alaska State Trooper from Chukchi."

"I guess I know who you are," Kelly said. "I hear you on Kay-Chuck sometimes, talk about catch people. How did you get here?"

"In the Super Cub. You looked at us when we flew over."

Kelly lifted his eyebrows. "But that airplane never land."

"I jumped out."

"Ah?"

Active nodded. "*Ee.*"

"You never use a parachute?"

Active shook his head. "I, well, I didn't have one."

Kelly was silent, digesting this. Then, "Pretty bum weather today. I never see a plane up here when it's this bad."

"Cowboy Decker was flying. Do you know him?"

Kelly squinted no, then his face tightened. He closed his eyes, laid the rifle on the cot and put his hand inside the wool shirt, feeling along his right side. Now Active could see that the silver gleam was a band of duct tape wrapped around Kelly's middle. He pulled his hand out, studied it, and seemed satisfied with the result. He looked up and caught Active's eyes on him.

"No more blood now, so I guess you never hit me too bad." He raised his right arm and rotated it gingerly at the shoulder, testing the side, wincing a little. "Why you do that anyway?"

"I thought you were going to run over me with your snowgo."

"Well, I think you're about to shoot me."

There was a long silence. Active gathered that Kelly, like himself, couldn't think of what to say next.

Finally Active spoke. "Why did you bring me in here? Why not just take off?"

"I'm shot, so I have to go back to my cabin, see how bad it is, fix myself up first," Kelly said. "But if I leave you out there, then maybe you'll wake up, find your gun in the snow, try shoot me again."

He stopped and smiled a little. "I'm shot, hurts too much to put you in my sled. I tie you on behind with rope, drag you to my cabin." The grin got bigger. "But I go real slow."

"My shoulder doesn't feel like you went slow."

Kelly shrugged, then grimaced like it had hurt his injured side. "I think your shoulder's already hurt before I tie you on. You scream when I pull on your arms, scream all the way to my cabin."

There was a silence. Active waited.

Finally Kelly spoke. "Anyway, I guess I wonder, why does a state trooper come all the way up here to my camp, jump out of airplane, try shoot me?"

Active studied Kelly's eyes and thought how to do this. Kelly seemed to want to talk. Ordinary people usually did after doing something terrible, like a killing. The stress was too much for them.

"Do you remember a man named Whyborn Sivula?" Active asked at last. "You brought him here a long time ago."

At first the calm eyes were blank. Then they widened in recollection. "Ah. Whyborn Sivula. He tell you, he tell you . . . what he tell you?"

"Will you tell me about Natchiq?"

"I don't know about that."

"You told Whyborn Sivula about him."

Kelly took a deep breath and gazed out the cabin's front window. It looked like milk out there, milk and flying snow. Active realized now how loudly the wind keened around the cabin. It sounded stronger, more violent, than when he had rolled off the ridge and into the willows and fired at Robert Kelly. Perhaps the storm was building again, as Cowboy had said it might. He wondered if the pilot would make it back to Chukchi in what would be a fierce head wind on the return trip.

Kelly swung his eyes back to Active's. "Whyborn told you about Natchiq?"

"A little. I know he was your grandfather. And I know he fought the *angatquqs* and made prophesies and then he started out for Barrow and he was never seen again."

"That goddamn Saganiq see him again, all right!" Kelly slammed his hand down on the bed, then winced from the pain. "He kill him up here!"

Active just lifted his eyebrows.

"I guess it won't hurt to tell you the rest of the story. Then you'll know how that Saganiq was." Kelly sighed and inspected his wound again. "By the time Natchiq start for Barrow, his first wife is dead so he—"

"What happened to her?"

"My dad never say, just that she die somehow. Her and Natchiq never have any kids of their own but they adopt these two little orphans, a girl name Enyana and a boy name Kiana. By the time Natchiq decide to go north, Kiana is already grown up and married to Point Hope girl and living up there with her family, trying to tell those people about Natchiq and his source of intelligence. This Enyana, she's really pretty, sew and cook real good, like to laugh, so Natchiq take her for his second wife. Him and Enyana, they leave for the north when springtime is starting, like now. They take maybe three-four dogs, but I don't know if the dogs are pulling sled, or if they're carrying packs. Natchiq tell everybody he'll go to Barrow, then Canada. You know the Eskimo name for Barrow?"

"I don't think so," Active said.

"*Ukpeagvik.* Mean 'place of the snowy owl' in Eskimo. Funny thing, ah?"

Active lifted his eyebrows. "The snowy owl was Saganiq's *kikituq* and Natchiq ate it, is what I heard."

"That's what the stories say, all right," Kelly said. "Anyway, Natchiq decide that him and Enyana will go up there to Barrow and they start out. After that, nobody hear anything about them for long time. Spring is over and summer is starting when somebody find Enyana on the trail few miles north of Chukchi. She's almost dead, nothing to eat for so long. Two of her dogs are lost, she eat the other two, then she eat the tops of her mukluks. They help her get back to Chukchi and she tell how she and Natchiq are up in *taggaqvik* and they stop to camp so Natchiq could get them some sheep."

"*Taggaqvik?* What's that?"

Kelly frowned at the interruption. "Mean 'place of shadows.' Now we call it Shaman Pass."

"The old-timers called it Shadow Pass?"

"Shadow Pass, ah-hah. So they're camped up there and Natchiq take two of the dogs and go out for sheep. Enyana wait and wait in camp, but he never come back. So finally, she go to look, same way he went. She look long time, never find nothing, till finally she see his snowshoes stuck in the snow. Then she have to give up because she's almost out of food and anyway, look like spring storm is coming down from the north and it's too dangerous in the pass. So she start back, but she almost die before they find her on the trail outside Chukchi."

Kelly eased off the bed, limped to the door, and looked out into the storm.

"So Enyana made it back to Chukchi?" Active said.

Kelly turned and picked up the pipe tobacco from the table, then eased himself back onto the cot. "Ah-hah, but she have real hard time." Kelly paused to load and light the pipe, then went on. "She's orphan girl, got no family except for her brother Kiana, way up in Point Hope. And now that Natchiq is gone, maybe dead, them people in Chukchi are afraid to help her too much."

"What were they afraid of?"

"That Saganiq," Kelly said, frowning at the name. "He's strutting around like a ptarmigan now, talking about how this proves Natchiq's magic is weak. Saganiq say he can't find his *kikituq*, maybe that little snowy owl of his fly up to Shadow Pass and fly into Natchiq's mouth and eat up his soul. So nobody will help Enyana. They think Saganiq got his power back."

Kelly fell into a brooding silence.

"Did Enyana go to Point Hope to live with her brother?" Active asked finally.

"No, she's too weak to travel and when she send word, there's no answer for long time in them days. They never have telephone or snowgos yet. So that Saganiq take her to be one of his wives." Kelly grunted in disgust. "She don't like it, because she think Saganiq or maybe his *kikituq* spirit, the snowy owl, is what kill Natchiq. But she got no way out and Saganiq is very powerful again. So she become his wife even though by now she know she got Natchiq's baby inside her."

Active thought this over for a moment. "Enyana was pregnant with your father?"

Kelly lifted his eyebrows. "My father, ah-hah. But he almost never live. That Saganiq, he's mean to Enyana all the time, always beat her a lot, especially when he find out she's having Natchiq's baby. He don't hardly feed her nothing until finally it's time for baby to come and she have to go off by herself like the women are starting to do again since Natchiq is gone."

"She had no one to help her?"

Kelly shook his head. "Not until her brother, Kiana, finally hear about it and come down from Point Hope. He still believe what Natchiq say and he don't care about the taboo or Saganiq. But Enyana, she's already in snowhouse, so weak from Saganiq starving her and beating her that she die having that baby, so Kiana, he take it to raise himself. That Kiana, he's my father's uncle. That's my father, Enyana's baby."

One hip was getting cold from contact with the cabin floor. Active shifted his weight to the other hip. "What happened to Enyana's body?"

"Her brother take her up in Shaman Pass, leave her on tundra in the old-time way, so animals and weather will take her back to the earth. But he build *inuksuk*, stone man, on that spot, right where this cabin is now. It's first *inuksuk* our family build in Shaman Pass, and it's still out there."

"Outside this cabin?"

Kelly pointed through the rear wall. "Ah-hah, on that hill back there. Then Kiana decide to stay in Chukchi so people don't forget about Natchiq and his source of intelligence. But it's real hard because Saganiq and the other *angatquqs* are back in power now and they scare everybody to stop talking about Natchiq, try to make them forget what he did. Anybody who knew him will never forget him, but they don't talk about him no more, and today hardly anybody even know who he was. His story die out."

"How did Saganiq end up joining the white man's church?"

"Not long after my father's born, white people come into the country," Kelly said. "Them missionaries show up and start saying some of the same things Natchiq did. At first Saganiq and the other *angatquqs* try to fight the missionaries and keep people in the old ways, but Saganiq finally figure out he can't win. That's when he join *naluaqmiut* church, take his name from that King Solomon guy in their Bible, and pretend to be a Christian. And he tell them my grandfather Natchiq's a false prophet! Hah! He's lot closer to being a Christian than that Saganiq ever was! But things are still hard for my father, Joshua—"

"His name was Joshua?"

"Ah-hah. When missionaries come in, that's what they name my father. Joshua Kelly. But things are still hard for him and his uncle Kiana that's raising him. Everybody's afraid of Saganiq again and they won't have hardly nothing to do with my father or with his uncle either."

Kelly moved to the cabin window and peered out. "So my father and my uncle finally have to leave Chukchi. They move up to Caribou Creek, where Enyana and Kiana first come from," Kelly said. "It's better there, but my father still have pretty hard time. A lotta people hear about how his mother and father die, and about Saganiq and everything, and they're pretty scared of them Chukchi *angatquqs*. My father stay alive by hunting and fishing like he learn from his uncle Kiana, but nobody will have nothing to do with him for long time because of his parents. He's over forty years old before he marry my mother, then I'm born few years later."

Kelly fell into another deep, wordless study and Active thought over what he'd heard. So many stories of death and loss and dislocation in the Arctic. Perhaps they explained the cheerful fatalism of the Inupiat, of the ones who didn't succumb to drink or suicide, anyway. Maybe it was either crack a joke or go crazy.

Kelly picked up his story again. "My father take me up into Shaman Pass lotta times when I'm still little, tell me about Saganiq and Natchiq and Enyana, try look for where Natchiq's body is hidden. That's what Kiana thought, that Saganiq killed Natchiq and caged up the body somewhere in this pass, so it couldn't go back to nature like it should." Kelly sighed. "My father die when I'm fifteen years old. After that, I can't think about them old stories anymore, and I never come up here for a long time, till I'm grown up and have kids of my own. Then I start dreaming I'm in Shaman Pass all the time. So then I come up here again, whenever I can, look for Natchiq, put up *inuksuk* anywhere I look."

Active shifted hips again and waited. Instead of resuming the narrative, Kelly stood and walked to the door in his mukluks, limping a little to favor his right side. He opened the door, knocked his pipe against the frame to empty it, and stood peering into the blizzard.

Active could see past Kelly to his dogsled, hitched behind the black Arctic Cat. It was packed for the trail, with the blue-wrapped bundle they had seen from the air still atop the load. The rig was already caked with a thin layer of snow. Active wondered how long he had been unconscious.

Kelly slammed the door, pocketed the pipe, and limped back to the cot, shaking his head. "Too stormy, I guess," he said, mostly to himself, as he settled onto the mattress. "Can't even see down the canyon now."

"Is that your grandfather on the sled?"

"Don't matter," Kelly said.

"Why is he still here? Why didn't you take him to Canada as soon as you took him from the museum? That's what your grandfather wanted, isn't it?"

"Don't matter."

Active looked around the cabin and noticed again the radio beside Kelly's cot. "You heard about it on Kay-Chuck, didn't you? You're all by yourself up here in Shaman Pass when you hear on Kay-Chuck how the *naluaqmiut* geologists found Uncle Frosty in the pass a long time ago and took him to Washington and how Victor Solomon was bringing him back to Chukchi."

"Goddamn that Victor!" Kelly pulled the pipe from his pocket and jabbed the air with it as he spoke. "Always talk about putting Uncle Frosty in that glass case! He's just like his grandfather, want to make my family little."

"I can understand how you'd feel. So you decided to come down to Chukchi and get Uncle Frosty out of the museum to see if he really was Natchiq. And then you found Saganiq's harpoon and amulet in the crate with him and that's how you knew."

Kelly was silent, looking lost in thought. Something was trying to swim up out of Active's subconscious. Then he remembered the records of the Henderson party.

"Those *naluaqmiuts* who found your grandfather?"

"Ah?"

"Did you know they found Saganiq's amulet in his mouth?"

"That piece of *anaq* Saganiq! Now I see what he mean when he talk about how his *kikituq* fly into Natchiq's mouth and eat up his soul." Kelly paused and smiled a little. "Maybe Saganiq can't forget how my grandfather eat up that owl, make him little." Kelly chuckled at the thought.

Active shivered again at Natchiq's genius for psychological theater. To the old-time Inupiat, the *natchiq*, the humble little seal, had provided food and fur, and oil for the stone lamps. Life itself. Natchiq had gone up against Saganiq with no magic, only words, and had climaxed the drama by eating an owl, the messenger of death and the *kikituq* of the great shaman.

Kelly looked down at Active on the floor. "You're trooper, you know *naluaqmiut* law about stealing, ah?"

Active lifted his eyebrows.

"After my grandfather is taken from museum, I hear Victor Solomon on Kay-Chuck again. He say he know who did it and he will find Uncle Frosty and put him back in that museum and police will put the thief in jail."

Kelly paused and his face blackened again. "He think I'm a thief! How you can steal your own grandfather? You're state trooper. You know *naluaqmiut* laws. How you can do that?" Kelly looked at Active and stared, waiting for an answer.

"He wasn't talking about you," Active said. "He told our police chief in Chukchi to arrest Calvin Maiyumerak for robbing the museum."

Kelly looked puzzled for a few seconds, then nodded. "I heard of him. He's the one try stop Victor Solomon from putting my grandfather on display?"

Active lifted his eyebrows. "And anyway, even a *naluaqmiut* court would probably have given Natchiq to you instead of Victor's museum if you could prove he was your grandfather."

Kelly was silent for a long time. "You mean I—" He stopped and shook his head. "I never think about that."

"None of this had to happen. You didn't need to steal your grandfather. And you didn't need to kill Victor Solomon. You did kill him, didn't you?"

Kelly was silent, his jaws locked.

"But why wait a day to kill him? That's the part I can't figure out. Why not just take off and keep going till you were in Canada?"

Kelly pinched the bridge of his nose and shook his head.

"Instead, you wasted that extra day, and that meant you got trapped up here by the storm and couldn't get away before I showed up. But why did you wait?"

Kelly's voice was light, reflective, when he spoke again. "Killing Victor Solomon—you think that's worse than putting my grandfather in a museum?"

"That's what the law says."

"*Naluaqmiut* law."

Active shrugged, white-man style. "Why did you wait a day?" he repeated.

Kelly shook his head, then rose and limped to the door. Snow whirled in when he opened it. The flakes fluttered to the floor and landed on Active's face. It looked as murky and white as ever out there, the wind still shrieking down the canyon and past the cabin. Active tried to guess what time it was. He and Cowboy had reached Shaman Pass by 8 or 9 A.M., he supposed, but how long had he been unconscious? He didn't know, but his inner clock told him it was around noon now.

Kelly shook his head, closed the door, and muttered, "*Arii,* no good."

He turned and sat again, but this time at the table in the center of the cabin. He looked down at Active, trussed up on the floor. "Your pilot, he'll come back when the weather gets good, ah?"

Active lifted his eyebrows. "With more troopers."

Kelly felt his side, looked at his fingers, and sighed. "Then I better go, I guess."

"You can't go in this weather," Active said. "And you're hurt."

"Can't stay either." Kelly stood and lifted the carbine off the cot. He put the muzzle to Active's forehead and looked down with his calm, resigned eyes. "And I can't let you tell about me."

Active tried to speak, but his tongue was paralyzed and swollen, blocking his wind.

Kelly pulled back the hammer on the carbine.

"You don't want to kill a trooper," Active finally managed to croak.

Kelly shrugged one shoulder. "I never want to kill Victor Solomon, either."

"Look," Active said desperately, "if you kill me they'll come after you the minute they get here."

Kelly tilted his head slightly, his eyes on Active's.

"But if you leave me alive, they won't be able to follow you.

They'll have to take me back to the hospital because of my shoulder."

Kelly lowered the hammer. "Left side, ah?"

Active nodded, and Kelly prodded the shoulder with the carbine's muzzle. Active winced.

Kelly reversed the rifle in his hands and raised it as high as his wound permitted. The calm eyes were the last thing Active remembered before the carbine's stock slammed into his left collarbone.

ONCE AGAIN, Active didn't know how long he was out, but this time he came awake cleanly and suddenly, speared out of sleep by the old pain in his shoulder, worse than ever, and a new one along his collarbone.

He lay on the floor for what seemed a great while, adjusting his position to accommodate his injuries, listening to the wind howl past the cabin as the pain subsided toward a manageable level. There was no other sound, no noise of a snowmachine, and he decided Robert Kelly must have gone.

Judging from the sound of the wind and what he could see of the sky through the windows above him, it would be tomorrow at the earliest before Cowboy could get back in with a plane. Maybe a whole week, as was entirely possible in the Arctic.

How long could he last on the floor? Already he was starting to shiver. Robert Kelly's oil stove still muttered in the corner, but the heat in cabins tended to stratify: suffocating at head level, but water would freeze in a bowl on the floor. And in a week, the stove would probably run out of oil.

He wriggled his hands. That jacked up the blaze in his

shoulder, but did nothing to loosen the tape on his wrists. Somewhere on his belt was a Leatherman, but not within reach of his fingers.

Then suddenly it came to him. Slowly, and with great care, he rolled onto his right side—the good side—and hunched himself sufficiently to bring his face down to his hands. He began to gnaw.

CHAPTER TWENTY

HE SPENT THE NEXT two days nursing the damaged shoulder, listening to the wind and Kay-Chuck, and wishing Robert Kelly had something in the place to read other than the *Alaska Hunting and Trapping Regulations* and a three-year-old copy of the *Anchorage Daily News*.

There was nothing to do but wait out the storm. He probed the burning shoulder, found a frightening number of knobs and bulges where none had been before, and rigged a sling to immobilize the arm. He took tea with some pilot bread and peanut butter he found on the shelves. When he went into the snow to take a leak, he found a cold-storage box nailed to an outside wall, and some dried fish inside it. He added the fish to his menu and found it warmed him from the inside, like a space heater in his stomach. He thought maybe it even made his shoulder feel a little better.

He opened his eyes on the third day and wondered what had awakened him. Then he heard it again: the rumble of an airplane engine, so far off he caught the sound only intermittently. Suddenly he realized it was the only sound. The wind was silent and the box of Sailor Boy Pilot Bread on the table was rendered nearly incandescent by a shaft of yellow sunlight.

He rolled out of bed, favoring the injured shoulder, opened the door, and stepped into an enameled landscape of blue and white and perfect stillness. The sun shone straight into his face, so bright that he had to narrow one eye to a slit and close the other completely to peer down the canyon. No plane in sight yet, but the engine sound seemed to be getting closer.

Suddenly the hair on the back of his neck prickled. He ceased all motion, held his breath, and listened intently. Nothing but the tiny, distant drone of the plane and that feeling of someone nearby.

He swept his eyes around the canyon. They came to rest, almost without his willing it, on an odd-looking pile of snow-plastered rocks on the hill just upstream of the cabin.

He walked over and floundered uphill through the snow, pulling himself along on the willows with his right hand.

The rock pile was maybe three feet high, a stack of flat stones with two longer ones near the top sticking out like arms. And crowning it, a round stone like a head. It looked like it had been there a long time. Where it wasn't snow covered, the stones were intergrown with grass and weeds, and covered with white lichen.

Active worked himself around behind Kiana Kelly's original *inuksuk* to look the same direction it did: down the canyon, out over the valley of the Angatquq, a field of white that stretched to the rolling hills across the river.

Still no sign of a plane and now no sound either. Perhaps he had imagined it, or it had been a Bush pilot passing through Shaman Pass on his way to the Arctic Slope.

He started down the hill and was almost back to the cabin when he heard the plane again, close and loud this time. He put his hand above his eyes and squinted down the canyon against the sun. Nothing, except that his eyes were starting to water in the glare. Then a big fat red-and-white metal airplane crossed the mouth of the canyon, convertible wheel-skis dangling beneath like duck feet.

Active recognized it as the Lienhofer Beaver, the craft he had suggested bringing, with backup, before Carnaby had gone cheap-ass and insisted on a look-see in the Super Cub first. He waved wildly with his right arm and saw the wings rock twice before the Beaver passed out of sight beyond the right wall of the canyon.

As the rumble faded and returned, Active strapped on a pair of snowshoes from the cabin wall and started downstream, gradually ascending the ridge that paralleled the creek. The Beaver passed directly overhead and he waved again. The plane made another looping turn downhill and then came straight in, flaps lowered for a landing on the ridgeline.

Active was waiting when the Beaver bounced to a stop on the snow and Cowboy shut down the radial engine. The doors popped open and out climbed Alan Long from the Chukchi Police Department, and Dickie Nelson, the trooper Active had wanted to draft for the trip to Shaman Pass in the first place. And Carnaby, towering over the others by half a head.

The trooper captain put out his hand. Active took it and Carnaby looked him up and down and said, "Did you really jump out of Cowboy's Super Cub?"

Not, "Hello," or "Glad you made it," but "Did you really jump out of Cowboy's Super Cub?"

Active thought it over, but couldn't see any way to dodge it. "Roger that."

"That how you hurt your shoulder?"

"Huh-uh." Active shook his head. "Robert Kelly did it when he ran me down with his snowmachine. Then he whacked it with his rifle butt while I was tied up on the floor."

"While you were tied up?" Carnaby asked. "Why would he do that?"

"It was in lieu of killing me," Active said. "I suggested that if I was dead, you guys would come straight after him. But if I was only hurt, you'd have to take me back to Chukchi for repairs. I guess he wanted to make sure I was hurt. Can you spare a pair of sunglasses, maybe? I'm half snow-blind already in this light."

Carnaby pulled a pair of mirrors out of his parka and handed them to Active, who put them on with an inward sigh of relief. "How's it doing, the shoulder?" Carnaby asked.

Active gave the right half of a shrug. "Sore. Swollen. Knobs sticking out in funny places. Dislocated, I think. Probably should be looked at pretty soon, all right."

"We've got a first-aid kit and Alan here is a paramedic. That's why I brought him. That and the fact he knows the pass. He's hunted up here some."

Active frowned in concentration, then said no thanks to the offer of an examination by Long. "I don't think I can get out of this sling and shirt and vest without passing out. And then I'd have to get back into most of it, which would probably mean passing out again, so all in all I'd rather not."

"Whew," Carnaby said. "Still pretty shocky, huh?"

"I think so, yeah," Active said.

"I think there's some codeine with Tylenol in here," Long said, swinging a backpack off his shoulder. "Want some?"

Active nodded and swallowed two tablets that Long handed him.

"Did you really jump out of Cowboy's plane?" asked Dickie Nelson, who had stepped behind the Beaver to take a leak. Dickie had knocked around the troopers' rural detachments all his career. He was short, wore a mustache, and was famous, and much ridiculed in secret, for a lush head of wavy brown hair that never got any longer, or any grayer. He was a mediocre cop, in Active's estimation, but a discerning connoisseur of Bush yarns. No doubt he scented a classic here.

Carnaby glared. "Save it, Dickie."

"Roger that," Active said.

Carnaby turned the glare on Active. "You feel up to briefing us?"

Active nodded and gave them the short version of all that had happened in the past two days.

"So he didn't actually confess?" Carnaby asked when Active finished.

"Come on," Active said. "There's too much that fits here. Who else could it be?"

"But you didn't actually see Uncle Frosty on his sled, right?"

"Well, no, not actually." Active half-shrugged. "Just a blue bundle the right size."

"And that one-day gap still worries me. Where was he and what was he doing for twenty-four hours? And why would he come back if he already had his grandfather?" Carnaby paused and the look of worry on his face deepened. "Shit! What if the museum burglar and Victor Solomon's killer aren't the same guy? Maybe all Kelly did was steal his grandfather."

"All right, there's some loose ends," Active said, uneasy again because Carnaby had once more made the same point as Whyborn Sivula. "I admit it. But he did knock me out and take off. We've got flight and assault on an officer, at least."

Carnaby pondered this, then nodded. "In for a dime, in for a dollar, I guess. Lots of dollars, unfortunately." He looked at Cowboy in the Beaver and shook his head before continuing. "So you think Kelly's on his way to Canada?"

"That's my guess. It's where Natchiq was headed when Saganiq killed him."

"Hell of a snowmachine ride."

"Kelly knows the country," Active said. "And judging from the load on his sled, he probably had enough gas to get wherever he wanted to go."

"And he's married into the Caribou Creek people?"

Active nodded.

"Well, they've all got relatives on the Canadian side. So Kelly could probably find somebody to stay with over there." Carnaby chewed on his lip and looked down the slope, toward the Angatquq River.

"Anyway, I guess we oughta get you back to Chukchi and have that shoulder looked at. Cowboy and Alan and Dickie and I can come back and see about picking up Kelly's trail."

"Pretty cold trail," Active said. "There were two days of wind and snow after he took off."

Carnaby nodded. "And this sun and warm weather aren't gonna help. Everything will just kind of glaze over."

"Let's go look now."

Carnaby chewed his lip again and squinted at Active. "With that shoulder and all?"

"The codeine is starting to kick in, I think. Another couple hours won't make much difference," Active said. "But you guys will have to do the shooting, if there is any."

Carnaby grinned approvingly. "I thought you might see it that way."

They climbed into the Beaver, Nathan riding shotgun beside Cowboy because he was the only one who had seen Robert Kelly, or his snowmachine.

Cowboy looked questioningly at Carnaby.

"Nathan says he can handle a little run up the pass to see if we can pick up Robert Kelly's trail," Carnaby said.

"All right," Cowboy said. He hit the starter and the old radial fired up, snorting and belching out blue smoke until it settled down to a throaty rumble. Cowboy pulled a headset from between the front seats and Active slipped it on.

Cowboy shoved in a little throttle, the radial growled, and the Beaver lumbered through a clumsy half-circle to face down the ridgeline. Cowboy fed in the rest of the throttle and in a few seconds hauled back on the wheel and horsed the plane into the air. He leveled off a couple hundred feet above the tundra and followed Robert Kelly's creek downstream toward the Angatquq River.

"Any ideas?" Cowboy asked through the headset.

Active studied the terrain beneath the plane. The wind had done its work. The long undulating snow ridges called sastrugas snaked over the tundra, leaving no sign a snowmachine and dogsled had ever passed by. "I don't see anything," he said. "Anybody else? Alan? Dickie? Boss?"

There was a chorus of negatives over the intercom. "How about we just fly up the pass a ways then?" Carnaby said. "That's probably the way he'd go, eh?"

"It's the only land route through the mountains anywheres around here, far as I know," Cowboy said. "We've got gas for maybe another forty-five minutes, max."

The pilot took the Beaver up to eight hundred feet, which, he explained, was the ideal scanning altitude. He continued downslope until they were over the Angatquq River, then rolled into a left turn and pointed them straight up the pass.

The plane hung in the air like a trout in a clear pool, the white landscape rolling away on either side, the blue dome arching overhead. As they flew up the Angatquq, the patches of scrub spruce and willow penetrating the sastrugas thinned out and the route into the pass became a broad valley of pure, rolling white.

But near the crest, the mountains crowded in from either side and soon Active saw a jagged, ice-walled canyon under the right wing.

"Angatquq Gorge," Cowboy said over the intercom. "That's where the river starts. Supposedly, there's a spring down in there that flows all year, even in the dead of winter. The snowmachine trail runs along the rim there."

Active peered through the frost on the window and saw what could have been a faint scratch along the lip of the gorge. The gorge petered out a mile or two below the summit, where the mountains opened out again into a broad, flat saddle of alpine tundra.

A few minutes after they started down the north slope of the pass, Alan Long spoke from the seat behind the pilot. "Isn't that a snowgo down there?"

Cowboy dropped a wing and they all stared down at the tundra. Active caught a glimpse of something that looked like a windshield and handlebars sticking out of the snow before they swept past it.

Cowboy brought the plane around in a graceful, descending turn and they passed over again, this time only a couple of hundred feet high. Now the picture was clearer. Definitely a windshield and handlebars, the rest of the machine and its dogsled discernible only as an oddly convoluted drift behind the windshield.

"Can you get us down there?" Carnaby asked.

Cowboy rolled the Beaver into another turn and lowered the wing flaps. In less than three minutes the plane was bouncing over the sastrugas to a stop by the buried snowmachine.

They piled out and used snowshoes to dig out Kelly's black Arctic Cat and dogsled, Active grateful to get a pass because of his shoulder. The other four—even Cowboy—grunted and heaved and it became clear in a few minutes that no frozen driver was under the snow. They found a rough shelter Kelly had made by turning the dogsled on its side and draping the skin of his wall tent over it. Inside was evidence he had occupied it for at least a few hours: an unrolled sleeping bag on a mat of caribou hides, a camp stove still set up for use, two paper sacks of groceries, one with the top half of the bag ripped away. Outside, three red jerry jugs of gas, a half-dozen plastic bottles of snowmachine oil, a small toolbox, a gas lantern, and the frame for the tent. Almost as one, they swiveled to survey the incandescent slopes around them.

"I guess it quit on him," Dickie said.

"Where's Uncle Frosty?" Cowboy asked.

"Kelly must have taken him along. A man carrying that kind of load, how far . . . in that blizzard. . . ." Active stopped and shook his head.

"Could he get through?" Carnaby asked.

"Cowboy, Alan, you guys have been up in this country before," Active said. "What do you think? Any shelter close enough that he could have made it?"

Cowboy spoke first. "I never saw any camps up here but Robert Kelly's." The pilot shook his head. "But I never saw that one before now."

Alan Long spoke thoughtfully, as if to himself. "Maybe if he made a snowhouse, it hasn't been too cold . . . but he was hurt . . . and that blizzard . . ." He paused, then shrugged. "I don't know. He knows the country, and some of these old guys— they . . . I don't know."

They all swiveled again to study the vast emptiness of the pass. Carnaby put Alan and Dickie to work on the snowmachine again and moved off by himself, presumably to think things over.

Cowboy walked a few yards behind the dogsled and took a leak, then kicked at something in the snow. "Hey," he yelled. "Look at this."

When the rest of them got there, he had uncovered a twelve-inch section of black rubber and metal cleats. "Looks like the drive track from his Arctic Cat," Cowboy said.

They dug it out and examined it. The track had obviously come apart on the trail.

"Never saw one of those fail before," Cowboy said. He

pointed to the edge of the track, where the break had started. "Looks like it was cut. Maybe he ran over something sharp."

"Huh-uh," Alan Long called out. He had returned to the snowmachine and was kneeling beside it. "I think Active shot his track. That's what started the break."

Long pointed to a bullet hole in the aluminum chassis of the machine, just above the running board. He took off his mirrors, put his eye to the hole, and peered in. "Yep," he said. "Lines up perfect with the slide rails. It was Nathan's Smith & Wesson that did this. It just took a while for the track to fall completely apart."

They all looked at Active, who shrugged.

"Now what?" Cowboy asked.

Carnaby pulled off his mirrors and pinched the bridge of his nose. "I'm pulling the plug."

At Active's look, Carnaby held up a hand. "I know, I know. But either Kelly's out there under the snow somewhere, or he's on his way to Canada, maybe lying low in the daytime and moving at night. Either way, we're not going to find him unless we bring an army in here. We'll put out another alert to the cops on our side of the border, and the Mounties in Canada, and they'll all watch for him. If he makes it through, we'll get him eventually. If not—well, then it's over. Case closed. There's no way to track him though this snow."

Cowboy, who had lit a cigarette, looked at the trooper captain in surprise. "Well, sure there is."

"Is what?" Carnaby asked.

"A way to find tracks under the snow."

"How?"

"With brooms."

"With what?" Active asked. "Brooms?"

Cowboy nodded. "Uh-huh. And you know who knows how to do it?"

Long, Carnaby, and Active lifted their eyebrows in the white expression of inquiry.

"Whyborn."

"Whyborn Sivula?" Dickie said.

Cowboy said, "Of course Whyborn Sivula."

He looked from face to face. "You don't believe me? Well, there was this kid named Archie Ramer who went missing out of Ebrulik a few years ago and I was called up there on the search. We found his snowmachine broke down on the trail, the tracks all blown in, no way to follow him, just like now. So they bring in Whyborn and he gets a bunch of brooms and hands 'em out and the guys from Ebrulik all start sweeping and pretty soon they find Archie's tracks under the blow-in."

Cowboy stopped talking and took a leisurely drag on his Lucky Strike. Active knew it was just to annoy them, and swore not to be the first to crack.

It was Carnaby who gave in. "Damn it, Cowboy, what happened?"

The pilot grinned. "Well, it takes 'em a couple days, but they finally track Archie to a snow cave, where he's waiting the thing out. He had pretty bad frostbite on his feet, but he survived, and he can still walk. He's got two kids of his own now, and they're both named Whyborn."

"Come on."

"Yep. Whyborn Louis Ramer and Rachel Whyborn Ramer."

"Whyborn Sivula," Carnaby said with a shake of his head.

"Let's go back to town and call him," Active said. "Cowboy can fly him up here to do a broom search."

Carnaby looked at Active and shook his head again. "Huh-uh. I'm not paying anybody to sweep this pass with a damned broom, Nathan. How am I going to explain it to Juneau?"

"Maybe Whyborn'll work cheap."

"He didn't charge anything to find Archie Ramer," Cowboy said. "All he wanted was his snowmachine gas."

Carnaby sighed. "Even so, Cowboy would have to fly support, right? Haul in gas, supplies, stove oil? Fly up to check on things once in a while? It's still going to cost plenty. Plus, there'd have to be at least one trooper along, and with you on the injured list, Nathan, we're pretty short right now. I just don't think I can justify it."

"Let's call it a Search and Rescue," Active said. He looked at Carnaby. "Then Cowboy's bill doesn't show up on our books."

Carnaby frowned, then nodded, finally. "Yeah, I guess I could write it up that way. You think Silver would go along with it, Alan?"

Jim Silver, as police chief, represented the city of Chukchi on Search-and-Rescue matters.

"I think he might," Alan said. "We're getting pretty close to the end of the fiscal year and we've still got a lot of Search-and-Rescue money left. Might as well spend it."

"But I still can't spare a trooper," Carnaby said.

"I'll do it," Active said.

"Injured like you are? Not a chance." Carnaby shook his head.

"They can fix me up at the hospital," Active said. "It hurts, all right, but it's probably just a bruised collarbone and a dislocated shoulder. I got a dislocation playing hockey in college and it's not much of a problem after the doctor, ah, reduces it. They put it in a sling, give you some painkillers and anti-inflammatories, send you home, and tell you to go easy on it for a couple weeks."

Carnaby snorted. "You mean like riding a snowmachine a couple hundred miles in the cold?"

"Cowboy can take me and my Yamaha up when he flies in

the gear," Active said. "If it's just short rides out of camp, I'll be fine."

Carnaby looked at the Bush pilot. "Can you get a snowmachine in the Beaver?"

Cowboy nodded. "Sure, If I take out the rear seats."

Carnaby pulled at his chin, considering. "I suppose. But, Nathan, you can't do any sweeping with your arm in a sling. Won't old Whyborn need some help in the broom department?"

"I'll come along," Alan said. "It's still my burglary case."

"All right," Carnaby said. "Let's go home, get Nathan to a doctor, and give Whyborn a call."

CHAPTER TWENTY-ONE

THE NEXT MORNING, COWBOY, Alan Long and Whyborn Sivula loaded the Ladies' Model into the Beaver, along with red jerry jugs of gas for the snowmachines, round cans of Chevron stove oil, and most of the other supplies they'd need in camp. Then Alan and Whyborn set out for Shaman Pass, pulling dogsleds with a wall tent and enough gear and food to hold them for a day or two in case one of the thousand vagaries of Bush flying kept the Beaver from getting in.

Active, his collarbone diagnosed as cracked but not broken and his dislocated shoulder reduced and immobilized in an official hospital sling, saw the two off, then took another painkiller, plus an anti-inflammatory, and napped in the bachelor cabin till Cowboy picked him up in the Lienhofer van at four o'clock. Soon they were back in the Beaver, the nose pointed across the Katonak Flats toward Shaman Pass.

The weather was still clear and calm and predicted to stay that way for while, according to Cowboy, who had gone over it with the briefer at the FAA Station.

When Active asked how long a "while" might be, Cowboy looked at him and grinned. "You never know."

The Beaver lumbered across the flats and nosed its way up the headwaters of the Katonak, the white saddle of the pass coming into view ninety minutes out of Chukchi.

Cowboy dropped down to four hundred feet, and they picked up the thread of trail left by the two snowmachines. They followed it toward the pass, the mountains to the west starting to throw blue shadows across the snow as the sun angled toward the northwest horizon.

As they climbed the snowy course of the Angatquq River, Cowboy's voice crackled over the intercom. "Check that out." He dropped the nose, swung to the right slightly and pointed at the tundra.

Active looked down and saw seven jagged flakes of obsidian sailing over the snow ahead of them. He turned to Cowboy. "I didn't know ravens traveled in flocks. I never saw that many together before."

Cowboy smiled. "See any shadows?"

Active peered down. Cowboy was right. The birds cast no shadows. How could that be, in this light? There was the sharp clear negative of the Beaver, sweeping across the tundra and rapidly overtaking the ravens.

Through some psychic window Active didn't know he had left open, a chill blew in and rippled down his spine, just for a moment. He was already figuring it out, feeling silly, when Cowboy spoke again.

"Those aren't ravens, they're ptarmigan. You can't see them against the snow, just their shadows."

Active watched until the shadows passed under the plane and vanished behind. He never did spot the white birds themselves.

"Spooky," he said through the intercom.

"I suppose," Cowboy said. "If it's your first time, anyway. You know, if you weren't flying, you'd never see that kind of thing."

"I suppose not."

"People who don't fly, they don't know how intimate you get with the country from up here," Cowboy said.

Active turned and looked at the pilot. Did the soul of a poet lurk under the bravado? "Good point," he said.

They overtook Alan and Whyborn just beyond the summit. Cowboy rocked the wings. The two men waved back and pointed down the canyon.

"We'll go on ahead and meet them at Kelly's snowmachine," Cowboy said over the intercom.

A few minutes later, Cowboy backed off the Beaver's throttle and started down. The ski marks from the day before came into view. Cowboy swung around to land uphill and grooved the Beaver into the day-old tracks. They began unloading the supplies, occasionally breaking through the crusted snow as they pulled gas, food, and gear out of the plane's rear compartment and set them down a few yards off. Finally, only the Ladies' Model was left in the Beaver.

Cowboy was grumbling about having to unload it by himself because of Active's shoulder when Alan and Whyborn pulled in and climbed off their snowmachines, stiff-jointed from the long ride.

A pretty little husky with one blue eye and one brown leapt off Whyborn's sled and bounded toward the plane, tongue out and a goofy dog grin on her face. She circled the Beaver twice, then stopped at the cargo door, barking joyously.

"That Kibbie sure like it out in the country, all right," Whyborn said as he flexed his shoulders. "She never get to go out much anymore."

Active watched as Kibbie raced to explore a little canyon that descended into the pass from the east. "I guess I didn't know a dog was coming," he said.

Whyborn shrugged. "She won't hurt anything. And she'll let us know if anything come around."

Active was about to say, "Like what?" when he noticed a caribou carcass on Alan's sled, neatly field dressed. He had the feeling the manhunt was getting beyond his control, turning into a caribou hunt and pleasure jaunt. All on the Search and Rescue tab, with a dog in camp for company. But he couldn't see any way around it, so he decided to keep his mouth shut.

Active watched the three other men horse the Yamaha out of the Beaver and onto the wind-packed snow. He straddled it, hit the starter, and drove off a few yards, out of Cowboy's way.

The pilot climbed into the Beaver, then spoke from the window. "I'll be back every three or four days, weather permitting, until you find him or Carnaby and Silver decide to give it up."

Active nodded.

Cowboy nodded back and shut the window. The radial engine rumbled to life. Cowboy nudged the plane through a big loop in the snow and came around to point downhill in the now well-worn tracks. The Beaver roared forward and lifted off into blue shadows.

The three men in the snow started their machines and drove the quarter mile to the mouth of the side canyon where Kibbie was now digging frenziedly in the snow. The dog had probably heard a lemming scurrying through its labyrinth of tunnels under the surface, Whyborn explained.

Even Active, a relative greenhorn, could see that the canyon was a good campsite. It would afford some shelter from the wind if Shaman Pass got another blow. Even now, the ever-present wind from the south was sifting a thin layer of snow along the floor of the pass, but it was calm here in the canyon. A fringe of willows along the creek made the scene look a little less sterile and hostile to life than the rolling snow desert in front.

Alan and Whyborn unloaded their sleds and decided, after some discussion, that Alan would haul over the rest of the gear while Whyborn set up the tent. Active asked what a one-armed man could do to help, and was advised to gather willows for the floor.

Alan took off with his empty sled. Whyborn untangled a bundle of two-by-fours from the pile of gear in the snow and went to work on the tent while Active floundered into the willows behind the camp. The brush was dry and leafless from the long winter, and it was cold with the sun out of sight behind the ridge, zero or so, he thought. The little trees snapped like icicles.

When he dragged his bundle back to camp, he found that Whyborn had assembled the two-by-fours into a frame and draped the tent over it. Already, the old hunter had dragged in his dogsled and positioned it along one side for sitting and sleeping. He was just setting up a camp stove made from the top third of an oil drum.

Whyborn poured in some stove oil from one of the Chevron cans, pulled matches and a wad of toilet paper from his pocket, and soon the tent was as warm as a house.

As Whyborn spread willows on the tent floor, Alan came in with a slab of fresh caribou. Whyborn found a skillet in one of the boxes still on his sled, while Active went out with a pot to scoop up snow for tea water. And soon Alan was folding his hands and saying grace over a dinner of caribou steak, pilot bread, and tea, topped off with dried salmon and seal oil supplied by Whyborn. For dessert, they found Oreos in one of the boxes Cowboy had brought. Active bit into one, and decided he couldn't imagine anything better for dessert in a wall tent in Shaman Pass, even if he did have to share them with two men who insisted on saying grace before they would eat.

Afterward, they discussed how to sleep three people on two sleds. Active suggested it wouldn't be a problem, because one of them would have to be awake at any given moment to stand watch anyway.

Whyborn frowned. "Watch for what?"

"Robert Kelly," Alan said.

"Hmmph." Whyborn's look made it clear he thought he was working with idiots. "No need for that. Kibbie will let us know if anybody come around. That Robert Kelly, he been coming up here since he was a boy. If he want to sneak up and shoot us, none of us will hear him, even if we're awake. But Kibbie will, all right."

Active bowed to this logic, and to his desire not to spend half the night watching the moonlight on the tundra.

After more discussion, they decided that Active and Alan would share one sled, while Whyborn and Kibbie shared the other. That settled, Whyborn lit a gas lantern and broke out a deck of cards and a cribbage board made from caribou horn. He and Alan began to play, using matches for pegs and the bed of Whyborn's sled for a table.

Alan's sled was still outside. Active left the tent and trudged past Kibbie, curled up in the snow beside the flap. The dog lifted her head and woofed ingratiatingly.

The sun rode well below the ridge opposite the camp now, drowning the tent in evening shadow. But as Active bent to unhitch the sled, the sun slid past a notch in the ridge, flooding the scene with shafts of horizontal light the color of blood. Active pulled the sled to the tent, worked it through the front flap, and went inside to unroll his sleeping pad and bag.

Whyborn and Alan were well into the cribbage game, seeming less tired out by their day on snowmachines than Active was by his ride up in the Beaver. As Active stretched out on the sled, he heard Alan asking, "You think he's out there somewhere watching us?"

"Who?" Whyborn asked. "Robert Kelly?"

"Naah," Alan said. "Old Natchiq."

From outside the tent Kibbie growled deep in her throat, nothing ingratiating about it this time, then whined piteously. Soon the dog's black nose came through the tent flap, followed by two imploring eyes.

Active sat up and was digging for his Smith & Wesson when Whyborn laughed and grabbed Kibbie by the ears. "You're not so tough when *amaguq* come around, ah? Smart dog."

Then the song began, high, cold, and lonely, sounding as if the wolves were just up the canyon behind camp. Kibbie, bold now in the refuge of the tent, howled back, a cry so powerful they covered their ears till she stopped.

"Will they, ah, cause trouble?" Active asked as the serenade went on.

"Maybe if you go outside to take a leak, you gotta watch Little Nathan," Whyborn said with the same kind of laugh as when he had grabbed Kibbie's ears.

Active grinned gamely and Alan chuckled as Whyborn dealt a new round. Suddenly the wolves fell silent, as abruptly as they had begun. Kibbie continued staring at the back of the tent, ears pricked, head tilted, and Active wondered in the deafening quiet if the animals were moving down on the camp. Then the dog's ears dropped back to their normal position and she curled up beside Whyborn on the sled.

Then suddenly she was up again, a half-whine, half-growl coming from her throat, this time staring at the front wall of the tent.

Active started to speak but Whyborn held up one hand and grabbed Kibbie's muzzle with the other. The older man's face was a taut skein of intersecting angles, reminding Active more than ever of the Inupiat's Mongol forebears. Several seconds ticked past, the only sounds the lantern hissing from the ridgepole and the tent stove muttering to itself.

Finally Whyborn relaxed and released Kibbie, who relaxed, too. "Thought I could hear something out there, but I guess not."

"Are the wolves moving around us?" Active asked.

"Must be, but I thought I heard a snowgo, way off. But I guess it was just the lamp or the stove. Kibbie, she must have heard them wolves again, all right."

Active frowned. "A snowmachine? Who'd be up here?"

"Maybe Robert Kelly?" Alan suggested.

Whyborn shrugged. "He might have another snowgo up here, in a trail camp, all right. But if he do, why is he still around this place? Seem like he'll be over in Canada by now, ah?"

"Maybe he had to leave his grandfather behind and now he's come back for him," Active said. He stepped out of the tent, letting his eyes adjust to the darkness. It didn't take long. The snowfields were flooded with moonlight and blue-green arches of aurora shimmered to the north. He gazed back up the pass. There—toward the summit. A flicker of light? The headlight of a snowmachine bouncing up the trail, back the way Whyborn and Alan had come? As he covered his eyes for a few seconds to make them more sensitive, he heard the tent flap open, sensed Whyborn Sivula coming out to stand beside him.

He uncovered his eyes and looked again.

"You see something?" Whyborn asked.

Active saw no light now, nothing but the slopes and folds of Shaman Pass, cold and empty in the moonlight. "Maybe a snowmachine light back up the pass there. Do many people come through here?"

Snow creaked under Whyborn's feet as he swung his gaze up the valley. "Not many. Too cold and too far."

Whyborn cleared his throat and avoided Active's eyes. "I'm sorry I never tell you all I know when you come to my house in Chukchi. I don't think my friend Robert Kelly ever mean to be a bad man. He don't need to be in your jail."

Another flicker of light caught Active's eye, and he glanced up in time to see a shooting star draw a thread of blue fire across the silent, salmon-colored sky above the opposite ridge. "Maybe the light I saw was nothing," he said.

"Maybe so."

Active was quiet for a moment, then looked at the older man. "I'm surprised that you came."

"When I think about how Robert Kelly's lost out here somewhere, I worry about his family," Sivula said. "His people should know what happen to him, never have to wonder all those years like with his grandfather."

CHAPTER TWENTY-TWO

THE NEXT MORNING, AFTER a breakfast of oatmeal and dried fish with seal oil and grace, Whyborn pulled Alan's sled out of the tent and hitched it to Active's Yamaha. Then he went to the heap of gear near the tent and dug out two ordinary household brooms, along with two pairs of aluminum snowshoes, and threw it all into the sled. He motioned Alan into the basket, stepped onto the runners at the back, and turned to Active.

"Alan and me will be out sweeping. Since you can't sweep with that shoulder, you could drive the snowgo, ah? Take us out to the trail, bring us back to the tent for lunch, pick us up at night, OK?"

Active nodded and straddled the Yamaha, started it, and drove to a spot Whyborn indicated about fifty yards ahead of Robert Kelly's Arctic Cat in its trench in the snow. The two men climbed out, strapped on the snowshoes, and grabbed the brooms.

Whyborn looked at Alan Long, who was staring at his broom in mystification.

"You never do this before, ah?"

Alan shook his head.

"Well, when somebody leave a footprint in the snow, it get hard like concrete," Whyborn said. "Even if it blow over, it's still under there."

Whyborn began trampling the crust, breaking it up with the edges of his snowshoes. When he had pulverized an area several yards in diameter, he began sweeping away the broken snow to get at the older layer underneath. Alan watched for a minute, then began sweeping, too.

Suddenly Whyborn stopped and bent down. "Look at this," he said, as Active and Alan hurried up. He pointed at two faint depressions, almost indiscernible in the field of white. "That's Robert Kelly, all right. That's his boot heel and that's his toe."

Active knelt beside the track.

"Go ahead," Whyborn said. "Poke it, you'll see."

Active gingerly probed the heel print with a mittened thumb. Whyborn was right. It was hard to the touch, as hard as pavement.

"We have to mark it," Whyborn said as Active stood up. "Maybe you could bring us some of those willows by the tent."

Active nodded, drove to the tent on the snowmachine, and went to work in the willow grove again.

When he had a couple dozen of the little trees lying on the snow, he ferried them back to the sled in only two one-armed loads. Snapping off the willows wasn't hard work, but floundering around in the snow was and he was sweating under his winter gear. He climbed onto the Yamaha and paused for a moment to catch his breath and cool off.

He gazed out at Whyborn and Alan at work with their brooms. The sky was bright and cloudy this morning, maybe ten miles an hour of breeze tumbling down from the summit. A cold enough day and bad enough light, white on white. The two men were the only nonwhite objects in sight. It would have been impossible to guess their size and distance if he hadn't known. They could have been dolls in the snow at his feet or giants across the pass.

It suddenly seemed preposterous. Tiny men with brooms, following a tiny trail of footprints through the blank expanse of Shaman Pass. He was tempted to call it off then and there, head back to Chukchi on the snowmachines, and wait for Robert Kelly to turn up across the line in Canada, or back home in Caribou Creek. Or for his corpse to be spotted on the tundra by some pilot flying through the pass on a summer day.

But Whyborn, with his quiet Inupiat capacity to do any job that needed doing with any tool available to do it, had already found a track. Active shook his head, started the Yamaha, and headed for that first track with his load of trail markers.

FOR THE next four days, Alan and Whyborn swept their way down the north slope of the pass. Active, his left arm still useless in the sling, did camp, cargo, and chauffeur duty on the Ladies' Model as the trail of willows crept onward. There were no more mysterious lights or sounds in the night, and he decided his imagination had been working overtime the evening they had arrived.

Cowboy Decker showed up just before twilight on the fourth day and was suitably impressed by the line of willows now stretching nearly five miles. He dropped off gas for the snowmachines, oil for the stove, and several boxes of food that Active hoped included more Oreos. The pilot loaded their trash and empty gas cans into the Beaver and rumbled away to the south.

That night, Whyborn pulled out the cribbage board and cards and shuffled for the first round of the game. "We could use some more caribou, ah?" he said as he dealt onto a sleeping bag. "Maybe we should go catch some tomorrow."

Alan's face lit up in one of his buck-toothed grins as he picked up his cards. "Sure, if we find the main herd we could even get some to take back to town with us."

Active, who was learning the game now, tossed his two discards into the crib and turned up the start card. He started to object, but realized his heart wasn't in it. The scrawny little spring caribou Alan and Whyborn had brought in the first day hadn't provided much meat. With Kibbie's help, they had eaten the best of it already. Only the tough and stringy cuts were left, and they would be gone in a couple more days. After that, they would be down to the canned meat in their supplies. "How far are they?"

"Not too far now," Whyborn said. "Around where Angatquq River runs into the Katonak, maybe."

Well, why not? They'd been at it for four days, twelve to fourteen hours at a stretch in the long spring light. A break wouldn't hurt. Active shrugged and said, "Sure."

"You could come, too, ah, Nathan?" Whyborn looked at him expectantly.

Active was tempted. It would be good to see the pass and the Katonak Valley up close, from ground level. Find the kind of intimacy you couldn't get from the air. But he shook his head. "I don't think so, with this arm."

The other two nodded and went back to their game.

Over a very late breakfast the next morning, Whyborn suggested it was time to move the camp farther down the pass.

"We should be closer to where we're working," he said. "Too much time running back and forth now. Look like a pretty good side canyon up about a half-mile from where we quit yesterday. Maybe you could go look at it today, Nathan. If it's good, we could move up there tomorrow before we start work, ah?"

Active nodded, happy to have something to fill the day. "Fine by me," he said.

Whyborn and Alan left the tent and began loading gas and a minimal camping outfit onto Alan's sled. When the load was bungeed down, they slung their rifles onto their backs, straddled their machines, and pulled away with Kibbie in her usual perch atop the sled, an expression of bliss on her face.

Active looked down the north slope of the pass as the engine sounds faded. A streak of gray-white was just visible on the horizon. Otherwise the day was perfect, blue and white as the one before. Even better: The south wind had died out and it was dead calm this morning.

As he stooped to enter the tent, he realized his injured shoulder was complaining for some reason. Maybe he had slept on it wrong? Then he remembered: He had forgotten to take the hospital's anti-inflammatories for the past couple of days. He found the bottle in his gear and took two with some of the morning tea.

By the time he finished cleaning up the breakfast mess, the familiar drowsiness from the anti-inflammatories was kicking in. Well, what the heck. A nap before the trek to the new campsite couldn't hurt. He started to go into the tent, then paused. The sun was so warm and brilliant.

He dragged Whyborn's sled out of the tent and stretched out on the hickory slats of the basket. He draped his right arm over his eyes to cut down on the light. Lassitude filled him up like hot oil and his muscles melted and then he was back with Cowboy that day they had seen the ptarmigan shadows flying up the pass.

The thought of a creature so at home in its element as to become invisible was more than he could resist, so this time he floated down from the Beaver and became one of the obsidian shadows himself. He sailed without effort past the Angatquq Gorge and over the summit and started down the north side of the pass, the joy of it blazing up and up inside him until he just had to let it out. But it came out as an ordinary human yell, not a ptarmigan cackle, and he awoke to find himself plain old Nathan Active again, not the least bit invisible, lying in Whyborn Sivula's sled with a cotton-dry mouth and the afterglow of ptarmiganhood fading inside him.

He sat up and looked around. It was cooler now, thin fingers of cloud reaching overhead from the north, a flutter of breeze, also from the north for the first time, plucking at the guard hairs of his parka ruff.

He checked his watch. Past two already, meaning his nap had stretched to two or three hours, not the couple of minutes it had seemed when he was a ptarmigan shadow. He went into the tent, finished the tea, and dug into the food box for some dried fish and Oreos. That didn't quite do it, so he ate two pieces of fried caribou left over from breakfast and felt ready to explore for a new campsite.

He hitched Whyborn's dogsled to the Ladies' Model and followed the line of willows over the series of gentle, terracelike bluffs that led down the north slope of the pass. As he crested the last terrace, a quarter-mile before the end of the willow trail, his eyes were on the cloud bank to the north, now a solid and unpleasant-looking gray-white mass that loomed halfway up the sky, with an awning of thinner, streaky clouds running ahead.

So he was almost on the snowmachine and the man sweeping the snow before he saw them. The man threw down the broom and sprinted for the snowmachine. Active gunned the Yamaha and bounced down the slope, fighting for control with his one good hand. The driver was yanking at the starter cord now as Active stormed across the flat below the bluff and steered the Yamaha straight at the other machine. With a little luck, he would be able to stop squarely in front of it and block the driver.

He saw that he was coming in too fast and reached across his chest to grab for the brake on the left handlebar, but too late. The Ladies' Model plowed into the other machine head-on. Active pitched over the windshield and into the other driver, and both ended up in the snow, with Active on top.

Active was digging under his parka for the Smith & Wesson and shouting, "State trooper! You're under arrest!" as the driver struggled to free himself when a huge shape launched itself with a roar from the sled behind the other machine. Active felt the dog hit his injured shoulder, then he was on his back in the snow with jaws clamped on his throat and yellow eyes glaring into his own.

Thanks to the parka hood, zipped all the way up into a snorkel, the dog's teeth didn't draw any blood, but the jaws were like a vise on his windpipe and he couldn't get air.

Finally he worked the Smith & Wesson free and put it up to the dog's neck and was thumbing off the safety when someone screamed, "Kobuk, let him go! Don't shoot, Nathan, I'll stop him! Kobuk, let him go!"

Calvin Maiyumerak fell onto Kobuk's back and got an arm under the dog's neck and began jerking. Gradually, the teeth slipped off Active's throat and finally he was free, fire snakes writhing in the injured shoulder again.

Maiyumerak led the snarling dog over to the dilapidated sled and made him lie down in the basket, then spoke softly into his ear. Active leveled the Smith & Wesson and watched as the dog calmed, the growls subsiding, the yellow eyes softening but never leaving Active.

Finally Maiyumerak straightened and turned to face Active. He was underdressed as usual, his skinny frame protected only by a snowmachine suit, a headband around his ears, and, yes, Active looked twice to be sure, the high-top sneakers.

Maiyumerak opened his mouth, saw the muzzle of the Smith

& Wesson pointed at his chest, and raised his hands. "Don't shoot, Nathan, I surrender."

Active shook his head in disgust. "That was your light up in the pass the other night, wasn't it? I wasn't just seeing things. What the hell are you doing up here?"

"I was caribou hunting and I—" Maiyumerak trailed off as he saw Active eyeing the broom abandoned in the broken snow a few yards behind the dogsled.

"Bullshit. You've been trailing us all week and you—you're after Uncle Frosty."

Maiyumerak looked over his shoulder at the broom, then back at Active. "Could I show you something?"

Active said nothing and kept the Smith & Wesson on Maiyumerak's chest.

"Don't worry, I won't try anything," Maiyumerak said. "Look, my gun's there." He pointed at the rear of his dogsled, where the stock of his rifle poked out of its scabbard on a rail.

"Let's go," Active said.

Maiyumerak led him to the cleared patch and pointed to a pair of oval depressions in the snow. They looked to Active like the toe prints of a pair of mukluks with *ugruk*-skin bottoms. There was even a fairly clear serrated line where the bottoms were stitched to the caribou uppers. But there was no sign that he could see of matching heel prints behind the toe prints.

Then Maiyumerak pointed to another pair of ovals in the snow a foot or so ahead of the toe prints. These were different. The bottoms were rounded and smooth, with no mark of a seam.

Maiyumerak stepped back and let Active study the tracks. Finally, Active shrugged his incomprehension.

Maiyumerak put the toes of his high-tops in the rear depressions and knelt. His knees fit squarely in the front depressions. He looked up at Active. "Either he stop to pray or he's real tired, look like."

"I doubt Robert Kelly would be praying." Active looked at the empty snowfields around them, imagining Kelly on his knees in the blizzard, ordering himself to keep moving while that voice at the back of his brain told him it wasn't worth the trouble.

Maiyumerak stood. "I could show you something else up there." He pointed ahead, at the mouth of a side canyon. Active nodded and they crunched forward, occasionally breaking through the crust. Maiyumerak followed his own snowmachine tracks into the canyon and up the bed of a little creek for a few yards. Finally he stopped and pointed through a fringe of willows. "See, somebody have a camp here."

Active couldn't see it at first, but eventually he picked out the silhouettes of several piles of gear under the snow, with blue tarp showing through here and there.

They pushed through the willows. Maiyumerak pulled back the tarps to uncover a snowmachine, several cans of aviation gas, a white wall tent with two-by-fours for the frame, three nylon backpacker tents, a barrel stove, and five waterproof duffel bags labeled A. RIVERS—CHUKCHI.

"Who's A. Rivers?" Active asked.

"Arnie Rivers," Maiyumerak said. "*Naluaqmiut* guide. Fly his hunters up here in the fall time for caribou and sheep, come back in the spring for bear sometimes. I guess he use this for his camp."

All was silent, except for the sound of Kobuk barking joyously somewhere out front. Probably after a lemming, judging from the tone.

The snow in Arnie Rivers's camp was pocked with tracks from Maiyumerak's high-tops. "Did you take anything?"

"I never touch nothing," Maiyumerak said.

From the looks of the gear under the blue tarps, Maiyumerak was telling the truth. But it still seemed unlikely to Active. "Why not?"

"I never have time."

"Why not?"

Maiyumerak squinted in reluctance and fished cigarettes and matches out of an inside pocket.

"But you had time to go out there with a broom and interfere with a trooper investigation?"

"I never interfere with nothing." Maiyumerak lit the cigarette, took a drag, and exhaled. The smoke drifted away on the breeze from the north. "I just want to get Uncle Frosty before they take him back to that museum."

"Uncle Frosty's evidence in a homicide. And he belongs to the tribal council."

Maiyumerak grimaced. "Not if they try put him in a case for tourists to look at."

"That's their business," Active said. "Why did you wait till now? You've been watching us all week, right?"

Maiyumerak nodded. "After I hear on Kay-Chuck how Robert Kelly take his grandfather and get away from you up here, then you guys find his sled and snowgo, I start to think he's probably dead, all right. Maybe I could come up here and find them, maybe at least hide Uncle Frosty before you fellas come back, except how am I going to find them? All Kay-Chuck say is, it happen in Shaman Pass. Didn't say if it was south side or north side, or even if it was up one of these canyons. Then I see Whyborn and Alan Long take off on their snowgos, all loaded up for a long ride, and I think maybe they're coming up here. So I follow them and then I watch you fellas every day to see what you will find."

"You've been camping by yourself up in these hills all this time?"

"I got Kobuk for company, all right."

Active shook his head. "So you've been coming down and doing your own search at night?"

Maiyumerak squinted. "I never sweep myself until today. That's when I see Alan and Whyborn take off to the south, look like they're going hunting. And you're asleep on the sled. I come down through this little canyon here and that's when I find this camp. Seem to me like Robert Kelly was trying to reach this place but he never make it." Maiyumerak pointed at the nearest trail marker in the line stretching back up the pass. "Robert Kelly and Uncle Frosty must be between here and that last willow, ah?"

Active studied the scene, and Maiyumerak's logic. "If he had Uncle Frosty with him. Maybe he hid him somewhere back up the trail. Or maybe he missed this place in the storm and walked right past it."

Maiyumerak was silent, looking along the line of willows. "Could be. But he know this country like his wife's *miluks*, from what I hear, and he have to go this way to get to and from Caribou Creek. I think he know about this camp."

Maiyumerak turned and pointed at the canyon wall. Like the gear, the *inuksuk* was hard to make out in the snow at first, but Active finally saw it. The little man stood on a ledge about twenty feet above the camp. His bottom half was buried in a drift, but he was mostly free of snow from the waist up. The dark frosted stones of the torso, arms, and head stood out clearly once Active's eyes focused on them.

Now it was Active's turn to shrug. "Maybe Robert Kelly put in the *inuksuk* before Arnie Rivers started camping here." He turned and looked out at the trail of willows leading down from the pass. Kobuk had stopped barking now, but was still digging furiously in the snow maybe a hundred yards out from the canyon mouth.

Active shook his head at the dog's boundless, if pointless, energy and turned his attention back to the problem of Calvin Maiyumerak. "I should arrest you for interfering with our investigation. But you're not worth the paperwork. Take off now, and I'll forget it."

Maiyumerak lifted his eyebrows, but didn't look convinced.

Active pulled the handcuffs off his belt and tapped Maiyumerak's wrist. " 'Take off now' means, 'If I see you again before this investigation is complete, you'll go home wearing these.' "

Maiyumerak jerked back. "*Arii!* They'll freeze my arms."

Active lifted his eyebrows and smiled. "Uh-huh. Now get— what the hell is that?"

Even as he said it, Active realized the unearthly howl was coming from Kobuk.

Calvin flicked away his cigarette. "Shit!" he said, and floundered through the snow toward Kobuk, who let out another howl.

Active burst through the willows. Kobuk was on his haunches beside his dig in the snow, his muzzle pointed at the sky. Calvin reached the spot first, looked into the crater, and knelt beside the dog. Active moved up beside him, looked down, and saw a shoulder, clad in a green corduroy parka, in the trench the dog had clawed out in the snow.

"Look like Kobuk find him for us, ah?" Maiyumerak said.

They began clearing away the snow around Robert Kelly. They worked in from the right arm, uncovering his torso, legs, and a frost-glazed face of dark marble, expressionless, the cut still visible over the brow. His arms were folded across his chest, mittened hands clasped as if in prayer.

As they cleared the left shoulder, they could see a blue shadow through the adjacent snow. They kept clearing until they had uncovered something man-shaped and man-sized wrapped in a blue tarp beside Robert Kelly. They stepped back and were silent for a time as the breeze from the north sifted snow onto the plastic.

"That's Uncle Frosty, ah?" Maiyumerak said finally.

"Has to be," Active said.

"Can we look?"

"Got a knife?"

Maiyumerak reached inside his snowmachine suit and came out with a big clasp knife. He opened it and passed it to Active.

Active knelt beside the blue bundle, cut away the ropes, and folded back the tarp. Uncle Frosty—Natchiq—was wrapped in caribou fur. Fresh caribou fur from the look and smell of it. Kelly must have removed whatever the Smithsonian had used for wrapping and replaced it with something his grandfather would be more used to.

Only the mummy's head was visible. Most of the hair was gone, and the skin was wizened and leathery from its long sleep in the cold, dry cave in Shaman Pass and in the Smithsonian basement. The eyes were open and empty, the lips drawn back in that ghastly grin Active remembered from the photograph. But something seemed familiar.

"They kind of look alike, ah?" Maiyumerak said.

Active looked back and forth between the two men and grunted assent. It was true. Natchiq had the same narrow, egg-shaped face as his grandson.

Active replaced Natchiq's blue tarp, then noticed a gleam from between Kelly's praying hands. Maiyumerak spotted it, too. "Look like he's holding something."

Active fumbled with his one good hand at Kelly's frozen hands, then gave it up in frustration. "See if you can get it out."

Maiyumerak knelt and forced Kelly's hands apart, then

pulled out an object wrapped in silver duct tape. "Look like he want us to find it. You want me to cut off the tape?"

Active nodded and Maiyumerak pulled out his knife again and sawed at the wrappings until the object inside was free. Wordless, he passed the Prince Albert can to Active.

Active thumbed up the lid and peered inside. A folded paper was all he could see. He started to pull the mitten and underglove from his right hand to fish it out but thought better of it as the breeze lashed his parka ruff into the corner of his eye.

"Come with me." He stood and trudged back to the snowmachines, Maiyumerak hurrying along beside him and asking, "What he put in there?"

When they reached the Yamaha, Active knelt and laid the tobacco can on the black Naugahyde of the seat. He looked at Maiyumerak. "I think it's a note. I want you to take it out and spread it on this seat and hold it down while I read it. And don't let the wind take it."

Maiyumerak squinted assent, bared his right hand, and gingerly pulled out the paper. It was a piece of brown grocery bag, Active saw, covered on both sides with penciled block printing. Maiyumerak spread it on the snowmachine seat and held it down as they both read it. "To whoever find me," it began.

My name is Robert Kelly and this man with me is my grandfather Natchiq the Eskimo Prophet who was kill early days ago by a bad *angatquq* name Saganiq. My snowmachine break down because it's shot by that Trooper Active so if you find us it mean we never make it out like I'm afraid will happen, that's why I write this note. I don't care what happen to me but please don't take my grandfather back to Chukchi. They will put him in their museum for *naluaqmiut* tourists to look at that don't know anything about him or what really happen early days ago.

After I take my grandfather from that museum in Chukchi, I go back to my camp in Shaman Pass, get ready to take him over to Canada where he was going when Saganiq kill him. That's when I hear Victor Solomon on Kay-Chuck, talk about how he knows who do it and they will put him in jail and my grandfather will still go in glass case for *naluaqmiut* tourists to look at. I never know he thinks Calvin Maiyumerak did it, so I think he's talk about me. That's when I decide to leave my grandfather at my camp and go talk to Victor, see if he will make a deal. I ride down to Chukchi again and ask some old lady on the street, where is Victor? She tell me he's at his sheefish camp so I ride out there and he come out of his tent when I drive up. He look pretty surprised when I show him his grandfather's harpoon and owl amulet and tell him who I am. Then he say, what I want?

I tell him it's time for our families to give up old fight, now it's modern times. I say, he can have Saganiq's things, put them on display in museum, I'll take my grandfather to Canada like he always want, then he will drop the case and it will be over. No more problems for our families.

Victor take that harpoon and the amulet, all right, but then he say he'll tell police about me anyway. He'll find my grandfather and put him on display in the museum and the police will put me in jail. My grandfather and me, we'll both be in cages, that's what Victor say.

That's when I think I'll just try to get away, go back to get my grandfather and hide him somewhere in Canada before police can catch me, hope Victor never find him. But Victor, he try stop me when I start to leave, hit my eye with his grandfather's harpoon.

So I grab that harpoon away and all of a sudden something tell me to stab him with it. I do it and Victor fall down in sheefish hole and seem like he's dead already when he hit the ice. I never mean to kill him but when he's dead, I'm not sorry. That's why I leave the harpoon and amulet behind, that way maybe if a few old people can still remember the stories about my grandfather and Saganiq, they will know what happen when they hear about how Victor is kill. I even put Saganiq's amulet in Victor's mouth, let him eat his grandfather's *kikituq*.

I know I'm bad man now, even if I never mean to do what happen. All my life, I try live new way. Go to school, get job, vote, pay *naluaqmiut* taxes. But when I'm out there on the ice with Victor, old-time Eskimo way seem right to me.

But my grandfather was a good man, never kill anyone or do any other bad thing all his life, try help them Eskimos at that time get ready for *naluaqmiuts* to come with their new ways. So that is why I ask you, if you find us, please never take my grandfather back to Chukchi.

And please call my daughters Louise Oomittuk in Point Hope and GeriAnne Carson in Barrow, tell them I'm found and that I loved them, and that I was not a bad man, except this one time.

Active folded the note, tucked it inside his parka, and dropped his sunglasses back over his eyes. "Well, I guess we know what he was doing that extra day," he muttered to himself.

"What?" Maiyumerak said.

"Doesn't matter." Active shook his head. "Let's get them back to camp. Cowboy can haul them out to Chukchi in the Beaver."

Maiyumerak didn't move. "Both of them?"

Active nodded, steeling himself against it.

"We could leave Uncle Frosty here like Robert Kelly say, ah? You got your man." He pointed at the trench where Robert Kelly lay beside his grandfather a few yards away.

Active shook his head. "Uncle Frosty is museum property and he's evidence in Alan's burglary case and my homicide. He has to go back."

"Alan don't have to know. I could take off with Uncle Frosty and hide him somewhere, and you could say we only found Robert."

Active pulled off his sunglasses and studied his reflection in Maiyumerak's mirrors.

Maiyumerak pulled them off and looked Active in the eye. "Please, Nathan?"

Active looked back at Arnie Rivers's hunting camp and the canyon behind it, then walked over to the trench.

"You don't need him for your case, now," Maiyumerak persisted. "And you're Inupiat. You don't want him in that museum for *naluaqmiut* tourists to look at. He belong out here."

Active looked at the pair in the snow. "It's not . . ."

Kobuk started barking again, his muzzle pointed south up the pass. They looked that way and at first saw nothing, heard nothing. Then Active picked up the distant hum of a snowmachine engine and saw a black speck moving down the slope.

Maiyumerak watched tensely until the rider was close enough to recognize. Then his shoulders sagged. "Too late now, anyway. That Alan Long would never do it."

Alan pulled in a few minutes later and shut off his Ski-Doo, staring in surprise at Maiyumerak. He walked over to the pit without a word, his eyes taking in Robert Kelly and the bundle beside him.

"Is that Uncle Frosty?" he asked, looking at Active.

Active nodded.

"Good." Alan stepped into the pit and pulled back the tarp for a look, then gave a satisfied nod. "Jim Silver never thought I'd get him back. Now we can close our burglary with the museum's property back where it belongs."

Active and Maiyumerak shot each other a quick glance, rolling their eyes. Active pulled the piece of grocery bag from his parka. "We can close the murder of Victor Solomon, too. Kelly left behind a note saying he did it."

"Really?" Long said. He took the note and read it over. "This is excellent. Damned fine police work, Active."

Active exchanged another eye roll with Maiyumerak.

Long turned to Maiyumerak. "What are you doing here, Calvin? Did you help Trooper Active find these guys?"

"Actually, it was Kobuk who found them," Active said.

"Smart dog," Alan said. He stepped out of the pit and, with Calvin, loaded grandfather and grandson onto the sled behind Active's Yamaha.

Active drove the Yamaha to camp with Alan and Calvin riding ahead on their own machines. When Active reached the tent, he saw four field-dressed caribou stacked in the snow, the purple-brown flesh already glazed with frost.

The three other men were huddled in front of the tent,

Calvin pointing at the cloud mass to the north and talking seriously to Alan and Whyborn.

"Calvin and Whyborn think we ought to get out of here," Alan said as Active walked up.

Calvin nodded and waved at the north again, in the direction of the clouds and breeze. "Storm coming. I heard it's real bad up here when it come from north side. We should go."

Active frowned. "Go where?"

"Not so bad on south side," Whyborn said.

Active shrugged. "Yeah, OK."

CHAPTER TWENTY-THREE

THEY PACKED A FULL set of camping gear into the sleds. Also, gas for the snowmachines and fuel oil for the stove. Plus the four caribou, plus Kobuk and Kibbie, who bounded onto their owners' sleds, wormed out hollows in the baggage, curled up with their tails over their noses, and closed their eyes. Finally everything was stowed except the corpses of Natchiq and Robert Kelly, now resting on the mat of willows where the tent had stood.

"Looks like we have to leave 'em," Maiyumerak suggested. "Cowboy could pick 'em up when he get everything else."

Active shot him a glance. "Not a chance, Calvin. Something might happen to them before Cowboy gets here."

"Like what? Nobody even know they're here."

"Somebody might come by."

"What you going to carry them in? You got no sled."

"We'll borrow one." Active turned and pointed at Robert Kelly's abandoned sled, still squatting in its trench with the Arctic Cat in the middle of the pass.

Maiyumerak squinted his unhappiness, but said nothing.

Active retrieved the sled with his Yamaha and they loaded the two corpses on, securing them not with bungee cords but with actual rope at Active's insistence.

Even with the four sleds, they left a fair pile of gear behind, with a note to Cowboy explaining their plan to wait the storm out in the best campsite they could find on the south side of the pass.

By the time they were ready to go, the wind was up to twenty miles an hour, Active guessed, with long streamers of snow slithering over the surface in a sugary mist.

Whyborn, as the senior hunter in the group, took the lead. He looked at Active as they prepared to start their engines. "You ever travel with a bunch of snowmachines in a storm before, Nathan?"

Active shook his head, the wind whipping the guard hairs on his parka ruff into his eyes.

"Well, we could put you second in line."

Active nodded, and Whyborn continued.

"I'll take the lead, then you, then Alan, then Calvin."

Active nodded again.

"So you should keep me in sight all the time, no matter what. If I speed up, you speed up. If I stop, you stop."

Another nod from Active.

"And you gotta look around every couple minutes, make sure you can see the other fellas behind you. You don't see them, you stop right there and wait. If they don't come up, you wait till I come back to you, then we will go back down the trail and find them, OK?"

Active nodded once more, with considerably more confidence than he felt, and they started off.

The temperature dropped as the north wind pushed air up the pass. The miniature thermometer on the Yamaha's key chain had read five above when Active pulled into camp with Natchiq and Robert Kelly; now it read five below.

Their only break was that the wind was behind them, not in their faces. For the first hour or so, they about matched speed with it, roaring along in an eerie bell of calm-seeming air, snowflakes whirling through it as the storm built up.

After that, the wind was faster than they were, hurling ever denser clouds of snow past them, the flakes dancing in the beams of their headlights. As the air thickened with snow, it became harder and harder to see the other machines, even with their lights on, and eventually they were no more than five yards apart. Whyborn cut their speed to ten miles an hour as he groped his way through the snow.

A little after six, Whyborn's taillight suddenly stopped bouncing and Active had to veer to the right to avoid hitting the leader's sled as the Ladies' Model coasted to a halt. They left their machines running, lights on, while they waited in the woolly twilight for Alan and Calvin. When they pulled up, everyone shut down and gathered beside Whyborn's machine. Active arrived in time to hear Whyborn say, "I think maybe we're off the trail."

Active peered around in the blizzard. The air was like milk now and with the machines stopped he could feel the full force of the wind. Forty miles an hour, maybe fifty. Temperature minus twelve by the key-chain thermometer. Chill factor? Better not to estimate. But how could Whyborn tell if they were on the trail or not? No feature of the landscape was visible.

"Yeah, I guess so," Calvin said. "Seem like we veer off to the right back there, start cutting across them snowdrifts at a different angle, all right."

There was a wordless moment that stretched on and on, no sound anywhere except the wind blowing past their parka hoods, the streamers of snow hissing over the crust.

"I guess I could take the lead," Calvin said.

Active almost protested, but stifled it in time. Whyborn lifted his eyebrows, and that was that. Maiyumerak, as usual, had been riding with just his snowmachine suit, a pair of leather work gloves, and a headband for protection, though he had replaced his high-tops with a pair of ancient Sorels. Now he went back to his sled and dug a parka and fur mittens from one of his boxes. He saw them watching, and his face split in his gap-toothed grin as he pulled on the extra gear. "Little bit colder today, all right."

He took the lead and they started off again. Maiyumerak veered left from the direction they had been taking before Whyborn stopped. Then, a few minutes later, he veered right.

Active couldn't tell for sure that anything was different, but now it did seem they were bouncing over the sastrugas at the same angle as before. At any rate, their speed picked up again.

They crested the pass a little after seven in gathering dusk. Active realized it was the crest only because Maiyumerak stopped the convoy and told them so, and said they would reach the gorge in another couple of miles.

Active checked his thermometer. Minus twenty now, the wind at least fifty and apparently still building. The cold was burning through his parka and Refrigiwear overalls, trying to get at his bones.

"When we get there, I'll stop again till you guys come up," Maiyumerak shouted over the wind. "Then I could drive through the bad part and walk back and take Nathan's machine through. Then Alan and Whyborn could come through, OK?"

They started down the south slope of the pass. It did seem that the weather eased slightly, as Whyborn had predicted. Less snow in the air, not quite as cold, visibility up to maybe a half-mile now, permitting occasional glimpses of the sea of cloud raging overhead. If he could see the clouds, Active realized, that meant little if any new snow was falling. The snow boiling around them must be an Arctic ground blizzard, picked up by the wind still building at their backs. It had to be pushing sixty miles an hour, he thought.

Below the summit, the pass narrowed toward the gorge, the sides pinching in and steepening until the trail was just a narrow bench along the brow of a hill. They rounded the hill and the gorge opened below them, vertical sides covered with snow and ice as far down as they could see in the murk.

Maiyumerak's taillight stopped bouncing. Active cut the Yamaha's engine and coasted to a stop beside him. Maiyumerak dismounted and walked over to Active, putting the snorkel of his hood against Active's to be heard over the wind. "That's the hard part up ahead," Maiyumerak shouted, pointing to a stretch where the bench narrowed even further. "I'll take my snowgo over, then come back and get yours and you can walk over. See them bushes sticking out of the snow there? You can grab them if you need something to hold on to."

Active peered into the murk and nodded. It didn't look as bad as he'd hoped. The bench did narrow a little more, but not so much that a snowmachine couldn't navigate it in reasonable safety, perhaps even a snowmachine with a one-armed driver. Another Arctic legend magnified in the retelling, no doubt.

Maiyumerak walked back to his Ski-Doo and Active watched as he raced toward the hard part. As the bench narrowed, Maiyumerak hit a small snowdrift that crossed the trail and his sled swung slightly downhill behind the Ski-Doo. Active's spirits lifted slightly at this. Maiyumerak gunned his engine and finished the crossing with the sled in a diagonal slide, snow spraying from under the cleated drive track, until he reached safer terrain where the bench widened again.

Active could just see him through the blowing snow as he

parked the Ski-Doo and started back toward them on foot, grabbing the dwarf willows in the snow to make it over the worst part of the trail.

Soon he was back, and straddling the Ladies' Model. "I'll take it over, then come back and walk across with you, Nathan."

Active looked down into the gorge, then glanced back at Alan and Whyborn, waiting a few yards back on their snowmachines, then decided. He turned to Maiyumerak and winked.

Maiyumerak pointed questioningly into the frozen depths of the gorge.

Active nodded.

Maiyumerak still wasn't certain. "Your snowgo, too?"

Active lifted his eyebrows and grinned.

Maiyumerak grinned back, started the Yamaha, and gunned it along the trail. He was halfway across when the sled hit the drift and swung downhill, as before. But this time the weight of the sled and its cargo seemed to be too much for the snowmachine. It churned to a halt, snow spewing from the drive track, and Maiyumerak flung himself off and grabbed a clump of dwarf willows. The Ladies' Model and the sled accelerated backward down the steepening curve of the hill, bounced into the gorge, broke into pieces, and vanished with Robert Kelly and his grandfather.

Maiyumerak picked his way back to where Active was standing, still staring into the gorge. Maiyumerak raised his hands and shrugged helplessly. "Sorry, Nathan, I just couldn't hold it."

Whyborn and Alan came charging up through the snow. Alan looked at Maiyumerak with a mixture of astonishment and outrage. "You ruined my burglary case," he said. "We'll never get Uncle Frosty out of there now and breakup will wash everything away."

"Them Yamahas never did have the traction of a Ski-Doo," Whyborn offered.

Maiyumerak said, "It sure was a pretty color of purple, though."

Active shrugged. "It died in the line of duty. The troopers will reimburse me." Then he asked Maiyumerak, "Think I could catch a ride up there on your sled with Kobuk?"

FIVE DAYS later, Active unlocked the bachelor cabin and stepped inside. It was warm, so the heat hadn't gone off while he waited out the storm in the camp Maiyumerak had found in a canyon on the south side of Shaman Pass. And the cabin smelled normal, meaning either that he hadn't left anything too gross in the garbage, or that Lucy had taken care of it while he was gone.

He slipped off his boots at the door, like everyone did in Chukchi, eased out of his parka and dropped it on the sofa. Then he dialed 9-1-1.

As he'd hoped, Lucy was at the dispatcher's station and took the call. "What do you want?" she said in her grumpiest voice. Cowboy had radioed in on the way back that everyone had safely weathered the blow in the pass, and Carnaby would have passed the news to Lucy that Active was on his way home. And her Dispatch console would have told her who was calling.

"There's an emergency at the bachelor cabin," he said. "I need some *muktuk* right away."

"Well, stop tying up this line and call Nelda Qivits."

"She told me only yours would do."

"My what?"

"*Muktuk.*"

There was a pause. Then, with the slightest undertone of surprise and delight, "*Arii*, that Nelda! She said that?"

"Yep. She said I should try out my harpoon on your *muktuk*."

Lucy gave a little cry that was half giggle and half yelp. "Is this an obscene call? This line is recorded, you know."

"Maybe you should come over and arrest me."

"All right, I will!"

EPILOGUE

NELDA QIVITS WAS WATCHING the *World's Funniest Animal Videos* when she heard the outer door of her *kunnichuk* open and slam, then a knock on the inner door.

"Come in!" she yelled, not getting out of her chair in front of the TV.

The inner door opened and there was that pretty Nathan Active, the *naluaqmiiyaaq* boy with winter in his eyes. This time he was carrying some caribou—a hindquarter and a backstrap, it looked like. He had never brought her caribou before, just money.

"*Arigaa*, Nathan, good to see you," she said as she hobbled over to take the backstrap. The tender meat along the spine was the best part of a caribou, in her opinion. Her stomach rumbled a little in anticipation. But she would have to wait, she saw. The meat was frozen hard. With a sigh, she laid it on her drain board to thaw.

"You could put that hindquarter in my freezer out there, ah? Then you sit down and I'll make us some sourdock tea."

Nathan put away the meat, stepped into the cabin, and shut the inner door. Then he sat at her little dining table, his eyes wandering between her tea making and a video about a wild crow that had adopted a kitten in some *naluaqmiut* town Outside.

"I hear on Kay-Chuck, you find that Robert Kelly, then you're trapped up in Shaman Pass in our blizzard last week, ah?"

"Yes, we were stormbound five days," he said. "I was with Calvin Maiyumerak and Whyborn Sivula and Alan Long. We had a good tent and a stove, so it wasn't too bad."

"Is that where you get the caribou, Shaman Pass?" She sat down across from him and sipped from one of the mugs.

"I didn't get it, Alan and Whyborn did, just before the storm hit. So we had plenty to eat, and there was still lots left when it was over. Alan gave me some."

"What you guys do up there in your tent all that time?"

"Ate and slept a lot, played cribbage. Alan and Whyborn told some old stories. Calvin showed us a lot of string tricks with his hands. And he sang a lot."

"Calvin sang?"

Nathan lifted his eyebrows in the Eskimo yes, which she liked. He was trying.

"What he sing? You mean gospel?"

"No, songs that he made up. He sang about how we found Natchiq and Robert Kelly, and he sang about how we lost them and my snowmachine in Angatquq Gorge. He made it all funny, somehow."

She shook her head in wonder. She had not known any of this about Calvin Maiyumerak. "He sound like a real old-time Eskimo, that guy."

"I guess," Nathan said.

"It was fun for you?"

Nathan paused like he needed to think this over, then looked at her with a surprised expression. "Yes, it was fun," he said.

"No problem with *quiyuk* now?"

He shook his head and his smile got bigger.

That knot over his brows was gone, she saw now. Not like

the other times, when he came in to tell her about the bullet dream.

"*Arigaa!* Then you had good dreams up there?"

He smiled. "No bullet dream. But I dreamed I was a ptar-migan flying through Shaman Pass. Was that a good dream?"

"Were you happy?"

Nathan's face opened up in a huge, relaxed smile. "Very happy."

"Then it was a good dream."

He took a sip of the sourdock tea and stood up. "I should go now. Lucy and I have to tell my grandfather a story."

"Your *ataata* Jacob?"

Nathan lifted his eyebrows.

"*Arigaa*," she said. "He'll like that."

AFTERWORD

The Real Natchiq

THE CHARACTER NATCHIQ IN this story is based on a real Eskimo prophet and social reformer who lived in Northwest Alaska in the nineteenth century.

His name was Maniilaq and Natchiq's life is drawn from his, the greatest difference being that Maniilaq was not murdered in the Brooks Range. Instead, he reached Canada, as far as can be determined, and his descendants reportedly live there today.

Natchiq's teachings and prophecies, as related in this story, are borrowed from the teachings and prophecies of Maniilaq, as set down in oral histories recorded by Eskimo elders who, as children, saw Maniilaq in the flesh. Maniilaq opposed the *angatquqs*, advocated better treatment of women, and tried to prepare the Inupiat for the waves of change about to wash over them.

Where he got his ideas and his information, no one knows, though it is possible he came into contact with Westerners— whalers or traders—in his travels through various coastal villages, and transformed what he saw and heard into the things he told the Inupiat of his day. As with Natchiq in this story, however, Maniilaq never explained the origin of his ideas, other than to say they came from his source of intelligence in the sky.

Relatively little has been written about this mysterious and fascinating figure, and much of what there is tends to exist in the shadow world of "gray literature"—material either out of print or never published, available only to the specialist or the determined or lucky generalist. However, at least two books that deal with Maniilaq in greater or lesser detail are in print, according to an Internet search at the time of this writing:

Maniilaq, Prophet From The Edge of Nowhere, Onjinjinkta Publishing
The Kotzebue Basin, Alaska Geographic Society

In addition, a useful chapter on Maniilaq can be found in *Tomorrow Is Growing Old*, an excellent history of the Quakers in Alaska (Barclay Press). That book, regrettably, is out of print and so falls into the category of gray literature. But it may be available in libraries or used bookstores.

In addition, an Internet search for the word "Maniilaq" may turn up useful information as more gray literature makes its way into the light.

Maniilaq's legacy of concern for the well-being of his people lives on today in the form of the Maniilaq Association, an Inupiat-controlled nonprofit corporation set up in the 1970s to provide human services in Northwest Alaska.

And Shaman Pass? There is indeed a real place in the Brooks Range where the wind is said to blow so hard it kills caribou. That place is called Howard Pass.

—Stan Jones
Anchorage
June 2002